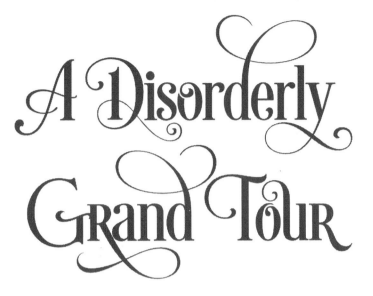

A Disorderly Grand Tour

VICTORIAN GRAND TOUR SERIES
BOOK THREE

LISA H. CATMULL

SALTAIR PRESS

To Barb,
and the countless NICU nurses and doctors
who work endless shifts to save lives.
Thank you for working days on end, talking all night,
and reassuring parents in our most difficult hours.

ACKNOWLEDGMENTS

I heard a new term the other day while listening to a deep dive discussion about Adam Grant's book, *Think Again*. The term's been around a while, but it was new to me: challenge network. Who do you have in your life that challenges you and makes you rethink things?

Instantly, I thought of my editors and beta readers. I ask them to lay it on me. Let me handle the ugly truth, and they respond in beautifully honest ways.

I've also been exploring what my "celebration language" is, like a love language. Rachel Mohr, a long-time friend and professional coach, has helped me embrace that feeling of exhilaration and the gratitude toward others that celebration engenders.

So, I'd like to acknowledge, first and foremost, Adam Grant and Rachel Mohr.

My challenge network: Michele Paige Holmes, Lorie Humpherys, Judy Olsen, Marianne Siegmund, David Catmull, and Sara Hacken.

My celebration stars: everyone in the challenge network, Richard Hacken, Heather Clark, Cindy Gunderson, Jessica Carney, Heather B. Moore, Maurine Walker, Tiffani Hacken, other family members, neighbors, cousins, friends who've sent flowers, Instagram followers, friends on Facebook, the Amazon reviewers who gush kindly even though we've never met, and other authors. Thanks for sharing this excitement with me. It lights me up and keeps me climbing this crazy mountain that I call writing.

My gurus: Allison Lane, Nancy Mayer, and Karen Pierotti. They are quick to answer obscure questions and are endlessly knowledgeable.

My inspiration: the LTUE writing conference 2021. You light up my life. Donna Milakovic's presentation on the Gallup/Clifton strengths blew my mind and strengthened the way I wrote my characters in this book. Nancy and Gordon Frye's lectures on costumes forever changed the way I write ballroom scenes and my understanding of crinoline hoops. Brilliant!

My research: HathiTrust Digital Library and Google Books, thanks for instant access to archaic slang words, dinner party menus, exercise books from the Victorian era, and so much more.

LIST OF FEATURED CHARACTERS

Miss Rachel Wickford
Mrs. Edith Wickford, her mother
Dr. Morrow, surgeon in Essex who cares for Mrs. Wickford

Colonel Curtis Loughton
Miss Alice Loughton
Mrs. Glenn, Alice's chaperone
Mr. Frederick Kempton

Lady Eleanor Shelford
Lord Shelford, Percy Hauxton
The Duke of Woodford, Guy Claybury
Lord Timothy Romford

The Duke of Lambourne, Colonel Loughton's grandfather

Frank, carriage driver/footman in Germany
*Herr Theodor Fliedner, the director of the Mainz Institute

*historical figure

Lady Agatha Goulding, nursing school trainee
Lady Clara Proutton, nursing school trainee
Lady Frances Billings, nursing school trainee
Miss Leonora Herbert, nursing school trainee
Miss Lydia South, nursing school trainee
Mrs. Isabella Phillips, nursing school trainee

CHAPTER 1

Florence, Italy
Early November 1856

Rachel inhaled the aroma of leather, parchment, and paper. Rows of journals and stationery sets crammed the orderly shelves behind the store attendant. Brilliant swirls of color adorned the thick gilded sheets of paper. The distinctive Florentine motif—blue, red, and yellow flowers erupting from green stems, all intertwined with a delicate feathered pattern in the background.

Perhaps a new diary was in order to record her class notes. She had filled nearly every page of the black leather logbook with sketches, diagrams, and details from lectures at the Mainz Deaconess Institute for training nurses. Perhaps she might get one of those to remember this visit to Italy for Lucy's wedding.

Her dear friend, Alice Loughton, examined a set of thick cream writing paper and envelopes with emerald-green flowers dancing along the edges. Gold stars intermingled with red, blue, and gold blossoms. The decorations matched the hazel green of her eyes. She hugged them to her chest. "Oh, Curtis! I must have an entire library of new journals and all of the stationery. Every design."

"Will that be sufficient?" Her brother's rich voice carried across the store. Colonel Curtis Loughton lounged against a wall, a lazy grin on his face. "It may last you a week. Perhaps two."

Alice put the stationery on the counter and began searching the shelves for other patterns. "And they have sheets of wrapping paper in all sorts of marvelous designs! Christmas is less than two months away."

Colonel Loughton stepped away from the wall and crossed the room toward the two women. "I'm surprised our gifts are not wrapped already."

Rachel turned quickly back toward the store attendant. If she pretended to study the journals, Colonel Loughton might ignore her.

"And which do you favor?" His deep voice sounded over her shoulder.

She could pretend she didn't hear him. Rachel tilted her head and pondered what size she required. Not too large, not too thick. She smiled at the store attendant and prepared to attempt her basic Italian. The attendant sized her up, then moved away to assist Alice.

"May I?" Colonel Loughton joined her at the counter. He'd spent the last two months translating the German lectures at the nursing classes for her. Evidently, he assumed she did not speak Italian well enough to make a simple purchase.

"Thank you," Rachel said, with as little sincerity as possible. *When will he learn that I do not want his attention?* "I can manage without your translation services."

Colonel Loughton raised an eyebrow. "Here, or in Germany?"

This was going better than she could have hoped. "Both. As much as I appreciate your kind services"—she knew her tone of voice did not entirely match her words—"Mr. Kempton can translate for us when we return."

She considered the row of journals and prepared to make her

selection, but the colonel interrupted her again. He scoffed. "Kempton can't do it alone. There's far too much to be done." He pointed to the hundreds of cards, envelopes, and leather-bound books. "As endless as this merchant's selection."

"Kempton has managed for the last two weeks," Rachel replied. "I'm sure he fared well enough while we were away." She smiled politely. Insincerely. Surely, he would understand.

Colonel Loughton studied her. She could not tear her eyes away without being vastly rude. She wanted to buy a journal and leave. The sooner, the better.

A slow smile crept across the colonel's face. "But Miss Nightingale's new school in London will require a full set of notes."

Rachel could not make out which color dominated his eyes today. The green? The brown? The gold? She needed to concentrate on the task at hand—dispatching the colonel as quickly as possible. She drew her mouth into a thin smile and her cheeks tightened. "I'm sure that would be helpful to her and the staff."

The colonel continued to maintain eye contact. "We'll need to transcribe Kempton's scribbles into a legible set. We should have been doing this for the last three months."

We? What was he suggesting? Perhaps he would not dare ask, if she did not offer.

She shifted her weight and darted a glance to the store attendant, who was still fawning over Alice. He refused to look elsewhere, and Alice was in raptures over the stationery. Rachel wouldn't get any help from either of them, if she wanted a diversion.

The colonel turned his attention to the rows of journals. "How are your notes divided?"

Rachel sighed with relief at the break in eye contact. The colonel's gaze was like that of a hungry tiger, waiting to pounce. "I don't recall at present." She'd not volunteer to spend any more time with him.

Colonel Loughton turned back to her. "Kempton will have three weeks of notes when we return. How would you suggest we organize them? How many journals shall I purchase? A rough guess, since you don't recall."

Rachel was caught. The colonel's golden-green eyes sparkled, as if he knew she was lying, and a smile played on his lips. He'd been sitting behind her during lectures for nearly three months. He probably knew her note-taking method as well as she did.

The colonel moved closer, a look of challenge on his face. Rachel took a deep breath, and the scent of shaving soap filled her senses. Perhaps she should answer quickly, buy her journal, and leave. "Four. I separate the notes by subject in the first. Remedies, poultices, and tinctures are categorized in another. Diagrams and illustrations in a third. Cases I attend are kept in a separate diary."

The colonel nodded and waved his sister over. "Alice, don't worry about your pin money. I shall pay. You as well, Miss Wickford." The attendant rushed over, his arms full of Alice's stationery, and immediately offered his services to the colonel.

Traitor. Rachel rushed to interrupt. "I can speak enough Italian to order my own journals."

"Yes, but it's for the school," Colonel Loughton said. "I will purchase these." He pointed to the shelves with journals and began speaking in rapid Italian.

Rachel huffed and let out a long breath. She hated condescension and pity. She rummaged in her reticule for coins. Funds had grown tighter since Papa's death, but she was still a gentlewoman, they still owned their estate in Essex, and she had more than enough money to buy her own diaries.

The colonel purchased five journals for each of them, identical in size, but with different covers: plain, orangish-brown leather for Miss Nightingale's new nursing school and the elaborate, paper-covered Florentine journals for her.

He should have asked her before making the purchases. What presumption, to imagine he knew best and could simply purchase journals for her. She had not stated any preference. True, he *had* purchased precisely what she wanted, but that only irked her all the more.

Rachel rolled the heavy coins back and forth in her hand. No one had ever paid such close attention to her before, and it felt distinctly uncomfortable. Had he been observing her while she shopped? Watching to see which she favored?

"Five diaries each? Was it necessary to buy so many?" She took her few coins, which now seemed ridiculous, and pressed them into Colonel Loughton's hand. "Four sections in one notebook would have sufficed."

Instantly, she knew she'd made a mistake. A large grin split his face. He pressed the cool coins back into her palm, closed her hand, and covered her fingers with his own. "We shall not return to Italy for some time, and I must ensure you are well provided for."

Why did she have to be wearing such thin, silk gloves in the Italian heat? She wished it were a pair of nice, thick woolen gloves for midwinter. His touch warmed her as if there were nothing between them.

Rachel quickly pulled her hand away and slid the coins back into her reticule. "Thank you, Colonel. How kind." She tried to make it sound sincere this time instead of breathless. She'd made a point of learning to speak in steady tones, so no one could ascertain her emotions. She was utterly failing at the moment.

Colonel Loughton's smile grew even wider, if possible. "You're right, Miss Wickford. My translation services *are* no longer required. I'm sure Kempton will do fine, now that there are only two of you." He gestured toward the exit, his arms laden with packages for herself, his sister, and the nursing school.

Rachel turned toward the door of the paper shop and inhaled the smell of ink and paper one last time. *Success.* Colonel Loughton would stop attending classes. Instead of sitting behind her to translate the German into English, so that she and his sister could understand the nursing lectures, he would stay home.

He'd copy the notes at night, and she'd hardly encounter him. They would no longer spend all day together and eat leisurely, long meals. Now he'd need the time to record and transcribe detailed medical diagrams. She'd be free of his distracting presence and able to concentrate on the one thing that mattered: learning how to help her sick mother.

Colonel Loughton considered her. "I'll occupy the chair that Lucy left vacant and copy the diagrams during class instead. I'll be able to copy your notes when there are no diagrams, and we'll still have plenty of time in the evenings after the lectures."

No. This was worse. Instead of sitting behind her, where his deep, rich voice rolled over her, he wanted the seat beside her? And then he wanted to spend the evening side by side at an intimate writing desk, comparing notes?

He raised an eyebrow at her, daring her to refuse. It was for Miss Nightingale.

"Alice can copy the diagrams, *General*," Rachel said. "We'll do quite well on our own." He hated it when she called him that. Perhaps the nickname would irritate him enough that he wouldn't want to spend the day with her. Excessive politeness had not worked.

The colonel simply smirked as they exited the paper shop. A hazy Italian afternoon greeted them. Clouds hovered menacingly in the sky, heavy with rain.

"Oh, I'm quite hopeless with anatomical sketches," Alice said cheerfully. "Curtis can sit between us all day. What fun. Shall we get a cup of tea before it rains?"

They darted into a nearby tea room. Most Italians favored coffee, so it was remarkable to find a shop serving tea anywhere at all. Usually the apothecaries sold the loose tea. Chandeliers hung at intervals in the narrow store. White-washed walls brightened the interior. Small wooden tables filled the space, their red velvet chairs and benches an invitation to intimacy.

Alice and the colonel settled themselves at a charmingly cozy table, just the right size for three people. Rachel looked for a way to avoid the snug seating for a while longer. She found it.

One long wall was filled with cakes, confections, rows of gleaming pots and porcelain cups, and assistants ready to serve tea. On the opposite side of the store, a long counter displayed glass jars of loose tea leaves and dried herbs. This was not just a tea shop–it was *also* an apothecary store. Rachel bit her lip. A paper shop and an apothecary in one day? Surely, she had stumbled into heaven. She examined the rows of dried herbs. There must be a hundred different varieties. Chamomile, calendula. *Grown in the Italian sun!* Imagine how vitalizing and healthful they would be. Something brushed against her arm. Rachel startled and turned.

Colonel Loughton stood at her elbow. He extended his hand. "I bought a few pens as well." He offered her one, then turned to the table behind him. He unwrapped one of her new paper-covered journals and handed it to her.

Rachel accepted it silently. She began to write the names of ingredients. "Are these—"

"Latin, yes. The handwriting is difficult." The colonel peered closely at the labels. "May I read the top shelf to you? Are you able to see them?"

Rachel sighed. She'd been discretely lifting her heels, attempting to gain a few inches, because the top shelf was out of reach. "Yes, please."

She kept her focus on the new journal, which cracked as she opened it for the first time. The ink sank into the thick, cream paper as she wrote the name of each herb in the tea shop.

The colonel peered over her shoulder, casting a shadow over the diary. "And what quantities do you wish?"

She didn't protest or offer to pay, but drew a column next to each herb. "One hundred grams of each? Thank you."

The colonel nodded and moved toward the counter.

Rachel sighed as he left, then slipped into a chair at the table with Alice. "Is he always like this?"

"So helpful?" Alice asked.

"No, so overbearing." Rachel contemplated the columns. An entire diary for herbs and remedies and tinctures. She wanted to hug it to her chest, like Alice, but she simply considered her lists. Some ingredients were heavier than others. Perhaps purchasing the same weight of each was a mistake.

"Yes," Alice said. "He thinks of everything."

Rachel studied his tall, imposing figure, made taller still by his silk top hat. The dark brown hair that hid beneath the hat, the broad shoulders and well-muscled arms, shown to advantage by the tight fit of his vest and coat. She could easily imagine him commanding his troops in the Crimea last year. She watched him pointing at jars, placing an order with the shopkeeper, and once again, paying for her.

Alice cleared her throat, and Rachel's gaze flew back to her friend. Alice was smiling at her. Rachel did not blush. She never blushed. "But you and I are not orderlies in his hospital or soldiers in his regiment to order about. We're women."

Colonel Loughton returned with the parcels. He set them down on the table as Rachel finished her statement. He shuddered. "And all the more terrifying because of it. Completely disorderly, the pair of you. I'd face hostilities against another opponent any day."

Rachel tried to hide her mortification at being overheard. She'd simply meant the comments as a jest, a way to cover her embarrassment at being caught admiring Alice's brother. Now she was even more discomposed.

A shop assistant delivered three cups of steaming tea, just as a light drizzle of rain began outside. Trapped, for at least half an hour. Mrs. Glenn, Alice's chaperone, had stayed at the *pensione* to read. Rachel should have done the same.

An assortment of tarts and pastries soon followed. Light meringue crusts, lemon custard, and chocolate cream. He'd selected her favorites. Somehow, that irritated her further. Handsome, well-bred, and considerate. This would never do.

She tilted her head toward the colonel and smiled. She spooned some sugar into her tea and stirred. "Are we enemies, *General*, merely because we are women, or because we are so 'disorderly,' as you call it?" May as well begin the assault.

The colonel didn't even react. The contest *was* beginning in earnest. "Depends." He stirred some honey into his tea and spun his spoon casually. "Did you or did you not declare war on all men?"

Rachel pressed her lips together. "On the institution of marriage, not on men." She took a tiny sip, letting the brilliant blue and yellow patterned teacup hide her face. "Alice and I are allies in this."

Alice shrugged. "I have no need to marry."

Colonel Loughton waited until the porcelain teacup rested back on its saucer, then leaned across the table to look Rachel directly in the eye. "In that case, Miss Wickford, yes. You have thrown down a challenge, recruited my sister away from me, disrupted my comfortable routine, and we are now on opposing sides of the battle." He settled back in his chair and watched her with a smirk on his face. "I have never backed down from a fight, and I intend to enjoy this campaign more than any previous one."

Rachel laughed. "You may as well concede now. Alice and I are determined, and we will accept your terms of surrender with grace."

The colonel studied her. "You underestimate the strength of my conviction and my love of order."

Rachel stirred her tea, willing it to cool faster. "Your sister knows your weaknesses. I have a spy in my camp."

Colonel Loughton crossed his arms. "I have time on my side. I need only wait, and you and Alice will soon tire of the struggle. Why fight against tradition? Thousands of years of history are against you."

Rachel took a sip of the tea, now cooled to perfect temperature. Just warm enough, but not too hot. "And I need only wait for you to grow distracted. You will soon accustom yourself to *my* ideas and abandon your battle altogether."

"Never reveal your tactics to your opponent," Alice warned. "Curtis has taught me that much." She smiled at her brother.

"Are you sure you have enough of each herb?" the colonel asked, rising from the table. "Shall I get anything else before we leave? Do you require more ergot?"

"There, you see, Alice," Rachel said.

Alice furrowed her brow and shook her head.

Rachel waved her handkerchief. "The herbs have already distracted him, and he's forgotten his objective. Signal your defeat now, Colonel."

"Buying the dry tea leaves *is* my tactic. I will reveal that much to you," Colonel Loughton said. He put one hand on the edge of the table near Rachel and bent down to speak directly to her. He caught her eye, then held her gaze before speaking distinctly. "I am not distracted in the least. On the contrary."

The scent of cedar shaving soap mingled with the aroma of lavender and other dry herbs. Rachel ducked her head and began to sort the brown paper bags to check which herbs she already had, but she couldn't help inhaling discretely to enjoy the smell. "Ah, trying to disarm us with kindness."

"More rosehips?" the colonel asked. "Perhaps more peppermint?" He grinned. "Some lavender? Or is it the cedar that *you* prefer?"

Rachel did not blush. She never blushed. She bit her lip. She loved the smell of his shaving soap, and he knew it, but she would never admit it. "Rosehip and peppermint will do for tea, and I could use more lavender for sachets," Rachel said, and continued to sort the brown bags, as though looking for something. "Yes, ergot for the deliveries is an excellent idea, if they have some."

"But I'm sure you love the scent of cedar, too. Perhaps they have cedar shavings or pieces for your wardrobe chests." Colonel Loughton grinned at her. "Or to put under your pillow." He moved away to the counter.

Incorrigible flirt. She should not have taken such a deep breath, but she loved the smell of cedar. If only he had not noticed. *Focus on something other than him.* The tea. Had he also noticed her hesitation when she hefted the bag of rosehips? They were so much heavier than the other leaves that one hundred grams meant very few herbs. She did want more rosehips, and he seemed to favor peppermint tea.

But the one thing Rachel did not want was this playful, light-hearted conversation with the colonel. She did not want to see his kindness toward his sister or herself. She did not want him to be thoughtful, considerate, and attuned to her every need, especially if it was a ploy, because she had just sworn a day ago never to marry him or any other man.

CHAPTER 2

Curtis flipped the ornate iron key over and over in his hand. The entrance to Lady Shelford's old apartments was situated on a landing between the staircase that led to his apartments above and Miss Wickford's apartments below. "Ready?"

He had imagined this moment during the train ride from Florence, Italy. With the Chelmsfords' wedding now over, he had had plenty of time to think as the passenger cars wound their way up through Italy, Austria, and into Germany. The mid-November rains had lashed at the windows, but the trains still ran along their tracks with mechanical precision. No blizzards or snow yet, but a chill winter wind greeted them at the Wiesbaden train station.

A cold carriage ride over to their apartments in the Old Town of Mainz, and now here he stood, ready to see three weeks' worth of work. He'd left Kempton with instructions to do far more than take notes while they were away. He needed a way to occupy his time during the upcoming winter months indoors, he needed a spectacular gift to surprise his only sister, and he needed a way to convince Miss Wickford to marry him.

Curtis slid the grooved key into the lock. He turned until the notches caught, and the key fell into place. He pushed the metal handle open and swung the door wide. "I present you with—my early Christmas gift!" He stepped aside to allow his sister to enter the apartment's entryway.

They crowded into the hallway. Mr. Kempton followed him and closed the door behind the small group. Alice glanced around and furrowed her brow, clearly searching for a package or box.

Curtis motioned to his sister. "The gift is in the drawing room."

Alice would love it. She loved anything and everything. He wanted to please Miss Wickford too, but he couldn't tell what thrilled her. She never displayed wild enthusiasm, nor did she sink into the depths of despair, both of which Alice did. There was something to be said for Rachel's steady, even temperament.

And yet, how could he woo her, unless he knew how to delight her?

Curtis glanced to the side. He couldn't read Miss Wickford's expression. Was she curious? She schooled her emotions better than any soldier he'd known. He wanted to shock Miss Wickford into betraying some emotion. Any emotion.

They reached the end of the hallway. This would do it. Surely, she would like this as much as Alice. He flipped the key in his hand again, then shoved it into his pocket. *Time to find out.*

Curtis strode ahead. "Ever since Shelford left, I've had my eye on this space. I've let the apartments between ours and yours and gained approval for a few modifications. Kempton has worked tirelessly while we were away to prepare this for us." He threw open the doors to the drawing room with a flourish.

Alice squealed and ran into the enormous drawing room. The last rays of a winter sunset cast a golden hue through the floor to ceiling windows. Vertical ladders were affixed to the wall at angles. Horizontal ladders intersected, creating rungs to climb hand over hand. Ropes dangled from the ceiling. A balance beam ran the length of one wall. In the center of the room, where the sofas had been, a thick mast ran toward the domed ceiling. A thick, solid board served as a landing at the top. Tall contraptions with pulleys attached stood at intervals along the length of another wall, some to pull weights by hand and others to strengthen the legs.

Miss Wickford advanced, running her hands over a set of pulleys. "What is it?" she asked. "I've never seen the like."

Curiosity. He had her attention at last.

Curtis relaxed in the doorway, his head resting on the doorjamb as he surveyed the room. "A gymnasium, built to copy the German model."

"What did you do with the furniture?" Alice darted about the room and returned to hug him. "I love it. Thank you."

"Kempton hid it." Curtis shrugged. "Shoved the furniture into the bedrooms or somewhere, I imagine."

Kempton held out his arms. "Do I get a hug?"

Alice laughed and went to examine the smooth balance beam. "Will you demonstrate?"

Kempton raised an eyebrow.

Alice scoffed. "The equipment, not the hug. Oh, may I try right away?"

"The equipment or the hug?" Kempton grinned.

Alice grabbed a climbing rope and swung it toward Kempton. It narrowly missed him. He dodged out of the way and caught it.

"The equipment, then." Kempton sighed.

Curtis laughed. "Shall we, Kempton? Before Alice injures you?"

Kempton flipped his hat off his head and spun it into the corner. They stripped off their jackets, tugged off their collars and cuffs, rolled up their shirt sleeves, and kicked their spare clothes across the smooth, polished wooden floor.

"Mine slid further," Kempton said.

"That is unfair," Alice said. "Why do men get to wear sensible clothing? I am expected to do this in a crinoline hoop?"

Kempton grimaced. "Then don't wear the abominable thing. The exercise instruction book has an entire chapter on what to wear. You'll find packages of clothing upstairs, as instructed in the manual."

"There's a book?" Alice's eyes opened wide.

Kempton grinned and handed a thick leather tome to her. "*Dr. Lewis's New Gymnastics for Men, Women, and Children.*"

"Shall we change?" Miss Wickford asked.

Curtis studied her figure. Perfectly shaped. The petite waist and the curve over the hips. "It's a shame. You look well as you are." He gazed at her. If he'd wanted a reaction, he'd gotten one. Finally.

Her cheeks were flaming red. The calm, unflappable Miss Rachel Wickford was actually blushing.

She would not meet his eyes, but her eyes traveled the length of his arms and chest. Only then did it occur to him that he had stripped off half of his clothing without a thought. He was with his sister, and they exercised together all the time.

Curtis rubbed the back of his neck. "I apologize for the casual attire. It's been a long day on the train, and I wanted to stretch. Thought you and Alice would want a go, too. I didn't consider your skirts."

If he were in London, he might worry more, but he was in Germany. They had four more months together in Mainz, and no gossips or social connections. It was perfectly natural to strip down to his shirt sleeves, or take off his shirt entirely, when exercising. If he wanted Alice to have this gymnasium, it meant allowing her friend to use it, too. If they all happened to use it at the same time, and he happened to show himself to advantage, so much the better. *All's fair in love and war, and this is a bit of both.* But he'd best keep his shirt on. There were limits to how much he could flout propriety, even in Germany.

Alice and Miss Wickford returned soon in casual Garibaldi blouses with snug waists. The loose skirts were much shorter than their day dresses, and their thick woolen socks showed a remarkable amount of leg.

Curtis swallowed. He had not even considered the ladies' exercise costume when designing a gymnasium. He had unknowingly handed his opponent a weapon for her arsenal. He tore his eyes away from the delicate ankles and stocking-covered calves.

"I can actually move my arms about in these blouses," Alice said. "How do these devices work? Shall I read a section?" She hugged Dr. Lewis's book to her chest.

"We've used all this equipment before," Curtis said. "Military training, gentlemen's clubs."

He and Kempton walked through the room, demonstrating the ropes, pulley machines, hand holds on the climbing apparatus, climbing pole, and balance beam.

Alice came and hugged him again. "You are the most considerate brother, and it is the most delightful early Christmas gift ever. I won't have to wrap it and write a card to myself from you." She smiled and moved away to try the balance beam.

Kempton held Alice by the waist and helped her onto the thin leather-covered beam. Her loose skirts fluttered as she pointed a leg and took the first step. Curtis wouldn't mind helping Miss Wickford onto the balance beam, when she wanted to try it.

He watched his sister extend her arms and move along the beam. *What if she falls?* Perhaps this had been a terrible idea.

Kempton scaled the rope ladder and ascended the platform, moving along to the pole. It looked like a pirate's nest on a ship. Why had he left Alice alone, without anyone to catch her if she fell? *She'll break her neck.*

"Must you wear those slippers?" Curtis called. "Are they sturdy enough? Perhaps without hose you'll have better balance."

"I'm doing well as I am," Alice called back over her shoulder.

Something brushed against his arm. Curtis tensed, a soldier's reflex, and turned quickly. Miss Wickford stood beside him, her hand resting on his upper arm. Her eyes widened. She dropped her hand to his lower arm, tried to speak, then she let go, as if scalded. She spoke to his shoulder rather than his face. "I'm sorry I startled you. I only meant to reassure you. She will not fall." Then she looked up at him, and her eyes took on that familiar teasing glint. "Stop fussing."

Curtis grinned. She was embarrassed. First, he'd flexed his muscle out of instinct, and she'd felt it. She'd noticed. Her eyes were still staring at the muscles in his upper arm when she talked to him. Then her gloveless hand had rested for a moment on his bare skin, where the shirt sleeves were rolled up. Perhaps that was why she had reached for his upper arm initially. His shirt covered it.

"I don't fuss." Curtis enjoyed seeing her discomposed, but his own heart was still pumping from the shock, surprise, and exhilaration of her touch.

Miss Wickford seemed to recover herself as she turned to investigate the hand holds on the wall. "I do believe she could outclimb you, even in her skirts, General."

Curtis grinned. She had thrown down the gauntlet. "Can you outclimb me?"

"Another challenge?" Miss Wickford asked. "Are you certain that is wise?"

Curtis folded his arms. "How do you feel about wagers?" He lounged against the wall, where a set of rungs and hand holds had been affixed.

"I'm in favor of wagers, when I'm certain to win. You first," Miss Wickford said. "I shall study your tactics and learn which hand holds to avoid."

Curtis trained his gaze on her. "You mean, which hand holds to use. A boon to the winner?"

"I've no intention of losing," she said. "I meant what I said. When you fall, I'll know which hand holds to *avoid*."

Curtis rolled his shirt sleeves past the elbow. He stretched and began to climb. He didn't want to lose his balance in front of Miss Wickford, so he took his time. His arms began to shake from the constant flexing required to hold each grip.

"Ahoy, down there," Kempton called. "The rope ladder is easier."

Curtis focused. A hand hold there. He reached, using his full height. He brought his leg up, beneath him, and found a foot hold.

Another hand hold, slightly to the side. He loved the challenge. Gradually, he made his way, higher and higher, until he reached the platform attached to the climbing pole and swinging rope.

He grabbed the ledge with one hand, scrambled onto it, and pulled himself onto the thick wooden board. The drawing room spread out twenty feet below.

Miss Wickford was nowhere to be found.

Someone tapped his shoulder.

"The rope truly is easier." Miss Wickford smiled. That tight, controlled smile, but he could see she was fighting a grin. A twitch on the side of her mouth gave her away.

"Very well. I lose. I shall pay you a forfeit." Curtis scooted across the narrow platform.

For the second time that evening, her eyes grew wide. She turned without a word, took hold of the rope ladder, and began to retreat.

It was working. He'd spent the last few months observing her carefully controlled responses. Nothing seemed to pierce her armor.

But her mouth twitched when she was pleased. Now he knew one more thing about the woman he loved.

He lingered a while, watching Kempton demonstrate how to use the pulleys. Alice paid careful attention, but Miss Wickford's eyes kept wandering to the platform. Perhaps she was not as indifferent as she insisted.

Because he'd seen her mouth twitch when he'd offered to kiss her.

CHAPTER 3

Rachel heard an apple crunch. Again.

She let out a long sigh and spoke quietly. "You cannot eat during the lecture, General. It distracts the other students."

She glanced around the room. A few of the other nursing students were watching the colonel. He wasn't exactly unobtrusive in a drowsy classroom filled with twenty-five women, all of whom had to be younger than him. Even when he wasn't eating an apple, his very presence was enough to turn any girl's head.

Colonel Loughton bent over his desk, swallowed his bite of fruit, and whispered to her. "I'm hungry."

His breath tickled her ear, and the now-familiar scent of cedar and lavender shaving soap hovered in the air. She tore her eyes away from the lectern, where *Herr* Fliedner was discussing principles of anatomy, to confront the colonel. His face pleaded with her, mere inches away, since the desks crowded together so close in the modest classroom. He had the hang-dog look of a puppy deprived of its favorite bone.

"You ate lunch an hour ago," Rachel whispered. "Roast beef. How can you be hungry?"

Colonel Loughton shrugged. He brought his apple up, ready to take another bite.

Rachel grabbed the apple. Her bare fingers brushed against his. She ignored the thrill of contact and pushed the apple away on the far corner of her desk, blocking it with her arm. She resumed taking notes.

Out of the corner of her eye, Rachel saw the colonel's hand, frozen in midair. He gaped at her. She repressed a laugh. No one interfered with the lecture.

Something soft tickled the edge of her hand. She shrugged it off. Listening to Mr. Kempton's translation while trying to take notes was hard enough.

It happened again, only this time the sensation traveled the length of her hand and back up. She shivered and pushed back her shoulders. Really, she wished she could wear her gloves and take notes, but the ink would ruin them.

She flexed her hands, shook her head, and continued. Rachel squinted at the board.

It happened a third time. Honestly. It tingled deliciously. What could it possibly be? She wasn't using a feather quill. She had a pen.

She spared a glance. Colonel Loughton's hand had traveled from his own desk onto hers. He stared straight ahead, feverishly copying a diagram, but the edge of his hand brushed against hers every time he wrote. On purpose.

"Use your own desk," she whispered.

"I can't see." A screeching sound echoed in the classroom as the chair legs scraped against the rough wooden floor. The colonel dragged his chair closer to hers, while every eye in the room turned toward her. *Herr* Fliedner paused in his lecture and looked up from his notes.

You can't see, but I can't think, Rachel wanted to say. She took the apple and gave it back to him. The colonel took a noisy bite. Better to let him eat an apple and distract the rest of the class than to take the apple away and have him distract *her*. If he was holding an apple, he couldn't also hold a pen.

Unless he held the apple in his left hand and continued to take notes and brush against her with his right hand.

There had to be another way to help her mother, one that did not involve this man. When Lucy invited her to Germany, Rachel had quickly agreed to go. Lucy required her emotional support, and Rachel had always wanted to learn more about nursing. She had not considered the colonel in her decision. She had paid him no attention. *Underestimating the enemy.* Classic mistake.

The colonel took another bite and chewed. Every bite took an eternity. Was there a noisier food anywhere? She set down her pen and closed her eyes. He would simply have to copy Alice's incomplete notes tonight. She couldn't think through the sound of his chewing.

"Apologies," he whispered, tipping his head toward her. She hated the feel of his breath on her skin. Well, she loved it, and she had to repress a shiver of delight, and she hated that she loved it. "I'll finish quickly."

Rachel took a deep breath. Her mother needed this. Something in this lecture might explain why Mama always felt tired or why she could hardly walk anymore. Nothing made sense. Mama had gotten sicker and sicker, and Dr. Morrow didn't have any answers.

Herr Fliedner might have the answers, but she couldn't hear them if the colonel ate apples all day long.

Rachel tipped her head to the side. Her cheek nearly touched the colonel's. "Can't you eat something quieter?"

Someone cleared their throat. Rachel turned her head. Alice and Mr. Kempton were watching her. Her and the colonel. Her *with* the colonel. They were grinning. Alice's eyes darted between Rachel and her brother, their cheeks nearly touching, their fingers nearly intertwined on the desk, their chairs pushed close together.

How did this happen?

Rachel set her jaw. She shifted in her chair, so that her back was to the colonel and her elbow blocked his hand from brushing against hers.

If the colonel was Napoleon, then she was the Duchess of Wellington. He might have the mind of a brilliant strategist, but she would hold a firm line against him. She would regroup and bolster her defenses. He would find himself crashing against his own Waterloo after the lectures when he came to dinner tonight. Because clearly, judging from the state of her notes, the pounding of her heart, and her inability to pay attention to the lecture, the colonel was waging war, and just as clearly, he was winning.

Rachel assumed a false air of calm as she waited for dinner with Alice and Mrs. Glenn. After Lucy left the nursing school to go to Italy, Rachel had complete charge of the household. When Alice asked to host a dinner, Rachel was delighted to step back and let someone else arrange affairs for an evening.

It had been a long afternoon at the Institute. Rachel picked up an embroidery hoop. Stitching soothed her soul. She had time before dinner, and she craved a quiet moment alone to think.

She pulled the needle through the linen in tiny, even rows. She could control her seams and stitches, just as she could usually control her emotions.

She'd spent years perfecting her even temperament. Ever since Papa died unexpectedly, she'd learned the futility of emotion. Emotions were pain, heartache, sorrow, regret, and disappointment. She and Mama got along well on their own. They spoke logically. There were no tears, no yesterdays, and no tomorrows. Only today, right now, and nothing more.

Rachel pulled a knot through the textured fabric and smoothed it. If only problems in life could be so easily resolved. They were best avoided. Keep things simple, straightforward. No entanglements.

She'd told Colonel Loughton that she would never marry. He knew. Alice knew. It had been *her* idea. Alice would never marry either, just as Florence Nightingale had vowed. Miss Nightingale believed God had called her to the work of nursing, and Rachel felt the same. All three of them were nurses, and they would devote themselves to the cause of healing and hope.

Not pain and heartache.

Rachel picked up the muslin and smiled in satisfaction. A perfectly ordered image. Everything according to design within the limited world of her embroidery hoop.

She would attend nursing school, assist Miss Nightingale for six months in London, and return home to care for Mama. It was a perfect design in her own narrow world, and nothing would entangle her or knot her stomach with grief.

She'd seen her friends, Lucy and Cecelia, deeply hurt. Love seemed like agony and anguish. True, their weddings were blissful and serene, but she couldn't erase the image, weeks earlier, of Lucy sobbing as Rachel comforted her. Lucy had barely been able to breathe, her stomach wrenched with the aches of betrayal. Was any happiness worth the price of that much pain?

Rachel had experienced enough sorrow for a lifetime already. She tied off the threads and cut the ends with a clean snip of her scissors.

Someone settled themselves beside her. Rachel started, and the scissors in her hand pricked one of her fingers. "Oh goodness! I did not see you."

"I'm so sorry." Alice's eyes filled with tears. "Allow me to bandage it."

Rachel laughed. "It's nothing." She wrapped her finger in her handkerchief and set her embroidery aside. Even perfect moments of peace could end in unexpected pain.

"Thank you for allowing me to arrange dinner. Mrs. Glenn wants me to learn how to run a household." Alice looked toward the door. "Curtis should be here any moment. He's never late for dinner."

Mrs. Glenn cleared her throat. She settled into a chair and

picked up a book. "You could be married in six months. No more dilly-dallying. It's a Season this year, and no more delays."

"Have you not had a Season?" Rachel asked.

Alice dropped her eyes. "Are you dreadfully ashamed to be my friend?"

Rachel stood. Her finger did ache a little, and she'd rather move about the drawing room to distract herself. "Relieved. I've never had a Season, either. I never planned to have one. I'm terrified to be presented at Court. Eighteen is not so old for you to be a debutante."

Alice hugged Rachel, nearly knocking her off her feet. "Oh, we'll go together, and we'll purchase our clothes together. This is more wonderful than I dreamt, but I shall turn nineteen during the Season."

"I suppose I didn't think it through, when I agreed to help your brother. I didn't realize going to London meant having a Season." Rachel pressed her finger into the palm of her hand. A little pressure made it feel better. "We are nearly the same age. I am as aged as you are, dear friend."

Alice slipped her arm through Rachel's, and they began to stroll around the drawing room. "Oh, you are quite young enough to capture any man's heart." She looked flustered. "But quite mature and capable of maintaining any household. Only look how well you are running the apartments here and managing the servants and dinners. Quite old enough. Oh, dear, have I offended you? My Season will be a disaster."

"No offense taken," Rachel said. "You shall manage, I am sure."

Alice sighed. "Curtis is *such* a romantic. He falls in love every Season without any difficulty. He's twenty-eight. Or is he twenty-nine? I've lost track. I've never fallen in love. Someone has fallen in love with him every year, and he's had the good grace to fall back in love with them. It never lasts, of course."

They walked with their backs to the doorway, over toward the window. Rachel felt a kind of sinking in her stomach. A passing fancy. Of course. She was the only woman in Germany. There was no one else for him to love. His infatuation would dissolve as soon as his feet landed in London.

But why should that make her feel off-kilter? No, it was her throbbing finger. *What a relief!* She needn't worry about hurting his feelings because she did not return them.

Alice turned toward her. "You look upset. Do you dislike him that much?"

Rachel could grudgingly admit a few of his good qualities, behind his back, to preserve her friendship with Alice. She had such a tender heart. They moved past the windows and turned back toward the drawing room doors.

"He's not entirely bad," Rachel said, looking down at her finger. She unwrapped the handkerchief and began to rewrap it. She'd never admit as much in person, but she could tell his sister. His sister would not get an inflated sense of self, as "the General" would. "Intelligent, devoted to his cause, dedicated to any duty that he takes up. So very kind to you. A real family man."

"I'm so relieved the escapades are over," Alice said. "Now that he's found you, he's finally ready to marry."

Rachel choked and began to cough. She cleared her throat, focusing intently on the handkerchief around her finger.

A high-pitched laugh burst out. Rachel's eyes flew across the room. Mr. Kempton was bent double, gasping for air, with one arm on the wall to brace himself.

The colonel relaxed against the doorframe, his legs crossed. His eyes twinkled, and he raised an eyebrow. "Fascinating conversation. I'm starving. Less talk, more dinner, little sister."

Rachel swallowed. How long had they been there? How much had the colonel heard? She'd been so occupied with tying the handkerchief around her finger that she'd paid no attention to the drawing room entrance.

Alice flew across the room to hug her brother. Mrs. Glenn set down her volume and cleared her throat. "Pair the couples to walk in to dinner, Miss Loughton."

Curtis held out his arm to Rachel. "May I escort you in to dinner, Miss Wickford? I'm not entirely bad." He smirked at her.

So he *had* heard everything she said about him. Rachel fought down a laugh as she took his arm. "Which is your good side? The right or the left? I do hope I will see your best side."

"You could never get on the wrong side of me," the colonel said in a low voice. His deep tones rumbled in his chest.

Rachel knew she was blushing. She never blushed, but she was blushing for certain now. She threw back her head and determined there was only one thing to be done. Stop talking to the insufferable, attractive, clever man who seemed capable of turning every jest and argument into an endearment.

CHAPTER 4

Curtis rolled up his sleeves. Sitting through lectures tested his willpower and patience. His muscles ached from disuse. He stared out the windowpane and onto the cobblestone streets below. Mists swirled off the Rhine River as the winds howled outside. Surely, this fog and rain would turn to snow any day.

The Germans were brilliant. An indoor gymnasium. He'd ask Kempton to install one in his London townhome as soon as they returned.

Curtis found a machine and tested the resistance. He pulled against the weights and felt his arms strain. He could hardly stand the tension in his own life. An entire day, sitting beside Miss Wickford, but hardly speaking a word to her. She avoided all conversation, answering him with only the most basic answers, and would not look him in the eyes.

Why would she vow never to marry? He pulled harder. He needed to feel something. His emotions were raw, and he needed something visceral, emotions put into action. If climbing poles and pushing against pulleys were the only way to do it, he'd spend all night in this gymnasium.

Curtis strode over to a horizontal ladder. He jumped and

grabbed ahold. He swung for a minute, then contracted his stomach muscles to bring his legs up. His body already felt better. He let his legs swing loose and began to work his arms, pulling his chin to the bar over and over.

She thought well of him. He'd caught her. Instead of the usual deprecations, she'd spoken kindly when she believed he wouldn't hear. So why was she on her guard and determined against him? What kind of men had she encountered in the past? There were plenty of scoundrels out there, but *he* was not one of them. Even she admitted that.

Blast. It was no good. Curtis dropped to the floor. He rolled his neck from side to side, stretched his arms over his head, and took a deep breath. He switched to the rope ladders and began to climb. He pulled himself up, hand over hand.

He'd never met a woman like her. That spark. Her fiery indignation, her wit, her determination, her curiosity. He hauled himself onto the landing above the drawing room and fought to catch his breath.

She loved nursing as much as he loved medicine. Never, in all his years in the *ton*, had he met anyone who cared about soldiers as much as Miss Wickford or Miss Nightingale did.

And Miss Wickford made his heart pound wildly, like it was doing right now. He gripped the rope and began his descent to the smooth marble floor. Did they have enough pads at the bottom? What if Alice fell? What if Miss Wickford fell? It was far too slippery.

Curtis slid part of the way and jumped to land on one of the thin, down-filled mattresses they improvised as landing pads. He fell. What should he try next? The balance beams. He needed to regain his equilibrium.

He had a choice. He could do what he'd always done. Move on. Forget her, and find the next woman to love. Or he could fight for her. Persuade her.

But Miss Rachel Wickford was not easily persuaded.

Curtis swung himself onto the beam and set his sights carefully on the pair of matching doors at the end of the room. He gained his balance and righted himself.

Soldier on. Steady on. He narrowed his gaze until it focused on a single point: the bronze doorknob. He took a step, then another. Was it worth the constant conflict and relentless rejection? He brought his foot forward, searching in mid-air, and felt it land on the solid leather-covered balance beam beneath him.

He grinned. He'd never met her equal and never would.

Curtis advanced along the beam, his eyes straight ahead. He'd already made progress in the last few weeks. He took another step. Perhaps she thought better of him than he knew. Nearly there.

The doorknob began to turn. His vision swam, and he rushed to finish. One false step, and he landed in a heap at the end of the beam. The down-stuffed pads were not nearly soft enough. Kempton should purchase more.

Laughter greeted him. Female laughter.

Curtis rubbed his hip. "Let's see you give it a try, then."

"And in a skirt, no less."

Rachel.

He scrambled up. He'd assumed it was Alice. "Miss Wickford."

She met him halfway across the room. "Loughton."

"Am I not 'the General' today?" Curtis tried to look commanding, in spite of limping slightly.

Miss Wickford looked him up and down, her eyes lingering on the rolled-up sleeves and upper arms. "Far too informal."

Curtis grinned. A chink in her armor. "And yet I still command your attention."

She glared at him.

"Shall we dispense with formalities? Please, call me Curtis." He was focused. *Soldier on.* Achieve the goal. The worst he could do was fall again.

To his surprise, she agreed. "Alice calls you Curtis when we are together. It's a bit wearying to think of you as anything else." She shrugged and studied the beam, running a hand over its smooth surface.

So, she was agreeing to call him by his Christian name, but she still wouldn't look him in the eye? She hadn't given him leave to call her by her first name. *Steady on.*

"May I help you onto the beam, Miss Wickford?" There were no gloves in the gymnasium, and this afforded him the opportunity to feel that perfectly curved waist. He'd imagined this too many times to believe it was happening.

Curtis wrapped his hands around the contour of her midsection. She inhaled quietly as he lifted her onto the balance beam, holding her until she steadied herself. She inclined her head, and he let go. Too soon, she had climbed out of his reach again.

She let out her breath. "Rachel, not Miss Wickford."

Progress. Curtis bowed. "Thank you. Since Alice calls you Rachel, I confess, I cannot help but think of you by that name." He watched for a reaction from her. Anything.

Rachel bit her lip and did not reply. Her eyes were locked on something across the room. If only she would focus on him as intently as keeping her balance.

Or could he throw her off-balance?

He walked to the end of the drawing room, then hesitated. He should not be in a room alone with her behind a closed door.

Curtis glanced up. "Is Alice coming?"

"Any moment," Rachel responded.

He shut the door. He'd listen for Alice and open it when she came. "I used the doorknob as my focal point." He stood directly next to it, waiting to see where her eyes would go. Would she look to him for her anchor point?

"No wonder you fell," Rachel responded. "Move aside, please."

Curtis sighed and opened the door. He walked the length of the drawing room and returned to the balance beam. Perhaps he could assist her when she dismounted.

"Stop hovering," Rachel said out of the side of her mouth. Her eyes were focused on a point somewhere across the room, perhaps above the door, her arms extended gracefully to the side.

"I don't hover," Curtis said, walking beside her each step of the way, in case she fell.

He'd never noticed her arms before. In the looser Garibaldi blouse, they were free to move about. They floated like—he didn't know what, he could only stare. Like branches swaying in the moonlight.

Her feet were so sure, so steady, *so barefoot*. No stockings today. Her ankles and bare legs peeked out from beneath those tantalizingly shorter skirts. It was remarkable, what women could do in skirts. She was rather daring to exercise without the wool or cotton stockings, and clearly more comfortable without them. He suspected this was not the first time she had exercised without her shoes.

They could never get away with this in London. If she were his wife, though, they could wear anything they wanted in a gymnasium of their own.

A weight hit his chest. *His wife*. A lifetime of this. She took another sure, firm step. She had nearly completed the length of the beam.

She would beat him again. She would probably outsmart him or outmaneuver him every time. He wanted this, and it was worth any risk. He only had to win once. It was time to increase his efforts, so he did not end the loser in this most important battle between them.

Curtis extended his hand to help her down. She looked around. There was no other way to get down. He put his hands on her waist and lifted her beside him, but she had to place her hands on his shoulders. They stood a breath apart.

And she hadn't let go yet. The quick twitch of her mouth told him she enjoyed it, yet she fought to hide it from him.

"There you are." Kempton's voice behind them startled him.

Curtis quickly let go of Rachel's waist, and she dropped her hands from his shoulders.

"You wear a corset, even in our gymnasium?" he asked her quietly, unable to forget the feel of holding her, even for a moment.

Rachel smoothed the waistband of her dress in a few places, checking for nonexistent wrinkles, once again avoiding his eyes. "A lady can exercise in any attire. She has more than one kind of corset. Ask Alice."

Alice had entered the gymnasium behind Kempton. Curtis's eyes had been so fixed on Rachel's waist that he hadn't seen them approaching until now. He could hardly pull his eyes away to greet them.

"But can she win a race up the rope ladder?" he asked. "Does she have a rope-climbing corset?"

Rachel pursed her lips. "I believe I already won that race against you."

Bang on the mark. Curtis moved forward. "And I neglected to reward you—"

She interrupted him. "Alice, shall I race against *you* today?"

Kempton and Alice had reached the middle of the gymnasium. Alice wore the same attire as Rachel, but she had stockings and sturdy boots. Those boots might be hard on the leather balance beam. Barefoot wasn't such a bad idea, especially when it meant he got to see Rachel's ankles.

"You installed four ladders? Kempton, that shows remarkable foresight," Alice said.

"No need to sound surprised." Kempton grinned. "Your brother ordered them, not me."

Alice laughed. "The truth will out."

"Shall we let the women start early? Give them a boost up?" Curtis asked. He moved around to where she stood and kicked the stool out of the way. He waited to put his hands on her waist again.

Rachel stared at him. "Do you want to race or not? Your rope is over there."

"A forfeit to the winner?" Kempton called out hopefully.

Alice looked at him scornfully. "In all the years you've known me, Kempton, have you ever won a kiss from me?"

"My luck is turning," Kempton said.

Curtis scowled at him. "Not while I'm watching. Not with my sister."

"Alice, you and I shall race while the boys argue. One—" Rachel began.

Curtis scrambled to get into position.

"Two…" Alice said.

Kempton came over and pulled Curtis down off the rope.

"Three!" Rachel and Alice said together.

The women began to climb. Curtis and Kempton wrestled to reach a rope, then started up. They climbed faster, but Kempton kept reaching over to pull Curtis's hands off. Curtis had to stop to retaliate and knock Kempton's grip free. By the time they finished, both women perched gracefully atop the ledge.

"Outdone, once again," Kempton said tragically, as he slid back to the floor.

"You shall never win a favor from me," Alice called to Kempton.

Kempton grinned up at her. "I shall never stop trying."

Curtis climbed down the rope. He growled at Kempton. "Oh yes, you will. If you lay one hand on Alice…"

"Whoa, Loughton." Kempton turned to him. "She's going to have a Season. Someone's going to kiss her, you know. It may as well be me. You already like me."

Curtis stared up at the ledge. A Season? They'd become so close, this group of four, taking classes together in Germany, but it would end in a few months. They'd return to London, and there would be other men interested in Rachel and in his little sister. In kissing them.

An intense urge to hit something overcame him. "We need to order a punching bag," Curtis said, "and boxing gloves. Could you?"

"Not on your life," Kempton said.

Curtis stared at him. "Bare knuckle boxing, then?"

Kempton shook his head. "You are crazy. Wreck this handsome face?" He patted his own cheeks.

Alice climbed down the wall, then Rachel worked her way along the hand holds. She could have been a soldier. These women, in their skirts, executed movements with more grace and skill than most of his men had.

Curtis looked around the gymnasium. Where could he go next? What would give him a chance to help Rachel again?

"Who made it to the top first, Alice?" Curtis asked. He approached them as they began using the pulleys to stretch their arms and legs.

They ignored him. It was hard to talk while doing the exercises. He waited for them to finish.

"Who's owed you a forfeit?" Curtis addressed Alice, but darted a sideways glance toward Rachel. He tried to look unconcerned.

Alice smiled. "Rachel won."

Rachel glared at her.

"Who lost?" Alice smiled at Kempton.

"Curtis did, certainly." Kempton swept his arm in a grand gesture. "Clumsy fellow. I beat him easily. I'm certain I climb better than he does."

"You cheat better than I do," Curtis mumbled. He appreciated Kempton's loyalty. He'd be happy for a chance to kiss Rachel or owe her any kind of favor.

Rachel's face broke into the widest smile he'd ever seen. "Wonderful."

Kempton and Curtis stared at each other. Alice exchanged a confused glance with them.

"I know exactly what I want." Rachel advanced toward Curtis, gazing intently into his eyes.

Hang it all. He knew that look. It never boded well.

She drew close and put a hand on his chest. He could feel it through his thin shirt. Perhaps he'd mistaken the look. Rachel's face was so hard to read.

But then her mouth twitched. *What the deuce.* She was enjoying herself.

"I want," Rachel said. She put her other hand on his cheek. "No. More. Apples. In. Class."

She dropped her hand, and her mouth twitched again. Hardly a smile, but he knew she was delighted. He had to pay her forfeit. He was going to starve to death, die of hunger every day during class, and waste away without her love. Or without a kiss.

But at least he might embrace her again. He quickly wrapped an arm around her waist before she could pull away, the satisfied look on her face changing to surprise. Curtis held her close, her arm trapped between them, searing him with her heat. "Is that the only forfeit I can pay?" He searched her eyes. It was a desperate gambit, but worth the undertaking.

She sighed, relaxing into his arms, and pointed to her cheek. Curtis pulled her close and kissed her cheek with as much passion as he could infuse.

Too much. Rachel pushed away with the hand on his chest. Curtis studied her for any sign of emotion. He grinned at her and raised an eyebrow, to see how she would react. She shook her head at him, as if he were a greedy child caught stealing sweets, but her mouth twitched, giving herself away.

Rachel had enjoyed the cheek kiss.

"No apples," Curtis said. "How do you feel about pears?"

CHAPTER 5

"I won't go without Alice," Rachel said.

"And I won't go." Alice crossed her arms. "You know my stance."

The women glared at Curtis.

"You can do very well with Kempton or someone else from the Institute." Rachel settled herself on a sofa. She arranged her skirts over her crinoline hoop. She'd much rather be wearing the exercise outfit.

"*Herr* Fliedner asked for you specifically, Rachel." Curtis paced up and down the drawing room. He had gone into military mode again.

This called for extreme measures. Rachel rang for tea. "Sit down, General."

He glanced at her and crossed to the floor-to-ceiling windows. The draperies were pulled back, and blue-grey winter light reflected from the streets below. The colonel put his arms behind his back, widened his stance, and began to brood. She could always tell when he was brooding.

"Staring at the snow won't convince me to accompany you." Rachel remained seated. Steady. Calm. Unruffled.

Curtis huffed. He clenched the hands behind his back into fists. Full Command Mode.

"Alice, be a dear, and inquire whether Mrs. Glenn might join us for tea." Rachel could see a direct attack might not work today. Curtis needed a nice, long talk to bring him around.

The maid brought the hot water and an assortment of cakes and tortes. Rachel went to the tea chest and looked through it. This called for a custom blend. Curtis needed something soothing.

"Would you care to try some of the herbs from Italy?" Rachel approached Curtis. She waited until she knew he could see her before she rested a hand lightly on his arm.

Last time she had done that without thinking, and Curtis had nearly jumped through the ceiling. He had incredible reflexes, as jumpy as any predator. Incredible arm muscles, too.

He looked pointedly at her hand and grinned. "Don't you prefer the bicep?"

How did he do that? It was as though he could read her mind.

"The loose herbs from Italy. Shall we make a blend?" She extended her hand. Surely, if she were extra kind, she could win her point.

Alice did not want to attend a birth. Rachel did not know why, but she knew that she did not want to go alone with Curtis. If Alice would not go, she did not want to go alone with the colonel.

He stared pointedly at her hand. He took it and wrapped it around his upper arm, instead of his elbow or his lower arm, and began to walk ceremoniously. She felt him tighten the muscle, flexing it.

Rachel bit her lip. He had made good use of the gymnasium. His arms were growing stronger. She dropped her hand, went over to the cupboard, and began to sort through the ingredients while she waited for the fluttering in her stomach to cease.

Alphabetical order. She had arranged the herbs in alphabetical order.

Curtis hovered behind, a few inches away. He reached across her, his upper arm brushing against hers. "The rosehip?"

"You need chamomile." *To calm down.*

"Hibiscus," Curtis said. "Mallow root."

"Honey with lemon." Rachel looked through the loose leaves. So many wonderful ingredients, but she needed a simple, soothing tea for today. For herself, as well as for him.

"Peppermint," Curtis said.

"Very well." Rachel selected the correct packet and put away the others. "So unimaginative. I was going to make you something wonderful." But it *was* his favorite.

She turned around with the brown paper packet of dried peppermint leaves.

"Peppermint sounds wonderful," Curtis said. He hadn't moved.

Well. At least he was distracted.

Rachel moved around him. Curtis followed her with his eyes, as if mesmerized by her every action. She could feel his eyes on her as she dropped the loose leaves in the pot and watched them settle to the bottom of the hot water. How many would this amount of water need? No one liked weak tea. She carefully considered the matter and tipped in a few more leaves until a hint of peppermint wafted up from the kettle.

When she went to return the packet to the cupboard, Curtis blocked her way. She ignored his lazy grin and moved around him to slide open the drawer and replace the tea. She had to think of a way to defuse the tension between them. Something he would not expect.

Rachel wrapped her arm around his upper arm, instead of his elbow. "Come, escort me to the sofa, General."

Curtis's grin grew to a smile. He adjusted her grip on his arm, fully and ridiculously flexing the muscle, and marched her across the room. She dropped his arm as soon as they reached the tea service, her stomach once again doing cartwheels.

Rachel realized her predicament as soon as Mrs. Glenn entered the room with Alice and looked about for a place to sit. If Curtis escorted her to the sofa, he would settle beside her. Walking past him again would have been a better blunder, over much faster.

Rachel waited to see if he would move away and find another seat. Alice was already settled comfortably on a chair near the fireplace. Perhaps he might join his sister. Mrs. Glenn found a chair near a book table. She could wait no longer. He was a true gentleman, and he would not sit until she did. Rachel sighed and lowered herself onto the sofa in front of the tea service. Curtis sat beside her, as she knew he would.

Very well. Perhaps she could use this nearness to persuade him to spare Alice and herself. Every time she looked at Curtis, he beamed at her. That needed to stop immediately. No one should talk seriously, or fall in love, unless they had a cup of tea in one hand and a plate of cake in the other. He was trying to do both without having either.

She poured the fresh peppermint tea into cups, stirred in sugar for herself, Mrs. Glenn, and Alice, and passed cups around. She spooned extra honey into Curtis's cup of steaming tea. The look of adoration on his face was an immense overreaction to the simple gesture. Tea should not warrant undying affection, and yet a warm cup of it seemed to inspire absolute reverence in Curtis Loughton.

The tea paired perfectly with buttery, crisp shortbread squares and chocolate torte. Cook had prepared bread and butter sandwiches as well.

Once Curtis had cleared his plate and Alice held her warm cup between her hands, Rachel felt it was safe to begin the conversation. "Tell me why you don't want to go, dearest."

Rachel took a sip of the soothing tea. Comfort flowed through her, a warm and steadying force. It tingled and soothed, all at once.

"Curtis is aware of my reasons." Alice's grip on the blue and white porcelain teacup tightened.

"Yes, but I am not." Rachel smiled.

Beside her, Curtis shifted, bringing him closer to her. She tried to focus on the conversation, not on his presence beside her. He was entirely too close. Curtis tensed beside her.

"You have to confront it sometime. Birth can be beautiful, and most births are safe and uncomplicated. I need you to see that," he said.

Rachel slipped another slice of cake onto his plate and refilled his cup with steaming tea. It would be better if he could not talk but would simply listen right now.

"Shall I?" Mrs. Glenn's voice rang out from the corner. "If it's too hard, Alice, I'll tell her."

"Yes, please." Alice sipped her tea and relaxed her grip. She set down her cup, then picked it up again immediately, cradling it with both hands.

Mrs. Glenn gazed over their heads, as if she could see someone who was not there, a phantom from the past. Her voice was uncharacteristically quiet and gentle. "Lady Jane and I were old friends, dear friends. I remember getting the letter, even now. I can see the handwriting." She paused. "Your father's hand was shaky, the ink running over the paper, the words scribbled in haste. 'Jane has passed. Please help me with Alice. I don't know what to do.'"

Curtis handed the plate to Rachel, and she set it down. He picked up a teacup but did not drink. He sat, his eyes unfocused, with his hand frozen in midair. Rachel took the teacup from his unmoving hands and set it on a saucer.

Mrs. Glenn continued. "Jane had passed in childbirth. When I arrived, her lady's maid told me the whole story. No one else could. No one else knew."

Alice had a hand pressed to her mouth.

"Alice witnessed the delivery—her father and brother were gone for the afternoon, and she refused to leave her mother's side, no matter how hard the servants tried. She insisted on staying to help her mother, along with the lady's maid, but the doctor could not arrive in time. There were complications, and both Lady Jane and the child did not survive," Mrs. Glenn said, her voice choking with emotion. "Alice doesn't want to attend births because they remind her of her mother's death and the loss of her younger sister. She was but seven years old at the time."

Rachel tried to convey sympathy in her voice, since Alice was across the room. "I'm sorry. I did not know how either of your parents died."

Beside her, Curtis hunched forward, cradling his head in his hands.

"Their father died about a year and a half ago, while the colonel served in the Crimea. It left Alice alone with me while her brother was in Constantinople." Mrs. Glenn's usual reserve had left her. Pain was etched in every line of her face. "Watching him lose his strength, nursing him through his pain, being with him when he died, was too much for Alice. She's sworn off sickrooms. I can't believe she agreed to come here or help with this school. She's an angel."

Curtis covered his eyes, rubbing his hand across his forehead.

"And the colonel missed the funeral." Mrs. Glenn closed her book and set it on the side table. "He's never recovered from that. Thinks he has to save everyone now, because he could not save his father. Miss Alice has done everything you've ever asked, but this requires too much of her, Colonel. She's not like you."

Curtis's shoulders shook.

Rachel knew he felt emotions deeply and could not fathom how much pain he must have felt when his father died. He'd been orphaned, left alone without any parents, and given all the responsibility for his sister. She, too, knew the pain of a father's passing, but she still had a mother who loved her deeply.

Alice watched her, as if hungry for someone to understand.

Rachel took a deep breath. "Dr. Morrow came one day to check on my mother's progressing symptoms. My father took me outside to play while they spoke, and he wanted to watch me climb our favorite oak tree. When I reached the top and looked over the grounds, Papa laid collapsed in the dirt. I slid down and ran for Dr. Morrow, but it was too late."

She turned to Curtis. "I vowed I would never climb again, but my mother insisted. When no one was around on the estate, she would take me to the old oak tree. We used Papa's old stopwatch, and she timed me until I knew I could always race down to her."

Curtis uncovered his eyes. Moisture glistened at the edges. He wiped it away. "That's why you beat me on the ropes."

She nodded. "Whenever I miss Papa, I climb into the oak and think of him. Mama rings her bell from her bedroom window after a while, and she records my time. Every time."

Curtis and Alice both looked through her, as though their minds were in dark corners of the past. Rachel cleared her throat. "It is an impressive time, since you asked."

Curtis glanced at her and smiled briefly, then looked steadily at his sister. "I'm sorry. I thought attending another birth would help."

"Advance. Steady on. Never retreat," Alice said, smiling at him. "I cannot face it, though."

Curtis spoke to the floor. "I can't go to the birth alone. I'm sorry. I truly am, but I require assistance of some kind. I cannot do everything. What if there are complications?"

Rachel wrapped her fingers around the still-warm porcelain cup and took a long sip of the tea. This was the heart of nursing: easing others' pain, whether it was the patient or her fellow practitioner. "Of course I'll go with you, Curtis, if Alice cannot." In the thickness of the pain, there was no room for flirtation or pretense.

Somewhere, a woman in poverty would give birth unaided, unless they aided her. Rachel could not leave Curtis to face the prospect alone, especially since he had mostly theoretical knowledge, and she was the one experienced in delivering children.

Alice glanced over. "There's more." She set her cup on its saucer, its contents undrunk.

"Go ahead, dearest," Rachel said. "Tell me your True Confessions. Pretend as though Lucy and Eleanor were here. Ignore your brother. Mrs. Glenn and I are listening. We may discuss anything you would want to tell us, if he were not here."

Alice's chin trembled as she stared into her lap. "I cannot wed, because I cannot be a mother."

Curtis fidgeted beside Rachel. She felt him tense, ready to pounce. He would only frighten Alice into silence. Rachel shifted closer to him, her hip and leg barely touching his, her shoulder gently pushing his back against the sofa with the smallest amount of pressure. She meant to shield Alice from him and block her from his view, while disarming the colonel. He responded to her presence instantly. She could feel him relax back into the cushions again. She kept her gaze on Alice, though intently aware of every minute movement of the man beside her.

"When you say you cannot," Rachel began, "do you mean that a doctor deemed you physically unable to deliver a child or that you face emotional obstacles?"

Alice stirred the untouched tea in her cup. "The latter."

Rachel sensed Curtis trying to talk. He shifted his weight forward, and his body tensed again. She rested her hand atop his, then applied the gentlest amount of pressure. Alice would not notice the gesture. He turned toward her in shock. She subtly shook her head and let go of his hand.

"Of course, dearest," Rachel said.

Alice's eyes filled with tears. "I've been so afraid to tell you, Curtis. I thought you would call me ridiculous."

Rachel caught his eye and nodded her head toward Alice. Curtis stared at her. Rachel jerked her head in his sister's direction again. Finally, his eyes widened.

He left the sofa and crossed the room to comfort Alice. He put an arm around her shoulders and looked at Rachel, a question in his eyes.

Rachel nodded and subtly mimicked a hug. Curtis bent down to hug his sister, and Alice began to cry.

Curtis stared at Rachel, wide-eyed, over Alice's shoulder. He seemed to have no idea what to say.

"A mother does so much more than just deliver her child," Rachel said. "Childbirth has its dangers, but most women survive. I understand your fears, and I will not ask you to attend any births."

Alice let go of Curtis. He rubbed the back of his neck. "I hate to see you give up marriage and a full life because of your worries. You have a tender heart, and you need someone to love you."

"Thank you for understanding, all of you. I'm quite over-whelmed. Will you excuse me? I want to write some memories of Mama in my new journal." Alice gave her brother another hug and left the room.

Curtis blew out a long breath. He settled back into the chair by the fireplace where Alice had been.

"I shall check on your sister," Mrs. Glenn said, smiling gently. "I cannot feel at ease unless I am by her side right now. Perhaps I can fill her ink for her as she writes or tell her my own memories."

Curtis nodded to her. "Thank you, Mrs. Glenn."

Alice's chaperone left the drawing room quickly. She tripped over her own gown in her haste. She righted herself and hurried out of the room. Her footsteps echoed through the corridor.

"Well done," Rachel said. She doubted Alice would write a single line. She and Mrs. Glenn could talk about her mother for hours, and Alice could cry as much as she liked in private now.

"I nearly told Alice she was ridiculous," Curtis said quietly. He scrubbed a hand over his face, tussling his thick brown hair.

"Yes." Rachel watched him. How she'd known, she couldn't say, but she could almost hear what he'd say.

It frightened her that she knew him so well, anticipated his thoughts, knew exactly where the hair would stand up when he ran his fingers through it. She fought the urge to run her own hands through it, smooth the tangles, unknot his pain.

"That could have gone so wrong," Curtis said. "If you hadn't been here, it would have been a disaster. I would have stormed around and insisted she come. I don't know what these 'True Confessions' are, but thank you for persuading her to confide in you at last."

"I cannot tell you any other True Confessions. They are a tradi-tion, among friends, and we never betray a trust. Once you have been admitted to the secret, you must keep it."

Curtis inclined his head. "I am honored to be allowed into your confidence."

"I wonder if *you're* hurting as much as your sister is," Rachel said.

Curtis searched her face intently. She realized she'd said too much, delved too far into his life, and allowed him too far into her own. She should *not* get involved in his feelings.

Her mouth twitched. She hated that it did that anytime she felt a twinge of emotion she could not subdue. It did not matter whether she was nervous or scared or happy.

"May I refill your tea?" Rachel asked.

"It's the hardest part of being a doctor," Curtis said. "They don't teach you this at *Herr* Fliedner's Institute."

"How to take tea with your patients?" Rachel tried to infuse some levity back into the conversation.

Curtis returned to Rachel and settled beside her. He spoke so quietly that she could barely hear him. "How to treat their minds and their hearts, Rachel, not their bodies. What am I going to do for my sister? She must marry. She cannot live with me forever. I want her to live a full life with family and children. I cannot allow fear to rob her of happiness."

He covered his eyes with his arm again.

"She is strong, Curtis," Rachel said.

He uncovered his eyes and looked at her, lost and unanchored, the weight of his care drowning him.

"She will heal someday. Your love and acceptance do more for her than any pushing or fighting ever will," Rachel said.

"Do they?" Curtis leaned toward her. "Would that change her mind?"

Alarm bells rang in her head. Alice's situation was too similar to her own, and now he stared at her with a mixture of hope and fear in his eyes. *Is it for himself or his sister?*

"You are a good brother to her." Rachel stood, trying to signal to Curtis that it was time for him to leave. "And a good doctor, one who considers the whole person, not just the illness."

"You do realize I can hear you this time," he said, smiling. "You're speaking well of me, and yet you know I am in the room."

Rachel shrugged. She walked to the doorway of the drawing

room. "I suppose I make mistakes on occasion."

"That's better," Curtis said. "I nearly thought you had developed a regard for me." He crossed the room to join her.

The hunger and need and pain in his eyes scared her.

She smiled. "We couldn't let you think that, could we, General? Alert me when the patient is ready, and I'll allow you to *assist me* at the birth." She included a hint of belligerence in her tone.

"That's the Rachel I know." Curtis's smile was natural and easy now, once their old rivalry was restored. "*I'll* supervise and *you'll* assist."

"You can supervise my supervision." She followed him to the front doorway, and they stood in the hallway together.

"I'm happy to inspect your performance." Curtis smiled appreciatively at her and raised an eyebrow. He took her hand and raised it to his lips.

Rachel's stomach tingled deliciously, and her breath caught. How did he always turn things to his advantage? She took her hand back, shaking it as if to erase the memory of his kiss. "Mind you keep your boots clean and your hands washed during that inspection. Pack your chloroform."

"You do admire me," Curtis said.

"Nonsense." Rachel put her hands on his chest and pushed him backward. How could he gather that from instructions to bring chloroform? "Leave. Go practice your rope climbing if you ever wish to best me." She began to close the door, decidedly *not* thinking about how firm and well-muscled his chest had felt beneath his coat.

Curtis put his foot in the door, his tiger-like eyes sparkling, more gold than green today. "Do you know? Your mouth twitches" —he grazed her cheek, her tell-tale cheek, lightly with his finger —"whenever I kiss you. I believe you really do admire me."

Rachel shoved the door closed, laid her back against it, and let out her breath. *He was right.* Had he observed her carefully enough to notice the mouth twitch? And now he knew that she enjoyed the kisses. Plural. More than one? First her cheek, and now her hand?

From now on, she would take care to hide her cheek whenever she was near him, and make sure he had no reason to kiss her again. Not her hand, or her cheek, or her lips.

She shook her head. *Never marry.* She'd sworn to never marry. Her mother needed her, many other sick women needed her, and she needed to avoid the kind of heartache that would come if she believed him. God wanted her to be a nurse, and she could not devote herself to two lives. She'd been called to this work, and marriage would only hamper her.

But even if she were tempted, she had to remember that men could not be trusted. He would change his mind when they returned to London. This was simply a ploy, and his behavior would change as soon as he was assured of her regard. He openly admitted as much. It was a campaign designed to win her affection.

Did she know the real man, or was it a mirage? Was this kind man real, or was he a hazy image, too good to be true, a trap to lure her forward? Once she went too far down the road, this perfect man would vanish. How would be behave once he believed she returned his affection? Would he treat her with disdain or lose interest?

He was persuasive, but he'd won over a woman every Season. She would not be another in his long list of triumphs. She could resist his charms, even if she did admire his many good qualities. How could she give up her promise to God for a bit of flattery? She enjoyed the attention. She like to banter with him. That was not a higher cause than caring for the sick.

She shook her head again. *Stop thinking about him.* He was probably smirking to himself right now, knowing that he'd left her in this state. She collapsed into a chair, haunted by the image of anguish and yearning in his eyes. Had she caused that pain for him?

Alice. She'd focus on someone else. Right now, Alice needed a friend to talk to.

And Rachel needed to talk with another woman who had no intention of ever marrying.

CHAPTER 6

Curtis recognized the scent of a man's cologne. *Confound it.* He scanned Rachel's drawing room. Had Alice invited guests? She had sent him an invitation for dinner. Mrs. Glenn insisted his sister prepare to keep house for him during the upcoming Season.

But had she gone that far? Kempton had arrived before him. Perhaps he had taken to wearing an archaic scent. No one except his grandfather wore *Albany* or *Mayfair*. Hardly any of his acquaintances wore cologne. Well, Shelford had that distinctive bay rum scent.

It had to be *Albany*. He'd bet his life on it. How many of the older officers favored that scent? The smell took him back to countless Army councils discussing the Scutari hospital. It almost made him sick as images of dying men, filth, and excrement flashed in his mind.

Alice, Rachel, Mrs. Glenn, and Kempton were in the room together, so why was Rachel huddled alone in the corner with a letter? Had she turned her back to him, or was he imagining it?

Curtis strode across the room. "Good evening, all. Rachel?"

She startled. Was she attempting to hide her letter? He could see her clutching it to her chest. The scent of *Albany* hung thickly around her.

"Letter?" Curtis asked. He slipped into the chair beside her, where he often sat to copy notes in the evening.

"Yes," Rachel said. She began refolding it, taking great care to sandwich the two sheets together. Her folds were meticulous, following each crease.

He watched her hands ply the paper with the skill of a practiced correspondent. She had dressed for dinner in a simple, but elegant gown, as always. She kept her face half-hidden, and he couldn't tell if she was smiling or not. Had she deliberately left the oil lamps unlit this evening? Why would she sit in semi-darkness to read?

"From home?" Curtis shifted his chair to the side, trying to get a better view of her face. The letter had to be drenched in cologne. The writing desk smelled like an old club, and it most definitely radiated from the paper she had hidden.

"Yes." Rachel finished creasing the letter, slipping it beneath the blotter on the writing desk. It was tight, tidy, contained. As inaccessible as Rachel. One look at her face, and he knew she would not let him read it. She pushed back her chair and walked to the window. She drew aside the curtain and gazed outside.

Curtis followed her. The formal evening dresses were a stark contrast to the day dresses she wore to the nursing school. Even with a shawl draped gently around her shoulders, Rachel looked equal to any woman among the *beau monde*. Superior. She held herself so dignified, so nobly, so serene. The dress's sleeves fell off the shoulders, revealing her neck and far too much else.

He followed her gaze outside the window. Better to focus there. There was nothing extraordinary beyond the windowpane: dusky twilight and the half-timber buildings across the way. Streetlamps flared intermittently in the darkness. They watched a young man climb a ladder, lift a pole, and light each lamp along the street.

"What news?" His stomach rumbled with hunger. How long would Alice wait to have dinner served?

"The usual." Rachel stared out into the black depths of evenfall.

Curtis felt his temper rising. "Who else wrote to you?"

Rachel turned to him. "Pardon?" Her icy glare warned him not to continue questioning her.

He wanted to persist, but he waited for an answer. Her elusive beauty haunted him. So distant. Out of reach, yet immediately beside him.

Rachel's arms stiffened. She always held herself so tightly when she tried to control her emotions. Well, she was wise, and he was not. He needed to know.

"While you are in Europe, I am responsible for you, as well as Alice and Mrs. Glenn. I've given my word to Shelford and Maldon. I've made arrangements with *Herr* Fliedner."

Her nostrils flared.

He knew he sounded pompous, but it was true. He would be accountable if any scandal occurred. It would not happen on his watch.

Curtis tried again. He lowered his voice, so that Kempton and the others would not hear. "If you are secretly corresponding with a man while unengaged, I wish you to tell me."

She continued to stare out at the street, her glare as icy as the frozen river below. A thought crashed into him. "*Are* you engaged?" Was that why she resisted his advances?

"I am not engaged to Dr. Morrow. Goodness, Curtis, you know me better than that." Rachel lifted her chin and met his gaze. "My letters are none of your affair."

He glanced aside at his sister. "Then why are you exchanging secret letters?" He kept his voice quiet, but firm. "If you and he are lovers—"

Rachel burst out laughing.

"How old is this doctor correspondent?" Curtis asked. Perhaps he had it all wrong.

Rachel returned her attention to the window. "A few years older than you, I imagine."

"Quite young, then." He did the math in his head. "Perhaps

thirty or thirty-two? How long has he been in practice in your neighborhood?" The perfect age to marry. *Double confound it.*

"Stop questioning me." Rachel's gaze seemed fixed on the evening stars, beginning to glimmer. "He is my mother's physician. We discuss her health."

"Is it common for a doctor to send scented letters to all his patients?" Curtis widened his stance and clasped his hands behind his back.

Rachel pursed her lips. "No more questions."

Curtis looked over her shoulder into the twinkling shadowland beyond the window. He drew a breath to speak.

Rachel turned to face him. Her eyes flashed with anger, but she spoke as pleasantly as ever. "Shall we join Alice?"

He hadn't expected her to treat him so politely, but this was Rachel. She would try to hide her anger. She would kill him with blandness and never let him speak his mind to her. She wanted no emotion, shown by her or spoken by him. She wanted everything as calm as the heavens outside, but his fears were raging, like comets with fiery tails shooting across the sky of his heart.

"No," Curtis hissed. "Not until you explain why you're hugging his letters to your chest and hiding them from me."

"Alice, I am absolutely famished. What divine dinner have you ordered for us this evening?" Rachel smiled up at him. That tight, false smile.

He narrowed his gaze. She took his arm, slipped hers through it, and said loudly, "What a gentleman your brother is." She tugged him forward and led him across the drawing room toward his sister.

Curtis seethed. She denied nothing. She hid everything. *This* was the real reason she had been so coy about marriage. She already loved another man. Of course it was another doctor.

Hadn't her friends said she spent time with Dr. Morrow? No, Rachel herself had told him that. She went on house calls alone with the man, just the two of them.

Curtis knew he'd regret his words or his actions unless he

reined them in. He clamped his jaw shut and did his best to return an artificial smile when Alice asked whether he was ready to eat.

"How shall I pair them, Mrs. Glenn?" Alice asked. "Who has precedence? Oh, I'll make a muddle of this. I'm too young. Why can't *you* run his household?"

Mrs. Glenn smiled kindly. "I am not part of your family."

"You're as good as," Alice said. "Been with me since I was born."

Mrs. Glenn patted her hand. "Yes, but precedence depends on blood and titles and a little bit of—" She looked between Rachel and Curtis. "Well, you'll need to take other factors into consideration when you pair couples to walk into dinner."

Kempton stood idly by. Mrs. Glenn collared him. "Mr. Kempton, for example."

"What have I done?"

Curtis laughed. "We'd like to know."

Mrs. Glenn dusted off his coat's lapels. "He's a decent dinner companion. Pair him with someone quiet. You consider not only rank, but desirability."

Kempton mocked an affronted look. "I'm merely decent? I'm more desirable than that."

Mrs. Glenn took Rachel by the wrist. "Miss Wickford's father was a Member of Parliament, am I correct?"

Rachel seemed to forget her anger. A look of surprise flitted across her face before her usual mask of calm descended again. "Yes."

"So, she is nearly equal to most ladies of rank. Higher than a mere gentleman's daughter, certainly, but a reserved dinner companion. You'd want to pair her with a more talkative gentleman."

"Please," Rachel said, and smiled. "Mrs. Glenn is correct, but you needn't worry about my status. I'll go in last to every dinner. I'm well aware that I have little social standing. It's of no concern to me. You may pair your other friends and give them more precedence if we ever eat together in London."

Curtis turned to her. "If?" The prospect of returning to London lost any charm for him.

"Will you not dine with us frequently?" Alice looked distressed. "How am I to manage the conversation without you?"

"You'll have Mrs. Glenn and Mr. Kempton, a decently desirable dinner companion. I daresay you'll manage." Rachel bit her lip.

Curtis wanted to tease her. He wanted to ask whether he was a desirable dinner companion, but he thought of the letter sitting on the desk behind them. He crossed his arms. Would Rachel really return to London when they finished classes, or would she marry Dr. Morrow? Why had she agreed to help Miss Nightingale?

And how often would he see her, once they returned to London?

Mrs. Glenn took his arms and uncrossed them. "And then you have your brother. He'll sit at the foot of the table. Regardless of his excellent conversation skills, pair him with the woman of most significance."

"Poor man," he heard Kempton mutter. Kempton exchanged a glance with Rachel, and she coughed. Or was she swallowing a laugh?

"It is true," Mrs. Glenn said, "that the colonel may undertake a great many dull conversations with matrons and scheming mothers. As head of the household, it is his duty."

"I've faced death. I can handle another Season," Curtis muttered.

Rachel laughed. "And you wonder why I wish to avoid the dinner parties, dear Alice. Your own brother compares them to a death march in the Army."

Alice's face dropped. How would she ever manage his household? It did not suit her personality. He needed a wife. He needed Rachel, for Alice's sake, as well as his own.

"Yours will be the talk of the *ton*," Mrs. Glenn said. "Now, let us go in to dinner."

"Yes. Curtis, if you'll accompany Rachel. Kempton, if you'll accompany me. Oh, dear."

Mrs. Glenn nodded. "You see, Miss Wickford, I shall go in last to every dinner, not you."

"But you are married and widowed. I am unmarried. Should you not precede me?" Rachel looked between Alice and Mrs. Glenn.

Mrs. Glenn shooed her toward Curtis. "But there is an element of choice for a hostess. Of course she may wish to pair the unmarried people together."

Curtis extended his arm to Rachel. She didn't move. He must have pushed her too far, if she refused to walk in with him.

"But surely you take precedence. Was not your husband also a Member of Parliament?"

Mrs. Glenn gestured toward Alice. "But your hostess has paired you, and you must graciously go in with the colonel."

"Your *highly* desirable dinner companion," Kempton said.

Rachel's mouth twitched.

Forget the country doctor. He could send all the letters he wanted. Dr. Morrow was far away in Essex, and Curtis was right here in front of her. He had the advantage, and she was not impartial to him. She thought him highly desirable.

Curtis threaded her arm through the crook of his elbow, and they led the way in to dinner. His stomach growled.

"Highly desirable," he whispered.

"Inexcusably impertinent," she whispered back.

"Decorated with military honors."

"Appallingly inquisitive." She stared straight ahead as they entered the dining room.

Curtis drew back her chair. As she seated herself and he pushed her chair in, he couldn't help bending over to whisper in her ear, "You are as radiant as the evening sky tonight."

He settled himself at the end of the table, smirking at her, as her look of anger was replaced by confusion. His sudden lack of antagonism had caught her off guard. *Steady on.* He had no intention of ceding the battle to this mystery doctor, whoever he was. Curtis had every advantage, and he would use all of them to discover more about his rival.

Blast. Curtis inspected the food on his plate, after serving Rachel and himself. None of his favorite foods, but all of the ones he disliked. He opened his mouth to complain, but just then a foot stepped on his.

Silk slippers hurt a surprising amount, with their thick leather soles.

He felt Rachel's eyes on him.

She jerked her head toward Alice and widened her eyes. When he didn't do anything, she mouthed something to him. He couldn't understand what she was saying. Rachel's mouth stretched into an unusually large smile. She turned and beamed at Alice.

"What a fine meal you've selected," Rachel said. "So many unusual delicacies. Ladies do not often get anchovies."

She turned back to Curtis and stared at him. Her cheekbones formed a natural line, defining the shape of her porcelain face. The softer candlelight in the room made her eyes slightly less angry than they had been in the drawing room. Her hair was drawn up in its usual intricately braided bun. Her mouth formed a perfect heart shape.

"Yes, indeed. What a selection of rare treats." Curtis smiled at his sister. "I cannot recall the last time I ate sardines. So...salty."

He knocked Rachel's foot with his boot. She choked on a sip, but recovered quickly. Two could play at this game.

After that, Rachel refused to engage in anything but trivial and tedious conversation during dinner, ignoring him completely. Evidently, she and Mrs. Glenn were sincere in their efforts to give Alice an authentic opportunity to prepare for the Season.

"And now you stand to signal to the other women that we shall leave for the drawing room. Catch the eye of the woman across the table from you as you rise. The colonel will then lead the men into the billiards room, or whatever room he wishes, where they will drink and smoke and behave abominably." Mrs. Glenn sniffed.

Alice stood. "Shall we excuse ourselves, ladies?"

Rachel waited for him. Curtis bent down as he drew back her chair, taking the chance to whisper, "You are as enchanting as the midnight moon."

She scowled at him as she rose. "And as fickle and ever-changing in its affections?"

She had him there. She was still smarting about his jealous accusations earlier. Perhaps the moon was the wrong comparison for her.

"The fixed and constant star in the heavens?" Curtis asked as Rachel walked past him without a glance. *And as distant and unobtainable, but I shall wish on my enchanting star, deuce take the blasted doctor. He can go to the—*

"You coming?" Kempton asked, a grin on his face.

Curtis shook his head to clear his thoughts. *Time for action.* "Why don't we join you, sister?" he asked in a voice loud enough to carry across the dining room. "I don't drink or smoke, and I hate billiards. Nasty habits only fit for a sailor. After dinner is tedium for me in London. I'm counting the minutes until I can return to you."

Alice turned and beamed at him from the doorway.

"He really doesn't drink," Kempton said. "Can't hold his liquor."

Curtis raised an eyebrow. "We don't need to go into the reasons *why* I don't drink."

Kempton doubled over in laughter. "Oh! The stories I could tell."

"But you won't." Curtis glared at him.

Kempton followed the women out of the dining room and into the hallway. "He can swear like a sailor when he drinks like one. Sing like one, too."

Curtis lengthened his pace to catch up to the others. "Shall we copy the day's notes, Rachel?" He was eager to restore the harmony between them and close the distance.

Now that he had eaten reasonable servings of every detestable dish on the table, he felt more like himself. They weren't delicious, but they quieted his stomach and allowed him to think.

She hadn't forgiven him for interrogating her, and he hadn't forgiven her for harboring hidden letters from another man, but he'd have to try another tactic to get a glimpse of the missive. He intended to know the contents one way or another, but he knew one thing. Rachel would not concede easily.

CHAPTER 7

Rachel tried to hide the letter she was composing, but it was difficult with Curtis attempting to read over her shoulder. Mr. Kempton argued about poetry across the room with Alice and Mrs. Glenn. Evidently, Mr. Shakespeare's sonnets and Mrs. Barrett Browning's sonnets were incomparable, and one must take sides. Kempton was staunchly on Mrs. Browning's side, while Alice and Mrs. Glenn argued for Shakespeare.

Curtis kept glancing at her paper. *The nerve of the toff*, to accuse her of a secret engagement.

"Do you require assistance?" She smiled sweetly at him.

Curtis met her eyes. His were so deep, with hints of green and brown now. "I can read your notes."

That wasn't all he wanted to read. He could hook it, and be off with him. Her private correspondence was, well, private. Rachel turned back to the cream and gold stationery from Florence. She began to write. *Dear Mama.*

A pen scratched on paper next to her. If Curtis would continue to copy the day's lecture into Miss Nightingale's journal, she could finally finish her letter. Christmas had nearly arrived, and she would miss Mama. They'd never been apart for the holiday, and to be spending months away from each other made Rachel question her decision to leave for Germany.

Can Mama handle the dizziness without me? Will the maids attend to her? She wanted to reread Dr. Morrow's letter about the new symptoms, but she knew it would draw attention. She'd never seen this jealous side of the colonel before, and he could be downright unpleasant. She'd been right to avoid giving her heart away, now that she saw the real man beneath the charming exterior. The domineering, controlling colonel who wanted to know every aspect of her business. *Dash it all*, not on her life.

She pushed away the anger to focus on the letter to Mama. A few more choice swear words ran through her mind. Must be Papa's cologne, reminding her of his extensive street vocabulary. As an orator, he felt it important to know the language and vernacular of every class in London, not just the gentleman. She smiled to herself. If Curtis knew the unladylike language with which she regarded him, would that scare him off? Perhaps she should let a few words slip sometime.

Do you wish me to visit home before the Season? I never thought to spend time in London. Where have you decided I shall live? We both know that you, Lucy's aunt Ellen, and Lady Barrington will decide my fate, not me. Hurry, quickly, before Lucy and Eleanor begin to barrage me with telegrams. I do hate to live on their charity, but I must board at one of their homes. Which shall it be?

Where shall I acquire dresses? You three must send me all the particulars of a fashionable wardrobe, again, before Lucy can take me in hand and buy it all for me.

She stopped writing. The scratching had stopped. She peeked sideways. The colonel's pen laid unused on the table.

Rachel shifted her body sideways and moved her arm to hide the paper.

As much as I love my dear friends, I prefer to pay for my gowns myself.

Curtis adjusted his position on his chair, shooting glances her way, as if to study her notes.

"Shall I read you the letter now, or do you prefer to wait until I finish?" Rachel asked. She pushed the sheet of stationery across to him.

"Oh, no, I can wait until you finish both," he said, pushing the letter back toward her. "I'm more interested in your letter to Dr. Morrow."

"Confound it." Rachel withdrew the letter from the corner of the desk's blotter.

The argument across the room ceased immediately, and Mr. Kempton arched an eyebrow at her. Rachel shot him a cool stare as she carefully separated the sheets of her mother's letter from the note Dr. Morrow had written.

Mr. Kempton turned his attention back to Alice, and the argument resumed.

She handed the detailed description of her mother's health to Curtis. "Go read the blasted letter and leave me alone."

Curtis grinned as he took the sheet of paper. He liked it when she swore. Of course he did.

Rachel blew out a breath. *Insufferable swell*. She tried to concentrate on finishing her letter, but Curtis didn't leave. He stayed beside her, reading carefully.

Rachel bent over her letter. *I'm sure Eleanor will want to buy them in Paris, as the Duke of Woodford has invited us to visit the embassy.*

She tried to imagine what else her mother would want to know.

I've never enjoyed myself more. Classes are thorough, and I love learning about each subject in so much detail.

But she missed her mother.

I shall hasten to return to you as soon as the Season ends, and Miss Nightingale's training course is completed. Or shall I visit you for Easter?

She bit her lip. What would it be like to stay in London? She glanced sideways at Curtis, still contemplating Dr. Morrow's thorough account. No, she already missed Mama.

With love, Rachel

She folded the note and began to consider how to respond to Dr. Morrow, with Curtis beside her.

"Decent chap," he said grudgingly, "for a country doctor. Knows a thing or two. Rummy old cove, he is." He set down the letter and crossed the room toward the sofas.

So he knew all the same vernacular as her father. He was a soldier, after all. She should have expected that.

Curtis settled himself onto the softest seat, stretching out his legs, crossing them at the ankles, and putting his hands behind his head. "Join me," he said. "Those chairs are the most uncomfortable in the room. Tea without sugar, they are."

"But the only ones near a writing table," Rachel said.

"Talk to me," Curtis said, smiling. "Write later."

"I'll join you, if you stop talking like a street rat." Rachel pushed her letter away. If she did not, he would only interrupt her anyway. She would get nothing done until he satisfied his wretched curiosity.

He closed his eyes and tipped his head against the wall. "You started it. I'm merely calling your bluff. Regular stunner, you are tonight." He opened his eyes to regard her dress appreciatively.

Rachel went to join him on the sofa. "By Jove, you're an ugly customer once you get started on the swear words."

Alice glanced over from her discussion, stopping mid-sentence.

"You were arguing the merits of a strict meter and rhyme scheme?" Rachel prompted her. "And do you agree, Mrs. Glenn?"

Mr. Kempton grinned. "She's called your bluff, Alice. We've been caught eavesdropping."

Alice's face pinked, and she turned back to Mr. Kempton and Mrs. Glenn.

Curtis grinned at her. "You know, I didn't think you could get any more beautiful, Rachel, until I heard you talking like a corned bloke." He sighed and put a hand over his heart. "I'm completely flummoxed."

"And you're acting half-rats like you've drunk a shandy-gaff. Stop wasting my time with this. I can talk circles around you. What did you want? I've got a letter to write."

Curtis couldn't look more lovestruck. Kempton laughed across the room.

"Blast it, Curtis! What did you want?"

He shook his head. "You are the most beautiful woman I've ever beheld. Tell me about your mother. When did the symptoms start?"

"That's better, you confounded toff. After she fell from our oak tree," Rachel said.

"I am in heaven. You have the voice of an angel." He closed his eyes and sighed. "Climbing with you, I presume?"

Rachel nodded her head, then realized his eyes were closed. If he liked the swearing, she would stop. "Yes, racing me, but she had to stop climbing after the fall. Instead, she began to time me with Papa's old watch after he died, trying to convince me not to stop climbing."

Curtis's chest stretched out beside her, an open invitation. She would fit so naturally. She folded her hands together in her lap, holding them tight.

"Initial symptoms?" he asked. His voice was serious now.

"Headaches. She slept a lot, kept forgetting things she used to know. The difficulty is that the symptoms began at the time that Papa died. I couldn't tell what was grief and what was a lingering effect for years. I still don't know."

"But now the dizziness, inability to change position easily. She's always had the pain?"

Rachel allowed herself to sit back, just a little, on the sofa. "Yes, even before the fall. The accident made it worse."

Curtis opened his eyes. He seemed surprised to find Rachel sitting beside him. He put his arms down and tried to sit up.

"Oh, stay comfortable," Rachel said.

He leaned forward, eyes blazing, his elbows on his knees. "What has been done?"

Rachel considered for a moment. "Powders for the headache. Laudanum at times for the pain or to aid sleeping, but she resists it. She prefers the clarity of mind that comes without it. Tea. A lot of tea."

"Has anyone helped her to stretch, move the muscles, loosen the areas of pain?" Curtis turned toward her. His deep, yet quiet voice rumbled in his chest, but soothed her. Like a gentle thundercloud. A quiet rainstorm on a warm spring afternoon. All the intensity concentrated and contained, but nonetheless powerful. She'd rarely seen this side of him: the focused, concerned physician. Not a trace of the clown from a few minutes earlier.

"Shall we install a gymnasium for her?" Rachel teased.

Curtis shrugged. "Yes, or a few pulleys at least. There is more that could be done, if I could speak with her myself and assess her surroundings."

"You are too kind," Rachel said. The last thing she needed was to bring him home to meet her mother. Mama would jump to conclusions, and Curtis would get more deeply involved in her life. "You could send instructions to Dr. Morrow. I can include them in my letter."

"Why didn't you tell me his blasted letter carried no hint of cologne?" He grinned at her and shifted on the sofa to face her. They were only inches apart and his broad chest had again become an open invitation. "It was your mother's letter, wasn't it?"

Rachel left the sofa and returned to the hard wooden chair by the writing desk. "My father wore *Albany*. She still has his bottle of cologne."

Curtis crossed the room and put a hand on her shoulder. "It is a wretched scent. He had terrible taste."

Curtis searched her face. "You understand that her illness is not your fault, simply because you were with her when she fell. Nor are you responsible for your father's death, because you were with him when he passed. You did not cause her pain, and you do not have to cure her. She chose to climb your oak because she loves you, and she wanted to help you when you were grieving. She would not want you to grieve further on her behalf."

Rachel felt dangerously close to tears. She shrugged his hand off, even though she enjoyed the comforting warmth and weight.

"You agree, though. The scent is awful." He settled himself and resumed copying notes.

She turned her back to him. "Never speak ill of the dead."

"My father wore *Mayfair*. Hate that odor, too." Curtis nudged her. "Admit it. You loved your father, but you hate his cologne, even if I saw you hugging that letter."

"I did not hug it." Rachel took out a sheet of ordinary paper to write to Dr. Morrow.

Curtis's pen began moving at a fast pace. Finally. He was working.

"You hugged it and hid it. Admit it," Curtis said. "You were probably coughing on the confounded odor."

She glanced over her shoulder. His head was hunched low over the journal, copying notes precisely, but efficiently.

"Truth be told, I prefer the scent of shaving soap," Rachel said, studying Curtis. "You have a beard again already, and it's only eight o'clock at night."

He kept his head low over the journal. "More evidence of my highly desirable status as a dinner partner." He straightened. "Do you like the smell of *my* shaving soap?"

She pinked and returned to her letter writing. "I hardly know what it smells like."

"You turned away on purpose, so I could not see you lie." Curtis put down his pen, left his chair and confronted her. "Tell me. Look me in the eyes and tell me what my shaving soap smells like."

"Kempton!" Rachel called. "Your highly desirable friend needs to go exercise in the gymnasium. He's pestering me. Will you please take him away?"

"Ha!" Curtis grinned at her. "You do know. You love cedar and lavender, do you not? Look me in the eyes and tell me I am wrong. Have I flummoxed you?"

Rachel turned her head. Curtis moved to the side. She moved her head the other way. He moved with her. She put her head down and bit her lip. He bent down to try to catch her eye. Finally she burst out laughing.

"Very well! It is *your* shaving soap that I like!" Rachel said, between gasps. "Will you leave me in peace to write my letter? Kempton! Hook it, why have you not taken this man away yet? He needs some exertion on the rope ladder. Have you not purchased boxing gloves yet? Give him a good slating."

Curtis lowered his voice. "You do admire me. Admit it. You said I am highly desirable."

"Dash it all, I enjoy *your* shaving soap. The *scent* is highly desirable. That is all I will admit." Rachel resumed writing to Dr. Morrow.

Kempton and Curtis laughed as they left the drawing room. She yelled after them. "Better yet, bare knuckles, Kempton! No boxing gloves today."

Curse that twitch. She needed to find a better way to disguise her feelings. Better yet, she needed to stop feeling them before she spent time any more time with the colonel.

And curse her cursing. She really should not let her temper loose or allow herself to speak so naturally. It had been a long time since she had spoken so freely with anyone, and of course, it only encouraged the colonel.

Word had arrived from the Institute that their patient was due to deliver her child any day, and Rachel knew she could not withstand an entire afternoon and evening alone with Curtis. The last time they had attended a birth, he had broken down in tears.

Every time she accompanied a midwife or doctor, she wondered at the beauty of the birth. It took all her training to focus on the mother and not get swept away in the emotion of the moment.

She'd have to keep Curtis occupied with other tasks: firewood, water, cleaning the home. Perhaps he'd be busy in other parts of the house, or he could spend time with the husband. Otherwise, they'd find themselves in a precariously intimate setting together.

When he'd looked at her with such compassion and concern tonight, she'd felt her resolve slipping. It was one thing to resist him on her own, but when he cared for her mother and spoke with such insight and gentleness, how could she withstand his draw?

She'd have to take things firmly in hand when the time came, make sure they were as far apart as possible, and focus on the mother giving birth, because if she dwelled on Curtis's kindness toward her own mother, she might forget all her resolutions and begin to fall in love.

CHAPTER 8

The hired carriage rattled over cobblestones toward Mombach as icy winds raged through the streets. Curtis tucked another wool blanket over Rachel's legs. "Is the brick still warm?"

"Stop fussing," she said.

"Men don't fuss." He secured the blanket. "Another brick? You may have mine."

Rachel laughed. "You always fuss."

"Will we arrive in time?" Curtis kicked the brick from beneath his feet and slid it toward her, then rearranged the blankets to keep it in place.

"They never call us early enough. Thank you." She eyed him. "I am quite warm, but you're shivering."

"Men don't feel cold," Curtis said. He pulled his coat around himself and blew into his hands. "Delivering a child in this blasted weather. I wonder how poor they are."

"Quite poor, if they can only afford the services of the Institute. Bless him, *Herr* Fliedner does so much good." Rachel snuggled into her blankets.

Curtis couldn't help the cold that penetrated his bones on this winter day, but Rachel's goodness and charity evoked a tenderness in him. A different kind of warmth settled into his heart.

"Stop looking at me like that," Rachel said. "Tell me about our patient."

"Thank you for braving the freezing wilds of the Black Forest to play midwife to some peasant that London society wouldn't recognize. They'd rather her child, her brat, drown in the Thames simply because they are poor." His voice choked.

"Curtis." Rachel's eyes sparked with defiance. "You're already crying, and the delivery hasn't even begun. We'll need more firewood than ever, if they have it, and plenty of rags. She'll require nourishing food. I've mixed some teas."

"Naturally, you made your own remedies for her." He could not imagine a better woman in the world. Who would spend Christmas Eve delivering a stranger's child?

"Confound it. I warned you. No more looks." Rachel glared at him.

Curtis arched an eyebrow. "Which of us sounds like a sailor?" He loved to banter with her and finally he was able to provoke some sort of response. "How can you assist me if I do not look at you?"

Curtis noticed every detail of her appearance. Her meticulously braided bun, carefully pinned up. Elegant, but practical, like Rachel. Her thoughtful, intelligent eyes, dancing with fire right now, but capable of so many emotions. And that heart-shaped mouth. His eyes lingered there for a moment.

Her face returned to its impassive mask. Rachel shifted on the seat, drawing the blankets up around her. "It may be a long night. I shall rest. Will you let me know when we arrive?"

Curtis watched her pretending to sleep. Avoiding his attention, really. He would bet that there were tinctures and syrups of her own making, as well as the loose tea blends carefully created. No other woman of the aristocracy even deigned to treat nursing with respect, save Miss Nightingale, and Rachel embraced it with her whole heart.

If only she would embrace him.

Steady on. Soldier on.

The carriage rocked gently as it made its way on the cobblestone streets. Streetlights flashed past, and a steady stream of moonlight filled one side of the interior.

Curtis tugged at the curtains to shield Rachel from the light, if she truly meant to sleep. Minutes passed, and he watched her head slowly droop. They rounded a curve and the path beneath them changed from cobblestone to pebbles.

I wonder how far it is. Curtis pondered how to wake Rachel before they arrived at the dwelling. It could be two more minutes or twenty. He had no idea.

He slid onto the seat beside her, studying the elaborate folds of her braided bun. What would her hair look like without the pins and braids and folds? He cleared his throat. "Rachel."

She blinked and looked around, disoriented. Perhaps she had taken a short nap after all. She closed her eyes, let her head droop onto his shoulder, and fell back asleep.

Curtis froze. *Does she know what she's doing?* He held his breath. Rachel didn't wake. He relaxed. Her head slid from his shoulder onto his chest, and she shifted to snuggle against him. Her blankets slid down to her lap, exposing her to the cold air of the carriage.

Definitely asleep. He stretched out his legs and crossed them at the ankles. He rested an arm lightly around Rachel and tucked the blankets around her. Her head rested on his chest, as natural as if they'd been married a thousand years. The steady rocking motion of the carriage tempted him to doze, just for a moment.

He allowed himself to relax. Rachel rested beside him, completely at peace, and the rightness of it all made his eyelids heavy. He let sleep overtake him.

Curtis heard a gasp, and something hard hit his chest. A hand. Rachel, pushing herself up. "What?" He heard the carriage door open and metal steps crunch as they hit the snow.

He looked around. Rachel sat beside him, eyes wide, staring.

"Nothing." She smiled a small, tight smile. "We have arrived."

Blast. He must have fallen asleep. It was so warm, with Rachel on his chest and the blankets covering both of them. How long had the carriage ride taken?

She wanted to pretend like that didn't happen. Very well. For now. A woman waited inside to deliver her child. He could save the entertainment for later, and quarrel about it when they rode home.

Curtis gathered his doctor's bag, pulled his wool coat around himself, and waited for Rachel to descend the steps of the carriage. Empty farm fields stretched in every direction. The family had carved a path through the thick snow to the door of the humble cottage. The entire dwelling was smaller than their drawing room gymnasium.

"Children don't wait for Christmas," he said in German, after introducing himself to the father and other children. "Please, take us to your wife."

But Rachel had already forged ahead, finding the tiny bedroom. She had arranged her things. He knew that look in her eyes. She was about to give him orders.

"Water. Wood. What else do you want?"

"Start with that, please." Rachel turned back. "Last time we both spoke English. My German has only progressed so far. I may need you to translate, if you'd be so good as to return every so often."

Curtis saluted her. "Yes, General."

She bit her lip, then turned back to attending the patient, who introduced herself as Bettina. Her husband, a farmer, met Curtis at the door of the bedchamber and issued instructions in German. The two men and the carriage driver, Frank, rushed to build up fires, boil water, and find rags.

"What else?" he asked when they finished. He was eager to check on his patient, be sure the labor progressed naturally.

"She's fine for now," Rachel said, guarding the entrance to the room.

Curtis could hear the children fighting in the other room. "Excuse me."

The father slumped in a chair. Frank sat awkwardly in the cramped room that functioned as kitchen, dining room, and drawing room.

"Long day?" Curtis asked.

The father nodded.

"Do your children like the snow?"

He nodded again.

"Let's go. Everybody out. Now." He used his strongest, most commanding voice. Four young boys looked up at him. Two were punching each other while the other two wrestled on the floor in front of the fireplace. "How can your mother give birth with all this noise? You need exercise. Outside. Get your coats."

The boys stared at him. "It's dark and cold. Papa?"

Their father pointed toward the door. "Go."

Curtis prodded and pushed and got them outside. He gestured to Frank to accompany him. Dusk had not yet faded on the empty fields. Perhaps the boys were also hungry. He'd find dinner for them next. Just then, a snowball hit him squarely in the back. He turned. "Who's the sharpshooter?"

The boys laughed. Curtis packed a loose snowball, nothing that would hurt too much but would make a spectacular explosion. Again and again, he methodically piled the snowballs while the boys watched him with a mixture of terror and awe.

He roared. "Attack!" He pitched the snowballs in every direction, making sure to hit all four boys. Just as he'd hoped, snow erupted in great puffs of white.

Frank took aim and hit him squarely in the face.

"Traitor!" Curtis returned a snowball at Frank.

Soon, the boys were pelting him from all directions. He dodged and evaded them, but with his height, he made an easy target. He made sure to fall dramatically every time they hit him.

After an hour or so, when his wool coat was finally drenched and the light had entirely faded from the twilight sky, he held up his hands. "I surrender." He took the smallest and put him on his shoulders, while Frank carried another boy on his shoulders. The boys cheered as they led them into the house.

While the boys changed into their clothes for sleeping, Curtis crept into the bedchamber.

"You make more noise than all four boys combined," Rachel whispered to him, glancing sideways.

"You could hear us?" He stripped off his coat. He'd meant to give Bettina some quiet, not merely move the source of the noise.

"Coat and boots outside," Rachel said. "Not in here."

He stepped outside the bedchamber and undressed down to his shirt sleeves. He folded the rest and set them beside the door. He took off his boots.

"Wash," Rachel said.

Curtis washed his hands and returned.

"The boys need dinner," he said. "They're ready for bed, but I suspect they're hungry, and Frank needs dinner as well. He found a small stable in the back for the carriage."

"You stay with her. I'll see what I can do. I brought some food in a basket for the family and ourselves." Rachel left the woman's side and came over to him.

"Of course you did." He gazed at her.

She put a hand on her hip.

Curtis shook his head. "I'm sorry. No looks. I meant to help the father," Curtis said. "He and I can feed the children."

Rachel cocked her head to the side and stared up at him. "Do you know how to prepare a meal? I don't mean it unkindly."

He crossed the room. "I can tear a loaf of bread into pieces as well as the next man. I did feed myself in the Army without you."

Rachel put her other hand on her other hip. "Surviving is not thriving."

"Perhaps you'll be more useful to him," Curtis said. "I'd like a chance to talk to Bettina, anyway."

Rachel left the room, and he settled onto the chair where she had been to observe the *Frau*. Normal, healthy signs so far, but the delivery had come earlier than expected, and she seemed quite large. He stoked the fire, drew the curtains tight, and began to observe the birthing pains.

Bettina was an experienced mother. She knew something was different about this pregnancy, having delivered four other children, and she had sacrificed to scrape together the sum for a doctor from the Mainz Deaconess Institute.

Her labor seemed as normal as the last birth Curtis had witnessed, except that Bettina wanted to regale him with stories in between her birthing pains.

Rachel returned in an hour, handing him a plate with thick slices of bread, cheese, and some slices of ham. He hadn't realized how hungry he was until the food was in front of him. Rachel thought of everything, even mustard for the ham.

She had warm tea for Bettina and another cup for him. Silence descended on the household. "Now we can get down to work," Rachel said.

Bettina began to question him, now that he had returned. Her pains had intensified and grown closer together. In between bites, he simply told her, "Twins."

Bettina rubbed her stomach, her eyes wide with surprise. "Really?" She collapsed against the pillows.

Curtis nodded, his mouth too full to answer.

Rachel's face grew serious. "Why didn't anyone warn us?" She brushed the hair from Bettina's eyes and held her hand as another pain passed.

"Has anyone seen her, or is this her only visit from a doctor?" He sighed. "The world needs more trained nurses from the Upper Class as well as the middle and lower classes. We need more women willing to help. Miss Nightingale's work is vital. My grandfather has financed this venture, supported Miss Nightingale, and sent me here. Thank you. When the other debutantes see you, this will erase some stigma."

Rachel was the epitome of perfection, the bravest and fiercest woman he had ever known. Confound it, he was looking at her again, and now she was avoiding his lovesick gaze. At least, he assumed it looked that way.

"That is the plan," she said lightly, glancing around the room. "But we both know it will take years to change Society's views, and I'm not likely to be welcomed everywhere I go."

Curtis searched her face. The firelight flickered on her profile. If she would just marry him, no one would turn her away. Every door in Society would be open to her. They could do so much good together. They believed in the same goals.

She turned back toward him. "I warned you to stop looking at me," Rachel said. "Go wash something. Eat your dinner." She turned her attention back to Bettina.

They worked all evening as the labor progressed. Rachel took charge, as he knew she would, but her views aligned with his. They'd studied together, they experienced it before, and they had discussed it at length. Last time, he felt helpless, like he didn't know what to do, and she had turned to the other women who attended the birth. This time, he had read everything *Herr* Fliedner recommended and brought the chloroform. He was determined to be useful.

"How is the pain? Do you want the medicine?" he asked Bettina.

She stared at him. "What medicine?"

Curtis took out the chloroform and allowed a few drops to saturate a cloth. He held it near her face. "It makes the birth easier. It will not hurt you or the child."

She scoffed. "I've had four boys. Why do I need medicine?"

Rachel gently wiped her forehead with a cloth. She spoke in the basic German she was beginning to learn. "It doesn't hurt. Hurts less." She looked up at Curtis. "She doesn't want it?"

Curtis shook his head. "She's never heard of it."

Rachel took the cloth from him and mimicked taking a deep breath. She exaggerated a sigh of relief. "Aaaah. Like sleep."

Bettina's limbs stiffened as a pain seized her body. "Yes," she said, looking at Rachel.

Rachel handed the cloth back to Curtis, who held it in front of her. Not too much, or she'd fall unconscious. Just enough. Bettina took deep breaths, glancing at Rachel, who nodded. "Like sleep. Good."

Curtis kept a close eye on Bettina, taking away the chloroform when she seemed to have had just enough. He watched her to ensure the labor pains continued.

"You have quinine, ergot, if needed?" he asked.

Rachel nodded. "I don't think she'll need any help with the labor. I have a tincture of black cohosh, too."

Curtis glanced away from Bettina for a moment.

Rachel was masterful in the sickroom, a fascinating blend of gentleness and efficiency. She rubbed Bettina's back, her eyes soft and caring as she checked for any signs of distress. How could he not love such a woman?

Bettina's pains grew stronger and stronger. Rachel massaged her limbs and talked her through the pain. Curtis held the chloroform close to her face again, giving her extra relief now that the labor had intensified. Bettina gritted her teeth, but nodded to show her gratitude. The pains came faster and faster, until at last a crown pushed its way through.

He checked to see that the cord was not wrapped around the infant's neck, then cleaned its mouth. The child cried immediately, a blessed sound. Rachel began to rub the child with lard, and he found a basin of water by his feet. He scrubbed his arms and hands again, until he thought they would be raw, then took the castile soap to clean the child. He took a soft cloth and gently dabbed with the soap to remove the lard and natural substances on the baby, making sure each tiny area of the body was thoroughly cleansed.

Finally Bettina held a precious daughter in her arms. Rachel waited near the foot of the bed for the second. Another wave of birthing pains seized Bettina, but Curtis did not dare administer more chloroform now that she had a daughter in her arms. He left the room to call her husband.

Rachel had insisted that he sleep as long as possible, but they needed extra hands now. The farmer quickly left his bed and joined them, his eyes wide at the sight of his new daughter. He rushed to Bettina's side, brushing her hair aside and taking the infant into his arms.

"Why is she still in pain?" he asked. "What's wrong?"

"There is another," Curtis said, watching Bettina closely. The final push should come any moment.

Rachel spoke quietly, "Curtis. Quickly. Don't alarm the parents."

"What is it?" he asked. He moved carefully to the end of the bed, speaking in English so they would not be understood.

"Meconium," Rachel said. "Just a little, but the second infant may be distressed." Her voice was level and calm, but her hands shook the slightest bit.

Curtis put a hand on her arm. "May I deliver this child? Will you attend to the mother? She must not be neglected now." Curtis nodded toward the side table. "The after-birthing tea. It's nearly time."

"You're right. Of course." Rachel glanced around the room. "But can I leave?"

Bettina's husband wrapped his arm behind her shoulder, supporting her, as the pains grew faster and stronger again.

"Yes, quickly. If you'll set the water to boil and return immediately," Curtis said.

Rachel left the room quickly, but without haste or any sort of panic.

Curtis sent a quick prayer heavenward, *Please, God, help us do all we can for this family,* then the head was pushing through and he had no time for thinking. There was a thin layer of green tar, but most was in the liquid around the child. He checked that the cord was not around the neck, dipped his hands into the lard, and spread it on.

Curtis laid the child on a blanket Rachel had left by the side of the bed. He washed his arms and hands quickly, lathered the castile soap, and began to scrub as though the child's life depended on it.

Rachel returned to the room. "Water's on." She walked calmly to join him on the other side of the bed. She seemed to take in the situation at once.

"Why is it quiet?" Bettina asked.

"It's another daughter," Curtis answered.

Rachel washed her hands quickly and began to scrub the infant, too, rubbing her back especially hard while Curtis cleaned every area of the child.

"She'll yell loud enough in a minute," Curtis said, meeting Rachel's eyes. In a lower voice he said, "I need cold water, just a little. Snow, anything. Something to shock the lungs, then we'll warm her."

Rachel again left the room quickly, but without haste.

Curtis finished cleaning the tiny infant, sweeping out her mouth. Nothing. He blew air into her lungs, trying to force a cry, and pressed on the chest.

Rachel returned with a small cup of cold water for the child and a cup of warm ergot tea for the mother. Curtis rubbed the baby girl vigorously, then blew air into her lungs again. Again, he pressed on the chest.

"What is it?" the father asked.

Rachel moved in front of Curtis to hide his efforts.

Curtis paused. "She's a sweet girl. Give her a minute to warm up, then she'll cry." He felt certainty fill him. *Steady on. Never retreat.* He continued to blow into the child's lungs and press on the chest as *Herr* Fliedner had instructed him. It would take. Just a few more tries.

"Rachel, will you please take care of the afterbirth?" he asked. "I've got this in hand. All will be well." He met her eyes briefly and was shocked at what he saw. *Fear.*

But the question seemed to startle her, and Rachel moved to take care of Bettina. He could hear her adjusting sheets, moving pails of water, and helping with the last parts of the birthing process.

It was down to the last resort. *Herr* Fliedner had recommended tipping the child upside down. He grasped the baby by the ankles and swung the head downwards. He brought her up again, cradling her in his arms, and took her to the fire to warm her.

"Another blanket. Do you have one?" he asked Rachel.

She left Bettina briefly to hand him a clean cloth, and he wrapped the infant. Curtis huddled in front of the fire, not caring that ashes were on his trousers, in his hair, everywhere. He rubbed the baby's chest and back until at last a tiny cry joined her twin's.

He wanted to cry with relief, too. He collapsed onto the hearth, warming the child. He needed to ensure she would cry again. She would live. *Thank you, God.*

Curtis leaned his head against the fireplace, cradling the child to his chest. Her cries were weak, and the breathing was faster than her sister's, but her lungs took in great gasps of air.

Rachel bent down to take the infant from his arms. She nestled the second twin in Bettina's arms, while the father held the first.

Curtis pushed up from the floor. He brushed off his trousers, collected the used buckets of water, and emptied them outside, again and again, while Rachel tidied the bedroom and prepared to leave.

He returned one last time, and Rachel eyed him. He didn't even know what kind of dirt and grime covered him, and she had such strict standards of cleanliness for the sickroom. "If you'll wash up, this will be the last bucket of water. Thank you."

He'd rolled up his shirt sleeves to wash thoroughly one more time. The exertion of working through the night, scrubbing the floors during the labor, and tending the fires, had left his shirt dripping and clinging to his chest.

"I'm sorry," Curtis said, aware that he looked more disheveled than the farmer did. His trousers must be covered in ashes from kneeling in front of the fires and tending them, as much as he had tried to keep the room clean. At least he'd scrubbed his arms until they were raw.

Rachel took in his appearance. Did she like what she saw, or was she appalled? Her eyes kept returning to his chest. He was exhausted and disheveled, the opposite of the London gentleman she usually encountered. Had she seen Dr. Morrow looking like this each time they delivered a child? Was this normal, or was she disgusted by him?

"You'll catch cold taking that water outside," she finally said, but she was the one shaking. The fear had never left her eyes, even though the twin now breathed and cried as loudly as her sister.

"Men don't feel cold," Curtis said, and he grinned at her. A little teasing might restore her humor.

Rachel hardly noticed the jest. She quietly collected the teacups and waited by the door. "Farewell, Bettina. Thank you. They're beautiful." She gestured toward the twins.

Bettina and her husband thanked them over and over, and Rachel left the bedroom.

Curtis grabbed the last bucket of water and stopped outside the door to dress. "Where is my coat?" All his things were gone. His vest, his cuffs and collar. Everything.

He followed Rachel into the parlor. His coat would still be soaking wet. Wool never dried quickly.

"By the fire," Rachel said, tipping the dishes into the small sink and beginning to wash them. "I asked Frank to keep an eye on it and turn it now and then."

Curtis wanted to wrap her in his arms and never let go. All his things were arranged neatly in front of the modest fireplace, draped on furniture that had been moved closer to the hearth.

Frank dozed on a sofa, his coat warming near the flames as well. In the middle of a delivery, Rachel still thought about the well-being of every member of the house, even the servants. She had made sure that Frank's coat as well as his own would be as warm as possible when they left.

In the half-minute it took to wake Frank and ask him to bring the carriage around, Rachel had shaken out Frank's coat and brought it to him. While Curtis dumped out the water from washing dishes, Rachel tidied the parlor.

He emptied the coins from his pockets and left them on a side table as they waited for Frank to harness the horses to the carriage.

He folded the vest and other clothes into a neat pile while Rachel emptied the last bits of food from the basket she had brought. There was a week's worth of food to feed the family. An enormous ham, loaves of bread, a large wheel of cheese, and apples. A bushel of glorious, crimson apples. He resisted the urge to pocket one.

At last he slipped into the mostly warm coat and followed Rachel to the carriage. The horses' breath blew clouds of ice in the air. He climbed the steps, ducked his head to get inside, and paused.

"Thank you," he said to Frank. "You've got good aim with snowballs."

"Them boys needed it," Frank said. "I'm not fired, am I, for impertinence?"

"I'll give you a bonus for working in the cold night air on Christmas," Curtis said, and continued into the carriage. He dropped onto the bench as Frank shut the door. A moment later, the carriage began to roll back toward Mainz.

Curtis tucked a blanket around Rachel, then sat across from her. He was chilled to the bone, but exhilarated. After years of working to save men's lives on the battlefield and in unsanitary hospitals, he knew that helping women give birth was his calling.

He shivered. "Why do I feel like I'm on top of the world? My teeth are starting to chatter, and I may not be able to feel my toes, but I swear I've never been happier in my life."

Rachel smiled, but it seemed half-hearted. "I love attending births." She still seemed shaken, and he wasn't sure why. The baby had recovered.

Curtis pulled a thick wool blanket around himself. He *had* intended to enjoy an argument with Rachel about falling asleep on his shoulder. She needed something to distract her from whatever had distressed her in the birthing room.

Or did she need to talk? Would she allow him in, just a little bit? His earlier teasing had fallen flat. He studied her. He would speak openly with her. She was in no mood for jokes or banter. "Did something upset you?"

Rachel squeezed her eyes shut.

Curtis steadied himself. She needed him right now. "That was frightening for a moment," he said.

Rachel nodded. "The only child I ever lost when I delivered births in Essex." She stopped herself. Now her teeth were chattering.

He longed to pull her into his arms and comfort her.

"She was delivered like that," Rachel said, and took a deep, shuddering breath. "Will you promise me that you will not tell Alice?"

"Yes," Curtis said. "I'm worried about you." He knew he was taking a risk. Rachel did not want him to get emotional, and he was barely keeping his feelings at bay. Could she hear it in his voice? "How can I help you right now?"

Rachel's lip quivered, as if she were fighting tears. She crossed the carriage and sat beside him on the bench, drawing her lap quilt around herself. "I don't want to be alone right now."

It took him a moment to recover from the shock, and then Curtis adjusted his own blanket so it came between them and shielded her from any lingering dampness from his coat.

"May I?" he asked and put an arm around her. He could feel her shaking. "You're safe. The child is safe. All is well."

"Thank you," she said. She settled closer to him on the seat. The shaking began to subside as she gazed up at him. "You were magnificent tonight." Rachel closed her eyes and lowered her head onto his chest.

The warmth of a red-hot fire exploded inside. Curtis rested his head on hers for this one moment of paradise on earth, not trusting himself to talk without crying. He pulled her blanket tighter, making sure it covered her completely, and tightened the arm around Rachel. He waited until she relaxed and the shaking stopped, then he allowed himself to drift into a blissful sleep.

CHAPTER 9

The carriage made its way carefully back on the snow-packed roads, over gravel and cobblestones, and finally to their apartments. Light reflected from the silver flakes, and the moon hung high in the heavens. Remnants of moisture-laden clouds drifted across the early morning sky as Rachel looked through the carriage's window.

With her head nestled on Curtis's chest, she could see through the pane on the side door. Sleep fled, though her eyes flickered open and shut.

They traveled through a shadowland, a place between sleep and waking, between dreams and reality. As the carriage rolled on endlessly, Rachel flitted between consciousness and rest.

Exhaustion called to her, making her lids heavy, but the heady elation of witnessing a birth pushed them open again. Her mind warred with her heart, and beneath it all, Curtis's warmth steadied her.

Had she really slept on his shoulder all the way from Mainz? She had a vague recollection of waking and tipping her head onto his shoulder herself. *Her* idea. Not his.

Bettina's delivery was a miracle. Healthy twin girls, despite the scare. It had been everything she'd hoped and prayed for Bettina, but everything she dreaded for herself. Working seamlessly with Curtis, watching him play with Bettina's boys, seeing his emotional depth, his compassion, his generosity toward the poor, were all too much.

And he'd saved the child's life, when she couldn't. She knew what that dark color meant, and she dreaded the possibility. She'd felt a fear that had frozen her, but Curtis had known what to do. He had known more than Dr. Morrow, because he'd studied every possible scenario with *Herr* Fliedner. He'd swung into action and persisted, relentless as always, until the child breathed.

If she ever were going to marry, she would want to marry a man like him. She sighed and shifted. If only he were like this all of the time. This wasn't real. Just as dreams vanished when she woke, her time with Curtis in Germany was a six-month illusion that would dissipate like the morning fog when they returned to London.

They would complete training in March, return for the Season, and things would return to normal. Best to remember that, but not too soon. The blankets were warm, and Curtis felt secure and real. Dreams always did.

Rachel woke well past noon. Alice let her sleep for hours after she and Curtis arrived home from Bettina's delivery. Rachel knew how difficult it was for Alice to delay Christmas morning celebrations, but that was the life of a doctor's family.

A row of neatly wrapped packages lay beneath a tabletop Christmas tree. Rachel recognized the creamy Italian paper adorning each gift. The tree above it had appeared overnight. Mr. Kempton and Alice must have spent Christmas Eve decorating it with Mrs. Glenn. Candles were affixed to each limb. Paper ornaments hung from the branches, and small bundles of nuts and candied almonds were tucked inside the tree.

How should she greet Curtis? He needed to understand that nothing had changed between them. It was Christmas Day. She must be kind. Oh, dear. Whyever had she allowed herself to sit near him last night?

The gentlemen joined them for a late luncheon. Curtis wore a perfectly starched collar and immaculate cuffs. His black coat and patterned vest were wrinkle-free and tightly fitted around his all-too-tempting chest. His trousers were pressed and fit snugly around the legs. He could not look more different than the man she worked with last night. Even his dark hair was perfectly in order. He could have graced any London ballroom in his attire.

He searched for her as soon as he entered the drawing room and came directly to her side. She inhaled. He had just shaved. *Why, oh why, oh why?*

He smiled down at her. "Happy Christmas."

Rachel bit her lip and gazed up into the depths of his eyes. They were a mixture of green and gold and admiration today.

He took a step nearer. Rachel swallowed. "Happy Christmas, Curtis." She smiled. "I'm famished."

She could drown in the endless regard she found there. Or love. Did she dare admit to herself that he loved her? *He* imagined he did.

Mr. Kempton cleared his throat. "Luncheon. We've waited long enough for you two."

Rachel turned around. "My apologies. Yes. Shall we? Thank you, Alice."

Oh dear. She was rambling. Slow down.

"Or presents?" Curtis grinned at Alice. "When have you ever been able to delay their opening?"

Curtis took a small, wrapped gift from beneath the tree and handed it to Rachel. "This was a supreme sacrifice."

Rachel tilted her head up at him. "I cannot imagine." She tested its weight in her hand. Heavy. Liquid sloshed back and forth. "Not brandy or rum for patients?"

Mr. Kempton snorted. "Heaven preserve us."

Definitely a bottle. She felt the outline through the paper. "Alice wrapped this for you," Rachel said.

Curtis scoffed. "Of course."

"Who do you imagine purchased it?" Alice asked. "Not Curtis."

"Kempton," Rachel said. "Am I right, Alice? Doesn't he do everything for your brother?"

Curtis was gazing at her, anticipation written all over his face. "Only the undesirable tasks."

"Like purchasing this," Kempton added. "His supreme sacrifice."

Rachel unwrapped the paper to find a bottle of *Albany* cologne. She laughed. "It's only a supreme sacrifice if you wear it, Curtis." She began to unstopper the bottle.

He backed away. "No, no, no. It's for your letters to Dr. Morrow, I mean, your mother." He winked at her.

She tilted her head and smiled at him. "Would you wear it for me?"

He shifted his weight and considered her. "What would I gain in return?"

She shouldn't tease him. He would get the wrong idea. She put the stopper back in the bottle. "Thank you. What a thoughtful gift. Mama will love receiving my cologne-soaked epistles. I shall scent my pillow, fall asleep, and dream of Papa every night." She smiled a genuine smile for him. It truly was kind.

She took an oddly shaped package from beneath the tree. "And my gift to you." Rachel held it out. Curtis's touch lingered on her fingers a moment longer than necessary. She backed away as he opened it.

An apple. She had saved one from the bushel she bought for Bettina. She thought it a delightful joke, and she and Alice had laughed when they wrapped it. Now, it seemed ill-advised.

"I shall owe you a forfeit, then, if I begin to eat apples in class again." Curtis came over to her while Alice and Mr. Kempton exchanged gifts with Mrs. Glenn.

"Oh, this is a special apple, just for Christmas Day," Rachel said lightly. "The ban on classroom apples still applies." She backed away, her legs hitting the sofa behind her.

Curtis advanced, tossing the apple up and down in his hand. "I shall relish every bite."

"Yes, do," Rachel said, her voice squeaking slightly. She cleared her throat and took a deep breath, which only made her inhale the scent of his cedar shaving soap.

"You're beautiful when you sleep," Curtis said quietly. His eyes traveled over her face. "Won't you reconsider, Rachel?" He set down the apple. "You know my feelings." He glanced sideways at the others and back to her.

He reached for her hand and intertwined his fingers with hers.

Rachel couldn't meet his eyes. Dreams evaporated in the harsh light of reality. Fathers died unexpectedly. Men changed their minds and broke hearts. Good humors gave way to jealousy and tyranny. She had chosen her path, and she would remain on it.

"I've devoted myself to nursing, like Miss Nightingale," Rachel whispered, studying the pattern on the carpet. "I'll help you establish her school, then I'll return to Essex to care for my mother." She didn't expect how much it would hurt to say it.

"We work so well together." The ache in his voice tugged at her as his fingers caressed her hand. "Marriage to a doctor would not hinder your ability to nurse others."

The image tempted her. Working side by side, delivering children together, as they had last night. But marriage would involve so much more than midnight deliveries. How could she neglect her own children to deliver others? How soon would the day-to-day responsibilities of marriage and motherhood consume her and leave no room for her to be a nurse?

She had never dared dream of a life like he described, and she did not think it existed. He would make promises now that he could not keep later.

"I'm sorry," Rachel said, finally meeting his gaze. She wasn't prepared for the pain she saw there or for how much she would miss Curtis when he untangled his fingers from hers.

Curtis bowed stiffly. "If that is truly what you wish." A dullness crept into his eyes, extinguishing the hope she'd seen.

He left the apple on the sofa and went to join Alice. She watched Alice open Curtis's gift and hug her brother. Curtis smiled half-heartedly at Alice, the lines around his eyes crinkling as he watched his sister's delight while trying on her new fur muff and hat. His love and devotion were evident, even when his own happiness was muted.

A tightness and longing pulled at her chest. He was such a kind brother and a thoughtful friend. She wanted to hug him, too, and thank him. He understood how much she missed her father and how much the cologne would mean to her. Even though he hated the very smell of it, he had purchased it for her anyway. Well, he had ordered Kempton to purchase it.

How could she not love him? Tears pricked at her eyes, and her throat felt tight. It was for the best. Whether she admired him or not, he would soon lose his fondness for her when they returned to London. He fell in and out of love so easily. Where would that leave her, if she allowed herself to lose her heart?

She knew God wanted her to be a nurse. If he also wanted her to marry, she needed to feel that. Once she married, there was no way out. It was forever, and she lost all her freedom. Curtis would decide what she could and couldn't do, and he was prone to ordering people around. What if he exercised his rights as a husband and prevented her from being a nurse? Who would care for her mother?

She'd always imagined she'd marry someone gentle and quiet, who never disagreed with her and allowed her to do anything she wanted. Someone more like Lucy's husband, Peter, not someone who enjoyed arguing simply for the sake of opposing her, like Curtis. He was stubborn, he meddled in her business without asking, and he contradicted her at every turn.

But he was magnificent last night and so devoted to the people he loved.

Rachel swallowed. "I might lie down again. I'm not recovered from our night's efforts."

Curtis wouldn't meet her eyes. She'd already lost his esteem.

Good. She could begin to rebuild the walls around her heart now. She moved toward the drawing room doors. A hand stopped her.

"May we send someone with a tray for you?" Curtis asked quietly. "Do you have a headache? Do you need any tea?"

Her throat tightened further. *I need you to stop loving me.* She turned around and met his gaze. He stood inches away.

She made sure her voice sounded steady and even. "Yes, please. Luncheon and a cup of tea would do nicely."

There was no anger in his eyes, only hurt and concern for her. He nodded.

"You'll miss the best part of Christmas," Mr. Kempton yelled. "The polar bear plunge. They do it in Mainz, too."

Rachel raised an eyebrow.

Alice sighed. "Curtis and Kempton strip down to their unmentionables and jump into a river to prove their masculinity every year on Christmas Day."

"Real men don't feel cold," Curtis said, smiling at her.

Rachel bit her lip. "Don't most people swim on Epiphany?"

"Why dive in only once? The freezing air makes the Christmas wassail taste better, but, Alice, leave the rum out," Mr. Kempton said. "You know your brother."

"Only cider and spices this year." Alice grinned. "You'll join us later?"

Rachel nodded, even though she doubted she'd ever be able to face Curtis again. He took her hand and spoke quietly, so the others could not hear their conversation. "Don't miss Christmas Day on my account. I swear, I'll never mention it again, if you are so set against me, Rachel."

She blinked the tears away. She could feel her wretched mouth twitch. He stared at her. She looked at the ceiling and a tear slid down her cheek.

"Rachel? Are you set against me, or against marriage? What is it? It's not like—like Alice?"

He deserved a reason. He deserved an answer. She couldn't give him one. Her mouth had given her away, and she didn't know what to do.

"You're not set against me?" He searched her face, holding her hands tighter.

"I have no plans to marry, Curtis." Rachel knew that was the truth. She could say that much.

He watched her carefully, and she saw the instant he realized the truth. She meant it. He let go of her hands, and a broken look entered his eyes.

Rachel carefully walked to her bedchamber, unlaced her slippers, slipped off the crinoline hoop supporting her skirt so she could lay on the bed, and took a deep breath. She had not cried since her father died, and she would not cry now. Stray tears did not count as crying.

She curled up and crushed her pillow to her chest. The thunderbolt that was Curtis tore her heart open, and a sob escaped her. A tear rolled down her cheek and another. She let the drops spill down her face until a knock startled her. She wiped her eyes and opened the door.

Curtis. With a tray. Of course. Her favorite dinner foods, a few meringues, a slice of chocolate torte, and a cup of peppermint-chamomile tea. He remembered what she liked and which foods to avoid. He knew which tea she'd need right now, and he'd gone to the trouble of steeping a custom blend for her. She wanted to throw her arms around him and kiss him. He was sunshine on a spring day.

"Thank you, Curtis. Truly." She knew her mouth was anything but a straight line. She accepted the tray and set it on her side table. "Thank you."

He waited a moment. "Off to the river."

"Real men don't catch colds," Rachel said. "Has your coat dried completely yet?"

He looked ridiculously handsome today, and he'd been irresistible last night. It didn't matter what he wore. Shirt sleeves or suit.

Curtis nodded. "Stop fussing."

A tear rolled down her cheek. "I am so, so sorry Curtis."

"I don't understand, Rachel, but I'll be here when you change your mind." He smirked at her. "I'm highly desirable."

Another tear fell down her cheek and another. "Yes, you are. Too much for your own good, you blasted, abominable man. I hope you drown in the river."

"Now I recognize my Rachel." Curtis extended his hand. "I love you."

Her mouth twitched. She took his hand.

"I know you love me. You don't have to say it. I'll be waiting." Curtis brought her fingers to his lips and kissed them. He turned and left.

Rachel shut the door and stared at the tray, yet another token of his love for her. *What if he's right? What if I love him? What do I do?* She cradled the porcelain teacup in her hands. Her head ached from not crying. She didn't cry. She never cried. She took a sip and allowed the warm tea to soothe her.

She refused to think or feel. She was still tired from last night. She would eat this light luncheon, nap for a few hours, and steadfastly avoid Curtis. *For how long?* She pushed away the thought, pushed down every emotion, picked up the fork, and slowly began to eat.

CHAPTER 10

Someone pounded on the outer door of the apartments. Rachel tied a wrapper around herself and cracked open the door of her bedchamber. The pounding continued.

"Who is it?" Alice rushed down the hallway, oil lamp in hand. Mrs. Glenn followed close behind.

Rachel coughed. She and Curtis had both caught colds from Bettina's boys. She hadn't noticed their runny noses at the time, but Curtis and Frank had both grown ill a few days after Christmas.

So had Rachel. Alice and Mr. Kempton kept casting her sidelong glances, as if dying to ask what had happened between her and Curtis. How had they caught the same illness?

Simply by being at the same house. But Mrs. Glenn kept smiling at her and winking. "The colonel is a fine man."

Rachel had kept to her room for the entirety of her cold after the teasing, but Alice and Mrs. Glenn had gone through a bout of sniffles as well. They probably caught it from Curtis, too.

Only a cough lingered now. Alice and Mrs. Glenn seemed recovered. They told her that Mr. Kempton had a mild case, but Curtis had it worst.

Rachel heard shouting and decided she best investigate. She was responsible for the leasing and condition of the apartments, not Mrs. Glenn. She blew out a breath.

"Where is that stunner?" Curtis's voice was loud enough to wake the dead. "I must see her."

Oh dear. He could only mean her. Rachel had avoided Curtis since Christmas. They hadn't seen each other for ten days. She avoided him during the holiday, then he grew ill, and then she did. Classes were due to begin in a few days, after Epiphany, and she'd been dreading it.

Rachel resigned herself to a confrontation. She entered the drawing room. Mr. Kempton supported Curtis, who looked terrible. He truly had a serious case of whatever illness they'd encountered. He looked feverish and worn. They were both wearing casual trousers and wrinkled shirt sleeves. Alice's face was as pale as her brother's, and Mrs. Glenn looked disgusted.

"You made him one of your concoctions, didn't you?" Mrs. Glenn accused Mr. Kempton. "Knowing what you know? Are you out of your mind? Raisins and licorice and rum?" She wagged a finger. "You can stay awake with him. I'll not bear the brunt of your mistake."

"No. I left him alone for one minute. That's it. I've been with him, night and day, for a week. I can't take any more. He's driving me mad. Pity me, woman."

Mrs. Glenn snorted. "You think a hot toddy cures anything."

"Would I do this?" Mr. Kempton tried to shrug Curtis off his shoulder, but he seemed to have fallen asleep on him. "He's the one who believes a rum toddy cures any illness. He's been singing for three hours."

"Good night to you." Mrs. Glenn looked at him. "Hide your alcohol better next time."

"Alice," Mr. Kempton pleaded. "You know I wouldn't."

"I don't believe I gave you leave to call me by my Christian name." Alice drew herself up. "Mr. Kempton."

Mr. Kempton scoffed. "I've known you how long? Everyone else calls you Alice."

"Is she here?" Curtis jerked his head off Mr. Kempton's shoulder suddenly. "Rachel. Confound it. Where is she? I must tell her something. It's urgent."

"He insists he's going to die," Mr. Kempton said.

Alice hugged herself around the waist. "Curtis always thinks he will perish, anytime he has a sniffle. He has yet to pass away, so I shall go back to sleep."

Rachel put an arm around Alice. "I see you're worried, but he's stubborn. He'll pull through."

Alice glanced at Mr. Kempton, then spoke to Rachel. "I'm no good in a sickroom. It reminds me of my parents." She rushed down the hallway, and a door slammed.

Rachel sighed. "Well, Kempton. He *is* half-rats. What did he mix? A shandygaff? I thought he didn't drink."

"By Jove! She *is* here!" Curtis turned to face her, swaying a little to find his focus. "It's very important."

"He darted out of the apartments before I could stop him. I'm sorry." Mr. Kempton tried to put an arm under Curtis. "Let's go home, Colonel."

But he wouldn't move, no matter how hard Mr. Kempton tugged or pulled. He walked directly to Rachel, stared deep into her eyes, and began singing. *"I am the very model of a modern major general. I've information vegetable, animal, and mineral. I know the kings of England, and I quote the fights historical from Marathon to Waterloo in order categorical."*

"He's soused," Rachel said. "Why does his breath smell like peppermint?"

"He wanted tea. He drank the rum hours ago." Mr. Kempton held Curtis up while he swayed from side to side. "He shouldn't still be drunk. No one else could stay drunk so long on so little alcohol. It's his particular gift."

"I like tea. Kempton's a regular brick. Made me an entire pot of it," Curtis said. *"There once was a ship that put to sea, and the name of that ship was the Billy o' Tea. The winds blew hard, her bow dipped down. Blow, me bully boys, blow."*

"This was urgent?" Rachel collapsed on one end of the largest sofa of the room.

"He sang the entire score of *The Pirates of Penzance* three times," Mr. Kempton said. "I'm going to kill him if I have to hear it one more time. Brick him over the head."

"Soon may the Wellerman come to bring us sugar and tea and rum," Curtis sang. His rich, deep voice reverberated off the walls. Good thing no one lived upstairs right now.

"He's had his rum all right," Mr. Kempton muttered.

Rachel studied him. "How long since either of you slept?" Their clothes were rumpled. Neither wore jackets, collars, or cuffs.

"Three days, at least." Mr. Kempton rubbed a hand over his face.

"The whale's tail came up and caught her. All hands to the side, harpooned and fought her, when she dived down loooooow." Curtis hit a low note and collapsed onto the long sofa, his arm flopping to the floor and his head resting in Rachel's lap. She could feel the song rumbling in his chest.

"I'll kill him, if you don't," she said. "How many verses to this song?"

Curtis looked up at her. "Do you like songs with a lot of verses?" He grinned. "I know the perfect song for you."

"The worst of it is that he doesn't believe you in the morning. Never remembers anything. We warn him, but he still drinks the rum. Every time he's sick."

"Go to sleep for a few hours. You can't go on like this." She was pinned to the sofa anyway, and she doubted Mr. Kempton had the strength to pull Curtis off. Perhaps Rachel could roll him off, if he fell asleep.

"Is he dangerous like this?" she asked.

Mr. Kempton yawned. "Only to himself." He collapsed onto a chaise by the fireplace, its back to the sofa. "Good night." He disappeared from view.

Rachel shifted on the sofa. She shoved some pillows behind herself and prepared for a long night.

Curtis sighed and stretched the length of the sofa, crossing his feet at the ankles. "Heaven. Ready for my song? I say, '*We'd be alright if Rachel married us*' or '*Having seven children wouldn't do us any harm*' and it goes on and on." He waved his hand in the air.

She stared down at him.

"Then the chorus, you see, you sing, '*Roooll the old chariot along*' and you sing the notes up high, and I go loooow, and we harmonize. Try it."

He began singing, and she couldn't fault his voice. It made her insides melt, especially when his deep voice hit the low notes. It was the words that upset her.

Rachel interrupted his second chorus. "Shall I have a go?"

He nodded.

"*Another night of sleep wouldn't do you any harm. Yes, another night of sleep wouldn't do you any harm. Oh, another night of sleep wouldn't do you any harm. Go back to your apartments now.*"

"You're terrible at this." He began singing again. "*Taking out your braid wouldn't do you any harm.*"

Right. She'd taken down the bun and brushed her hair out for bed. She only wore a simple braid. Why had she taken pity on Mr. Kempton?

Now she understood Mrs. Glenn and Alice. *Hide the rum better, Kempton.*

Why did he even keep rum in his room at all?

Rachel studied Curtis while he sang another chorus. He couldn't breathe very well. Lying down was all wrong. He needed to sit up. She could hear the congestion in his chest. He needed to drink more tea. What had Curtis and Kempton been doing the last three days? The last week?

Not taking proper care. Jumping into freezing cold rivers on Christmas Day.

"*Sitting up wouldn't do you any harm,*" Rachel tried to interject.

"No, here's a good one," Curtis said. "*A tender little kiss wouldn't do us any harm. Yes, a tender little kiss wouldn't do us any harm. Oh, a tender little kiss wouldn't do us any harm, and we'll hug each other, too."*

He shifted to look at her. "That's my favorite so far."

"How clever." Rachel smiled at him. "Time to sleep."

Curtis collapsed again, his head in her lap, his eyes fixed on the ceiling. "I don't know any tragic songs. Sailors didn't teach me any on the way to the Crimea."

Rachel put a hand hesitantly on his forehead, checking for fever of course, and ran her fingers through his soft hair. He wouldn't remember this tomorrow. He needed to fall asleep. And a nurse's instincts told her that he would relax and sleep sooner if she soothed him. At least, that's what she told herself. It was a strictly *medical* decision to run her fingers through his hair. Not at all emotional.

Curtis closed his eyes. In the corner by the fireplace, Mr. Kempton snored loudly, though Rachel couldn't see him. She combed her fingers through Curtis's thick hair again, gently, like she did when she helped her mother or Lucy with a headache. Not at all sentimental on her part, but his hair did poke up in all the places she knew it would.

"Farewell and adieu to you, fair Rachel Wickford. Farewell and adieu to you, lady of mine. For you've given orders we'll never marry, even though you are simply divine. I guess I can write my own tragic songs." Curtis tilted his head up to her. "That one's about Spanish ladies, but I made it about you."

Rachel rested her hand on his head. What should she do with him? He was a hopeless romantic. Had he believed himself so sincerely in love with the other women?

As if he could read her mind, Curtis began speaking again. "The most tragic part…" He covered his eyes with his arm. "I've kissed, I don't know, a dozen women, but I didn't love any of them. The only woman I've ever loved won't kiss me. It's a wretched way to die."

Rachel ran her fingers through his hair again. "You'll recover."

She could feel his shoulders shake with emotion. She pressed the back of her hand against his forehead. "You may have a fever developing. I've had this same illness, and I survived. It's merely a cold, but of course you've taken it to the extreme. Your polar bear plunge did not help."

"I used to think." Curtis laughed. "I used to think that when you called me 'General,' you were really saying, 'I love you.'"

Rachel pulled her hand away from his head.

"I didn't even mind it so much." Curtis turned toward the sofa's back.

She could hear him struggling to get air. "I don't like the sound in your lungs. Sit. You can hardly breathe."

"The sooner I die, the better." Curtis rolled back onto her lap and gazed up at her. "Who will you marry? Woodford? Dr. Morrow? Romford? You could kiss me once to grant a dying man's blasted wish."

"No one, Curtis. I'll marry no one, and there's no point in kissing you. You're not dying, and you won't remember it in the morning."

He adopted a roguish air. "I can make it unforgettable for you."

Rachel bit her lip.

"Always so stoic. You're more stubborn than any man in the Army." Curtis played with her braid. "Why are you set against marriage? We could have been magnificent together. The two of us, a force to be reckoned with. I need a duchess."

Rachel stared at him. "Why?" She took her braid out of his hands.

"Grandfather won't last forever, and my uncle's daughter has no children." He shrugged. "I'll be a marquis soon, and the heir."

She settled back against the sofa. Curtis? A marquis and the heir to a dukedom? She had no place in his highly decorated and aristocratic life. Simple, plain, poor Rachel. Barely on the edge of respectability all these years. She and Mama clung to their position in the gentry through the goodwill of their friends, careful budgeting, and grace.

What kind of confounded lifestyle did he lead in London?

Curtis reached over her shoulder and began to play with her braid again.

"Where's your townhouse? Do you have your own or live with your grandfather in London?" Rachel asked.

Curtis wove his fingers through her hair, untying the ends and beginning to undo the weave. "Park Lane, Piccadilly. South end, closer to Hyde Park Corner. Grandfather thought I should have my own address on my calling card, near the Duke of Wellington. Army address, you know."

Her braid was rapidly unraveling. He lived in the most expensive, exclusive, fashionable part of London.

Who were his other friends and associates? He was friends with the Duke of Woodford, after all. That should have alerted her to his true social standing, but she had paid no mind, since Eleanor was also acquainted with the duke, and the duke was so unassuming. But a duke *was* a duke, and she was only a gentleman's daughter, without a title. Eleanor's father was a Peer, and they were members of the aristocracy. Sometimes Rachel forgot that she and Eleanor really should not be such close friends.

And which women had Curtis courted? Who were Alice's friends in London? No wonder his clothes were of the finest quality. She would not attend dinners at his home, with his grandfather in attendance. What could she wear that was suitable to impress a deuced duke? And his uncle, a marquis?

"I love your curls." Curtis ran his fingers through her hair. "I wondered what your hair looked like."

Rachel didn't care how ill or tired he was. She was going to push him on the floor and let him sing sea shanties all night. She arranged her hair behind her back. "I'm going back to bed, and you require sleep. Will you please seat yourself so you can breathe?"

"What is there to live for?" Curtis met her gaze.

"You are the worst patient I've ever attended," Rachel said. "You won't mind my instructions, you sing at the top of your lungs, and you're morose."

Curtis pushed himself up halfway. "Melancholy."

"I'm through." Rachel tried to push him off the couch.

He didn't budge, but he rolled over and put a hand on her face. "I know." His chin quivered. "Just tell me why."

He was out of his mind. Feverish. Kempton said he never remembered these episodes. She may as well explain her reasons to him, so she could get back to sleep sooner. Curtis always required reason and explanation. Even when drunk, he wanted long, drawn out conversations.

Rachel gently removed his hand and tried to settle back onto the cushions, but she could not get comfortable with him clasping her hand as though it were a lifeline to a sinking ship. "Marriage means heartache. It means bondage. It's giving up everything I know, and it's permanent. I cannot undo it. It's forever, for eternity. I cannot change my mind. Once done, it cannot be undone. I am at the mercy of my husband's whims. If he says I cannot nurse, I cannot nurse. If he says I must do something, I must do it. It is the loss of freedom and autonomy. He can order me about, like a general." She smiled down at him. "And I must obey."

Curtis wove his fingers through hers. "You would never stand for that, Rachel. We both know that. What makes you think I would be so cruel or uncaring? I love you. Marriage is joy, and I won't settle for anything less than forever with you. I've already named our seven children," Curtis said. "Four boys and three girls. Maybe we'll have a set of twin girls, like Bettina."

Rachel sighed. His grip was firm, and his thumb traced circles on the back of her hand. She was beginning to grow accustomed to the feel of her hand in his. She relaxed into the sofa.

Curtis smiled at her. "Do you want to know their names?" He shook his head. "Hang it all, I know there's more to it than this. You're not afraid to have children, and you're not afraid to defy me. You create more disorder in my life than anyone ever has."

She pulled her hand away from his. "Because you'll change your mind and break my heart."

"Why would I change my mind?" Curtis searched her eyes. "I

could never hurt you. I would hold your heart safe, if you would give it to me."

Rachel saw the truth in his eyes. In this state, he couldn't lie to her. He believed it, and he ached with that knowledge. She was causing him the same kind of pain she had sworn to avoid for herself. She was hurting, too. What good was her vow to never marry?

She studied him. "You fall in love every blasted year, then love someone else the next."

"Not like this. It's never like this." Curtis sat up further and turned to face her. The glow from a gas lamp warmed the room.

Something palpable hung in the air between them. She loved him, and he loved her. She didn't trust him to always love her, and she knew she'd never fit into his world, but just for this one moment, for one more dream, perhaps she could let go. Perhaps she did not have to be alone.

She ran her fingers through her hair, separating the curls he professed to love, allowing the long locks to cascade down her shoulders. He watched her, riveted by her every motion.

"Change. My. Mind." Rachel smiled at him and leaned forward.

Curtis stared at her in wonder. "By Jove. You're serious."

Rachel wrapped her arms around his neck, then his mouth was on hers. She closed her eyes and entered a magical world, where she could give her heart and her love, and no pain existed.

Curtis paused to catch a breath, and hungrily returned for more. He shifted on the couch, sitting up now, reaching for her. He ran his hands through her hair, kissing her again. He wrapped his arms around and held her tight.

"Rachel." He spoke her name softly.

She glanced at the corner. If Mr. Kempton woke now—but no, he still snored loudly, invisible on the chaise. She could linger in the shadowland for a moment longer. She ran her hands over Curtis's face, along his cheek, and down to his lips. He kissed her again, crushing her to him as if he would never let go, and resting his head atop hers.

"This is a fever dream, isn't it?" he asked. "The men at the hospital in Scutari hallucinated. It seemed so real for them."

Rachel traced her fingers down his arm, finding a ragged white line. "What's this? A scar?"

Curtis closed his eyes. "I wasn't always behind the desk at the hospital."

"You weren't on the battlefield?" Rachel asked.

Curtis laughed without humor. "I wasn't supposed to be, but there were so few doctors. How could I let men die?" He unrolled his wrinkled shirt sleeves and tugged it down to cover the scar.

Rachel took his hand in hers and rested her head on his shoulder. "You cannot put yourself in harm's way to save others." It was clear that the scars were more than physical. Even in his current state, Curtis could not bear to talk about the war.

He wrapped an arm around her waist. "Stay with me. The end must be near. I want to behold your angel face as I'm dying, confound it."

Rachel allowed herself one more moment, where their love was fixed in the constellations, and nothing would eclipse it. But the gas lamps flickered on the side table, and the illusion twinkled into faery lights, unknowable and uncertain.

"Sleep, you corned bloke. You're merely sick." She managed to slip out from beneath Curtis.

He watched her every move. She pushed him backward. "Rest." She bent over him to adjust the cushions. He caught her around the waist and pulled her down for another kiss, running his hands through her hair again.

She nearly lost her balance, falling into him, into love, and righted herself, her heart beating wildly.

"You *do* adore me," Curtis said, running a finger lightly down her cheek and caressing the corner of her mouth. He ran his fingers through her long hair once again, trying to pull her back toward him.

"Highly," Rachel replied. "I might even love you." She retreated to a chair across from the sofa, where she could observe him. Out of reach, but within sight. Safest for now.

Curtis squirmed around, readjusting the pillows so he could watch her, and pulling his long legs onto the sofa. Finally, he settled into a deep sleep, but Rachel did not.

What if she let go of her fears? What if Curtis could love her always, as he believed, and not change his mind? She relaxed into her chair. They could work together, attend patients together, share carriage rides and kisses. She would have Alice as a sister, for life.

What if he did not order her about, but allowed her a degree of independence?

Perhaps she could risk the heartbreak, because not taking a chance hurt too much. What would a life *without* Curtis be like? The last ten days had been some of the worst of her life, reminding her of the first few weeks after Papa died. She missed the confounded colonel too much.

She watched him sleeping on the sofa. The gentle bear of a man. Always attuned to her, putting her needs first, taking her to Italy to watch her friends marry, helping her study at the Mainz Institute, fussing over her safety in the gymnasium.

And then at times he was quarrelsome and domineering with his good intentions and anxieties. She knew how to bring him around when he overstepped himself. She had never met a better gentleman, and she could not imagine a better husband. Going through life together, side by side.

If only she could be certain that she could do both, that she did not have to give up nursing in order to marry him. Her heart whispered that a life married to a doctor would not impede her work, but could be a glorious confluence of their interests and their passions.

Her fears imagined a life spent at home, watching him leave while she stayed behind, frustrated. She could lose herself in his cause, supporting him, but never being allowed to nurse the needy or help the sick herself. Helping him could consume all her energy, leaving none behind for her.

But her heart hammered louder than her fears tonight. She left her chair to brush his damp hair away from his face. His handsome, kind face. His forehead was warmer now; the fever had taken hold.

Rachel studied his features, so gentle while he slept, before going to get a cold compress for his forehead. Let him sleep. Let Mr. Kempton sleep. She would see things through tonight, and there would be time enough to decide in the morning.

CHAPTER 11

Curtis groaned as light flooded into the room. "Why did you open the confounded curtains?"

"Two days is long enough to sleep," Kempton said. "You should be fine now. I've barely cracked them open."

Curtis ached all over. "What happened?"

Kempton gestured toward a tray with a mug of steaming tea. "Someone sneezed on you. Rachel sent up some tea. You've drunk nothing else for days."

Rachel. She'd broken his heart on Christmas Day, and he'd not seen her since. She'd hidden in her room, and then they'd fallen ill. He'd thought of nothing but her for days while he rested. He vaguely remembered a fever, but the last few days were a blur.

Curtis sipped the tea. Chamomile and mint with honey and lemon. Thoughtful of her. *Why is she so blasted thoughtful?* "What day is it?"

Kempton ripped open the curtains all the way, letting the light shine directly in Curtis's eyes. "January sixth. Epiphany. Ready for another swim?"

"Not today. I'm barely recovered, but I could use a stretch. Meet me in the gymnasium?" He took another swallow of tea. It warmed his chest and soothed his throat.

"I wasn't serious. You've been delirious for days. You're in no shape to race, swim, or do anything else." Kempton eyed him. "Change your shirt sleeves and wash up, and I may let you sit in the drawing room."

Curtis looked around the room. His coat hung over a chair. His collar and cuffs lay somewhere else. "Did I banish the valet as well as all reason and common sense?"

Kempton collected other used cups from the side table and set them on the tray. "As usual, you thought he would catch the plague from you. Shall I send him in?"

Curtis laughed. "Tell Carter it's safe to return." He shook his head. Why could he never remember what happened when he was ill?

The valet helped him wash, found a pair of clean trousers and shirt sleeves, and helped him shave.

Curtis felt nearly recovered, except for a lingering cough. Rachel's tea must have helped clear the congestion from his chest.

He staggered into the drawing room and collapsed onto a sofa. What had hit him? Flashes of feverish dreams flitted in and out of his memory as he rested his head against the wall. Rachel, long tresses flowing over her shoulders. Rachel, kissing him. Rachel's hands gently caressing his face and the relief of a cool compress on a searing hot forehead.

He felt ashamed of the images his imagination had conjured up while he was ill. He wouldn't be able to look Rachel in the face next time he saw her. It felt so real. He'd wanted so desperately to believe that she loved him, that his mind had played tricks on him while he was sick.

The Crimean Fever. He groaned. He must have it. The hallucinations, the chills, the aches, the sickness. It was a life sentence. Miss Nightingale had it. Friends of his suffered. It meant years of recurring fevers and aches.

It meant the end of his ability to deliver children. He couldn't risk spreading the fever to expectant mothers. They could lose their pregnancies if he spread the illness to them.

And had he exposed Rachel to the Fever? No one knew exactly how it spread, and it might be contagious. He had spent time alone with her in the carriage, in close quarters, where no air could circulate. He had kissed her hand and her cheek. He'd put his arm around her, letting her rest her head on his shoulder. Had he condemned her to a lifetime of aches and pains and fevers, too?

The door to the drawing room opened, and Rachel entered with Alice and Kempton. His sister rushed over and greeted him, but Curtis winced at the sound of her voice.

Rachel moved over to close the curtains halfway. "How are you today?"

Curtis straightened on the sofa, glad he'd changed into a clean suit. "Well." His head pounded, and the room swam in front of him. He dreaded this conversation. How could he get rid of Alice and Kempton?

"I'm so relieved," Alice said.

Curtis wasn't in the mood for small talk or any kind of talk. He wanted to crawl back into bed and sleep for another two days. He had the heartbreaking task of warning Rachel that she might contract Crimean Fever, and he did not relish it.

"What have you eaten?" Rachel asked. "Kempton, he needs food."

Kempton grinned at her and left the drawing room.

"Alice, could you help him with the tray?" Curtis asked. It was a thin excuse to be alone with Rachel, but hopefully his sister would understand him.

Alice smiled broadly and left the drawing room.

Plunge right in, like a frozen river. Curtis rubbed a hand over his eyes.

Rachel went to the window and closed the curtains all the way. "Are you still sensitive to light?"

Curtis nodded. "This blasted headache. Please, sit down. I have something serious to talk with you about."

Rachel settled herself next to him, unusually close. He wished he could enjoy it, if his head would stop pounding.

Rachel rested a hand on his arm. "Shall I get the lavender oil?" She reached the other hand up and gently touched his temple. "A few drops would help right there."

The feel of her fingers on his skin distracted him so much that he nearly forgot the painful conversation ahead of him. Instead, memories of her touch flooded him. Her hands, exploring his face and his lips. He shook himself to clear the recollection of his delirium.

Rachel was resting against his shoulder, almost, and seemed so concerned about him. "Or a compress?"

Curtis steadied himself. "I need to say this quickly."

Rachel withdrew her hands.

He tried to focus on her face. "I must ask you not to attend any more live births, and I will do the same."

She stared at him.

"This illness is the Crimean Fever, contracted when I served in the Army. It recurs over and over again, unpredictably. I thought I had escaped, but I'm afraid it has struck. It puts expectant mothers at risk, and I cannot be near them. I may have passed the illness to you, Rachel, and I'm so sorry."

Her face remained impassive.

"There is no way to know if you will contract the disease. This is my first instance of it since the war. It may lay inactive for months. I did not know it could lay dormant for years."

Rachel tilted her head to consider him. "Years? This is the first occurrence?"

Curtis took her hands. "It is devastating, I realize."

"It's not Crimean Fever," Rachel said. "We all had the same illness. Alice, Kempton, Mrs. Glenn, and I have all been ill with trifling colds in the past week. Yours was simply more severe."

Images of Rachel's long, flowing hair flashed in his mind. Kissing Rachel. Rachel looking at him with loving eyes as she traced lines down his arm. He shuddered. He could almost feel it now.

"No, I've never hallucinated like this before." Curtis felt emotion rising and tried to keep it at bay. "I'll help the school in other ways, do anything Miss Nightingale asks, but I cannot make in-person visits to expectant mothers or deliver children any longer. It endangers the unborn child."

Rachel let go of his hands. "Hang it all, you're just sick with a cold."

"I must ask you to do the same," Curtis said. "Train the nurses and allow the others to deliver the babies. It's not safe for you to practice in person anymore."

Rachel stood. "Theoretical knowledge only goes so far. I must work *with* the nurses to truly train them. They and I must attend births together for me to teach them."

Curtis rested his head in his hands. He was a healer, and he had made others sick. "I would never have exposed you to this if I had realized I was ill."

Rachel tossed her head back. "No."

Curtis stared at her. "I must insist."

Rachel walked to the edge of the drawing room. "I'm going to finish the course. I'm not leaving Germany until I've completed it. You can return to England, if you'd like, and Kempton can translate for me."

Curtis couldn't imagine leaving her. "I'll stay, but I must register my concern at your choice."

"You drank a rum toddy after jumping in a river when you already had a cold," Rachel said. "That's your only illness. You don't have the Crimean Fever, and I will not stop nursing because you are delusional."

Curtis joined her by the door, slightly unsteady on his feet. "That's quite a statement." He tried to look imposing.

She narrowed her eyes. "It's the truth."

"Rachel," he pleaded. "This illness causes unspeakable pain for years. I've seen what it does to people. I hate to think that I might have done this to you. We cannot work together again to deliver children." He lowered his voice, so that the butler would not overhear them.

"I cannot be…"

Curtis couldn't help himself. His eyes flitted to her lips, as if the delirium had been as real as it had felt.

Rachel's eyes widened. He rushed on, before she guessed his true thoughts.

"I cannot be close to you or spend time alone with you again. What if you have not contracted the disease yet, but I make you ill? I cannot ask you to put yourself in harm's way to aid others."

Rachel smiled sadly. "You know I won't stand for being ordered around, General."

General. She clearly thought he was overstepping himself again. He only had her health in mind.

Rachel drew on her coat. "And I won't have you use my own words against me."

Confound it. It was deuced hard to think through this pounding headache. When had he used her own words?

Kempton and Alice appeared in the hallway with a tea tray, laden with luncheon.

Rachel moved away from him and toward the door. Her face was flushed.

"Leaving so soon?" Kempton asked.

"I hate to disturb your fragile friend's recovery." Rachel sniffed. "I will not concede this point, Curtis."

"You're a danger to the children," he said, "and I am a danger to you. I cannot stress how strongly I disagree." He tried not to clench his fists in frustration. How could he protect her if she would not listen or believe him?

"I am a danger?" Rachel glared at him. "The only danger in this house is Kempton's rum." She stormed out the front door.

Alice stared at him. "How dare you call her that!" She ran after Rachel.

Curtis went back into the drawing room and dropped onto a sofa.

Kempton set the luncheon tray down. "What the deuce do you think you're doing, treating Rachel like that?" He looked ready to kill.

Curtis groaned. Kempton didn't know about the carriage ride or the conversation on Christmas Day. "Things have passed between her and me that you are not aware of. It was a hard conversation. Let it alone."

Kempton advanced, his face stone serious for once. "Things have passed between you and Rachel that *you're* not aware of. You owe her an apology."

Anger, frustration, sadness, and exhaustion mixed in his chest. Curtis's body ached from the illness. "Leave it alone. You don't know what you're talking about."

"You're off your chump," Kempton said. "Don't ever talk to her that way again, or I'll knock your block off."

"Look," Curtis said. "You and Alice have nothing to lose. You never intended to practice medicine. You're both here to help train others in the school, but Rachel and I—"

Deep breaths. *Steady on.*

"What are you talking about?" Kempton asked.

Curtis ran a hand over his face. "The Crimean Fever. I've contracted a contagious disease, and I had to ask Rachel not to nurse or deliver any more children."

Kempton huffed. "That's a bit of first-rate nonsense. It was a wretched fever."

Curtis laughed without humor. "I wish it were so, but I assure you. I saw many men in the Crimea and after. I have spoken at length with Miss Nightingale, who has the illness herself. It manifests months later."

Kempton shoved the luncheon tray onto a table near him. "Eat. Rachel's right. You're not thinking straight." He left the room, shaking his head.

Curtis was the doctor. He had supervised the nightmare they

called a hospital in Scutari, when The Lady with the Lamp had arrived to sort it and begun to set it to rights, scrubbing the floors, setting up the new kitchen, and insisting on clean linens. He still had nightmares of the battlefields, the wounded, and the diseased men.

He knew what he knew, and he would never tell anyone about the hallucinations he'd had of Rachel. If he told Kempton, that would convince him that Curtis had been truly out of his mind. Rachel kissing him? Only in his dreams.

It was the Crimean Fever, and no one could convince him otherwise. He'd protect everyone else, even if they didn't believe him. He would stop visiting patients and begin copying notes upstairs in his own apartments in order to keep his distance from Rachel. Dinners were fine, but no more quiet moments together.

And he'd never marry Rachel or anyone else. He laughed at the irony that *he* was making that choice. He could never inflict this pain on her, and he would never risk intimacy with someone he loved so dearly. He could not allow anyone else to contract the illness from him, and especially not her. It was for the best that she had refused him on Christmas Day. The thought stung.

Soldier on. Two more months of training. Two more months of being with her, but not being able to be near her. He'd have to find something to focus on instead of her.

He tore off a piece of a roll and began to eat alone in the drawing room. A long, lonely life stretched ahead of him, and a sense of frustration pounded through the headache. Rachel would unnecessarily risk the lives of infants because she didn't believe him. *No one* believed him, but time would prove him right.

CHAPTER 12

Mid-March 1857

Rachel brushed aside the familiar pang of disappointment as Curtis escorted Mrs. Glenn into the waiting carriage. Rachel followed her in and settled into the far corner. He'd rented the largest, most luxurious, six-person carriage, as if he needed room to isolate himself from her, even when they traveled.

He'd distanced himself from her for the last two months, and now it was time to return to London. A telegram had arrived shortly after Curtis recovered from his fever. The queen had appointed him to serve on a commission with eight other men. Miss Nightingale had recommended him personally to study sanitation conditions in the Army and report to the House of Commons in August.

Curtis seemed delighted with the opportunity to be useful in a reclusive way. He spent his evening hours upstairs preparing the report, while Mr. Kempton transcribed the notes, charts, and diagrams from the nursing school. Meals were short, so the men could work.

Rachel felt detached, like an outsider watching a parade. She would not change her ways or stop what she was doing, but she hated the distance between them. Now, they would return to London and go their separate ways. She'd help train the nurses at Miss Nightingale's school, and she did not know when she would see him.

It was best that she had prepared herself for this. Men changed their minds. Curtis had promised that he would always want her to work as a nurse, but it hadn't lasted a week. He had made promises he could not keep.

He'd been just as domineering as she'd feared. If she'd been married, he might have been able to insist that she stop her schooling. As it was, he had tried to order her anyway, and she'd had to defy him and lose his good opinion to continue.

Crimean Fever. Of all the blasted things. It was a simple cold with a nasty bout of delirium. She'd nursed him through it herself. She should know. What would it be like to be married to someone who believed himself dying when he merely had a cold?

Or who held her future, her funds, her property, everything in his control, when he was clearly unreasonable himself?

Then the telegram arrived, and he abandoned her completely. Perhaps he realized how far beneath him in social status she really was. *The queen herself.*

Her heart ached. For one or two moments, she had let herself hope. In the obscurity of darkness and the anonymity of nightfall, she caught a glimmer. It was *indeed* a faery light, leading down a false trail.

She had tried. She gave him a chance, and she gave him her heart. She trusted him with it, and he had not kept it safe.

She watched Paris roll past, the great buildings not so different from Mainz. She tried to pick out which architectural details might distinguish France from Germany to distract herself as the knot in the pit of her stomach gnawed at her.

She'd not felt right for two months. Curtis despised her for taking risks. He thought her dangerous, unsound, and unreasonable. He'd never want to marry someone like her, and she could never marry someone so imperious.

He'd spent two months avoiding her. On the few occasions when she saw him, he treated her with the same polite detachment she had shown to him previously.

Now she knew how much it hurt. Rachel bit her lip. He sat across from her. They'd had dinner together sometimes, but never really been in close proximity since the night he'd been ill.

She darted a glance at his face and back out to the cobblestone streets and the smoke drifting from chimney tops. Curtis was watching her without any of his usual humor, but with a steady, thoughtful gaze. Almost as if he didn't see her, but had his mind elsewhere. She glanced back at him again, letting her gaze linger for one moment. These were their last minutes together, after studying in Germany for six months.

"Where will you live, Miss Wickford?" he asked.

So formal. Rachel folded her hands in her lap. "With Lord and Lady Shelford."

"I will miss you," Alice said.

Rachel smiled over at her.

"Will you miss me?" Mr. Kempton raised an eyebrow at Alice from across the carriage.

She cast her eyes down to her lap. "You're always with us, so I shall have no reason to mourn your absence."

Mr. Kempton bellowed with laughter. "Oh, you've trained her well, Mrs. Glenn. She's ready for a Season."

Mrs. Glenn smiled demurely. "You'll have many gentlemen try to needle you, Alice. Your response was perfect. Downcast eyes, but perhaps a more evasive response."

Alice looked up, a mask of confusion and worry. "But he never leaves us alone."

Mr. Kempton roared with laughter again.

"Less truth, sister." Curtis winked at her. "I can't be having pistols at dawn every day."

Mrs. Glenn smoothed her skirt. "Gentlemen may pursue you for your wealth."

"I know." Alice sighed. She peered over at Rachel. "Perhaps it was frivolous of me to fear marriage. It is my duty, and I shall take it up." She smiled over at Curtis, but her chin trembled.

So Alice was attempting to convince Rachel to change her mind about marriage. Did she not realize it was her brother who was set against Rachel, and not the other way around?

"Men will pursue you for other reasons." Mrs. Glenn glared at Mr. Kempton. "They will try to get you alone, force their advances on you."

"Kempton would never accost me. We only jest with one another," Alice said. "Curtis has been alone with Rachel numerous times."

Rachel turned her head back to the window to watch the rooftop smoke curling up to join the clouds. Perhaps it was time to stop listening to Alice's conversation.

"But your brother does not pester her with unwanted proposals," Mrs. Glenn said.

Rachel's eyes flew to the colonel's. Her heart beat faster. A mixture of pain, anger, and sadness reflected in his eyes, but his mouth was set. She hoped hers was as well.

Mrs. Glenn continued. "She is a nurse, and your brother is a doctor. When they attend to a patient, there is nothing improper in their conduct. The patient is the chaperone. There is always a third person with them. They are never actually alone."

"I wouldn't mind having Alice assist me the way Rachel nursed Curtis." Mr. Kempton raised his eyebrows at Alice again.

Curtis turned so quickly that the carriage rocked on its axle for a moment. "I'll knock *your* block off."

Rachel covered her mouth and stared out at the passing buildings. *What did Kempton know?* She needed to talk to him as soon as they arrived at the embassy.

Curtis's hands were balled into fists. "Don't ever talk about Rachel that way."

Mr. Kempton slid along the seat, away from the colonel.

"And I did not give you leave to call me by my first name," Alice said. "Miss Loughton will do nicely."

Heavy tension filled the carriage.

Alice gestured across the carriage at her brother and Mr. Kempton. "Will you come to dinner often, Rachel? You cannot leave me alone with these two animals."

Rachel turned to face Alice. "You're most kind."

Mrs. Glenn, who sat between them, nodded. "Miss Wickford's answer is the proper response to any number of questions, Alice. Remember that, and you'll do fine without me. I shall miss you."

Alice laid her head on Mrs. Glenn's shoulder, and Rachel watched them. Alice would be lost without her chaperone, but Mrs. Glenn had not visited her sister for a year. Alice would have to brave the Season without her chaperone or mother or parent or anyone but Curtis. She'd have to take her maid with her everywhere or accompany friends.

Mr. Kempton and Mrs. Glenn tactfully resumed a quiet argument about poetry.

"You didn't answer her," Curtis said, leaning forward and speaking softly.

Rachel met his eyes, and he searched her face. The emerald green of his paisley vest reflected in his eyes, and the gold in his tiger eyes nearly disappeared today.

"You made it clear you wish to keep your distance from me. The heir to a dukedom does not need a country girl at his dinner table." She pressed her lips together to control her mouth and her emotions. He had avoided her at dinner for months now. As dearly as she loved Alice, she would not go where she was unwelcome or where she did not belong. It would be uncomfortable for all concerned.

Curtis half-turned his back to the others in the carriage, as if to shield their conversation from being overheard. His voice was low and urgent. "What do you mean?" He glanced over at Mr. Kempton and Alice, still arguing whether Fanny Brawne was worthy of John Keats. "I do not *wish* to keep my distance, Rachel." He rubbed a hand on the back of his neck. "Do you think I haven't missed you?"

Rachel felt a tug of longing as the fierceness of his green eyes pierced her. "You said we cannot be near one another, lest I fall victim to your Fever. You will have plenty of others courting the favor of a new marquis, whether he is ill or not."

Curtis stared at her. "I haven't told anyone about my grandfather's or my uncle's failing health." He lowered his voice still further. "Even Alice and Kempton don't know yet. Imagine my Season if anyone knows my cousin is barren. They'll hound me."

She thought back on the night of his fever and their shared kisses. He was afraid he'd spread his illness to her that night, but had other concerns developed? Did he now attribute her sudden change of heart to her knowledge that he would soon be heir to a dukedom?

But he seemed not to remember their conversation. How could that be? Why would he worry that she might also have Crimean Fever, if he didn't remember that evening? She'd assumed that Kempton was wrong and that Curtis had a full, clear memory of that evening after all.

But now she wasn't so sure. Did he recall her brazen invitation to kiss her? She could not meet his eyes, and something like a blush crept up her face. She did *not* blush. She never blushed, but her face felt unusually warm.

His knee brushed against hers as the carriage went over an unusually rough patch in the road, and he folded his long legs to the side. "How do you know I will be the heir? That doesn't make sense. Most women who found out would—"

He looked over at her and seemed to notice her pink cheeks. He tipped his head back and covered his eyes with his hands. "I'm sorry, Rachel. Miss Wickford. My apologies."

This was the tortured Curtis she knew from the night of his illness. For a brief moment, it was as if his true self emerged. She had not seen his real heart in months. He still seemed hurt by her refusal, yet he was angry with her for not believing his illness was real. It was as if he still longed for her approval, but she knew he disagreed with her choice to continue nursing. He wanted nothing to do with her.

Or did he still care? Was there any chance that he doubted his own diagnosis? It hurt to try to understand. She had gone over it again and again for weeks, and she was weary of the heartache.

Why would he ask her these questions unless he had forgotten their confounded conversation? How much did he remember from the rum toddy and the fever?

She nudged his knee with her own. He uncovered his eyes. She pretended to watch out the window. Finally, he caught on, and casually stretched, then rested his arms on his knees. He studied the countryside out the window, his head close to hers, where they could talk casually.

"I won't tell a soul," Rachel said quietly to him, her lips barely moving. She pretended to watch the other carriages rolling past on the streets, but she could see his face in the reflection of the glass.

Curtis glanced over at her. "How?"

"You talk in your sleep," she said, "and when you're drunk."

"I don't get drunk," he said. "I hold my liquor well. When have you seen me asleep?"

Rachel bit her lip. They sat so close, their heads nearly touching as they looked out the carriage window. It was the closest they had been in months. She glanced down at his chest and his broad shoulders, invitingly near to her. Her shoulder bumped against his as the carriage rode over another rough patch in the road.

Curtis grinned back at her and dropped his voice to a whisper. "Kempton and Alice lie about the alcohol, but I'll grant the sleep talking." He gazed at her, his eyes softening for a moment. She could almost hear him telling her again how beautiful she looked when she slept.

"You're an ugly customer when you sleep," she said quietly, settling back in her seat, away from the cedar and lavender scented invitation to tell too much and to feel too much.

Curtis barked out a laugh, a genuine deep laugh, and Rachel smiled at him across the carriage. It felt good to tease him again.

The carriage slowed and stopped. Curtis waited for her to descend the steps, hovering behind her. She could feel his eyes on her. She hadn't really answered his question, and she was fairly certain they both knew it. She needed time to figure out how to respond before Curtis confronted her.

He remembers, he remembers not. If only she could find a daisy with some petals to pluck, perhaps that would answer her question.

"Kempton, may I have a word?" Rachel seized his arm and began to walk with him toward the magnificent entryway of the embassy.

"Sorry about the nursing comment, Rachel," Mr. Kempton said, rubbing his neck. "I didn't think."

"What exactly did you see?" Rachel asked, narrowing her eyes.

"Heard. I kept my eyes closed. That chaise didn't allow for much snooping."

"Not that you didn't try," Rachel said.

Mr. Kempton's sheepish grin did not console her. "I just heard a few suggestive sounds between my snores."

She pulled him aside as they waited with the others in the grand lobby of the building. "You were awake?"

"You honestly imagine anyone could sleep through *his* singing?" Mr. Kempton nodded his head over toward Curtis. "I may have dozed off here or there. I didn't hear your conversation, just his songs and, uh, perhaps, it grew too quiet for a few moments."

Rachel looked over. Curtis was glaring at them.

She took a few steps farther away from him. "What must you think of me?"

"That you're in love with him," Mr. Kempton said. He turned so that both their backs were to the colonel. "You and I both know that, but he doesn't. Look, he'll come around."

He *wouldn't* come around. He was the most obstinate man she'd ever encountered.

"He won't accept the simple truth that he's not ill. You heard him that day. He was unreasonable and overbearing." Rachel looked over Mr. Kempton's shoulder. Curtis's glare was still smoldering. "I won't tolerate it. He said he would remain constant, and he has already changed his mind."

"I'm sorry. He's a rummy old cove, and we both know that, too." Mr. Kempton looked over his shoulder. "Suppose Alice will ever change her mind?"

Rachel followed his gaze to Alice, miniscule in the center of the towering marble entryway. Mr. Kempton's look had a little too much yearning in it. Curtis lounged against a column next to her, his eyes still trained on Rachel and his arms folded. She could see the scowl from here.

"Do you really want her to? If she actually ever agreed to any of your ridiculous schemes, what would you do?" Rachel asked.

Mr. Kempton considered Alice. "Turn the opposite way and run." He spun his hat and tipped it back on his head.

They laughed.

"If you would tell Curtis how you really feel," Mr. Kempton began, "that might cure his fever in a hurry."

Rachel laughed. "If you would keep him away from rum. I told him it was a cold, and he didn't believe me. No, I don't fit into his life. It's better this way. Leave things as they are."

Mr. Kempton took her hand and peered at her. "But it hurts me to see you both unhappy. Why do you both keep insisting you are fine without my interference?" He sighed dramatically and affected a sheepish look. "I solemnly swear I will never buy another bottle of alcohol as long as I live, no matter how many patients think they require it. I only keep it for them. I will give Alice the key to every bottle in the house. Unless *you* need it?" He smiled suggestively. "Perhaps you prefer him in that state?"

Rachel returned the smile. "No matchmaking."

She heard sharp, precise footsteps approaching. Rachel dropped Mr. Kempton's hand and whirled around.

"May I escort you to your friends?" Curtis's jaw was set. He glanced between Mr. Kempton and Rachel, his hands clenched into fists again. "Lord and Lady Shelford have arrived."

Rachel rested her hand lightly on Curtis's arm, and they crossed the lobby in silence. "I don't like the way he was looking at you," Curtis finally said, "or talking about you or holding your hand."

"Thank you for your interest in my affairs." Rachel pressed her lips together. "But I am no longer your concern. Lord Shelford is here, and he shall be my guardian now. Please don't knock Kempton's block off." Why was he suddenly jealous, when he had scorned, despised, and avoided her for the last two months? He still treated her as though he were responsible for her. As if he still cared.

Eleanor rushed to greet her. Rachel let go of Curtis's arm. It was over, finally. She would see much less of him in London, and in formal circumstances. They would not ever be alone together again. She told herself it was relief she was feeling.

But Curtis remained at her side, stiff and formal, and not at all at ease, making it hard to feel relieved.

Eleanor hugged her. "Oh, darling! Tell me everything!"

Lord Shelford greeted her. "Are you two engaged yet?" He pounded Colonel Loughton on the back.

The Duke of Woodford joined them, looking curiously between Rachel and Curtis. "Loughton, old man, catch up on everything?"

Rachel didn't know what to do, except stay silent. Curtis scowled. They could ascertain the state of their relationship from that.

"Are you acquainted with Lord Romford? Only bachelor in London who is older than me?" The duke motioned toward a handsome, sandy-haired gentleman.

"By a mere six years. Come now. There must be others." Lord

Romford bowed and took Rachel's hand. "Pleased." He turned to Alice. "Miss Loughton, always a pleasure."

Alice blushed and stared at the marble floor of the entryway. Mrs. Glenn prodded her. "Pleased to see you again, Lord Romford."

Alice was going to struggle during the Season. Rachel wished she could be there to help her through it.

"Shall we take tea in the garden?" The duke gestured toward a set of doors leading to the back of the embassy. "My mother will meet us there."

They strolled through the cavernous marble entry, past columns and pillars, chandeliers and footmen, a bustle of people coming and going everywhere. They wound their way through a richly deco-rated corridor to an expansive patio with tables set for afternoon tea.

After they settled themselves at an iron-wrought table, perfect for outdoor entertaining, Rachel hastened to ensure the duke understood her relationship with Curtis. "The colonel and I are not engaged, Your Grace."

Lord Shelford smiled. "Not engaged *yet*, eh?"

Next to her, Curtis stiffened in his chair.

"No reason to delay. Bliss awaits you, old man." Lord Shelford sent an affectionate gaze toward Eleanor.

Woodford glanced between Rachel and Curtis. He, at least, seemed to sense the true nature of things. "Ah. In that case, Romford and I shall not be the only seasoned bachelors in London after all," the duke said. "Kempton, Loughton, and I are old class-mates. Eleanor's brother, Dunmore, was our comrade in arms, as well as Shelford's older brother, Spencer."

"Worst group of troublemakers Eton ever saw," Kempton said affectionately.

"Or Cambridge," Lord Shelford added. "Although John and I did our best to live up to your reputation."

The duchess began to pass around plates with exquisite French pastries and cups of tea. Rachel caught Eleanor's eye across the table, but her friend merely studied her curiously. She looked down at her lap. *Disaster*. Percy was blunt, and Eleanor would not rescue her. Why had Mama thought they were the right chaperones for the Season? But would she rather live with Lucy and Peter, who were still enjoying their Grand Tour? They would not return for several months more, and she would not be able to help Miss Nightingale. There was no other choice.

She hated living on others' charity. She kept her tight smile in place. Show no emotion. Let the conversation flow around her, since she could not think of a way to redirect it. *No response is the best response.*

Rachel sipped her tea. Bland. She'd prefer to mix her own blend.

Beside her, Curtis coughed and put down his cup. He didn't like it, either. Rachel found a tureen of honey on the table and slid it toward Curtis.

He spooned some into his tea.

Rachel stared out at the gardens. The mid-March wind chilled her, and she shivered. Curtis took her shawl, which had slipped down, and guided it back up onto her shoulders.

Thankfully, the duchess was more adept at conversation than she was.

"Who will present you at Court?" the duke's mother asked Alice, who seemed terrified to be addressed directly. She could not have been softer spoken or gentler, yet Alice was almost in tears. "How old are you, dear?"

"Eighteen." Alice stared into her tea.

Curtis cleared his throat. "I'm certain my aunt, Lady Abridge, will beg for that duty."

Rachel knew that Alice was probably thinking of her mother, who would have presented her had she not died, and trying not to cry.

The duchess tried to catch Alice's eye. "Perfect age for a Season."

Alice stirred her tea and took a long sip. Rachel knew that trick. She wouldn't have to answer, if she were drinking tea. Her Grace turned her attention to the Shelfords. "Is Lady Octavia determined to have a Season, Percy?"

Lord Shelford groaned. "She attended half the events last year. I cannot keep her at bay any longer, though she's only sixteen."

"Yes, that's what Arabella tells me. Your mother is delighted." The duchess smiled graciously.

"It'll send me to an early grave," Lord Shelford said.

"Shall I prepare for a wedding, then?" the duke asked. "One week or two? How long will it take Octavia to marry?"

Eleanor looked at the duke shrewdly. "She will be hard to please. Octavia craves the excitement of the Season, but she has no plans to wed soon."

The duke nodded. Curtis shifted uncomfortably in his seat, his long legs bumping into Rachel's skirt, then quickly shifted back the other direction. Any mention of women with no plans to wed was a rather awkward subject just now. Rachel turned toward Mr. Kempton to avoid the colonel's gaze.

Mr. Kempton caught her eye. "We are indeed old classmates, Miss Wickford. Do you remember the polar bear plunge, Woodford?"

He shook his head. "You didn't do that again."

"They cut open a hole in the Rhine. You should have joined us." Mr. Kempton shivered. "Glorious Christmas Day."

Now Rachel shifted uncomfortably in *her* chair. She'd rather not recall that day, and she was sure Curtis was trying to forget it, too. She picked up her teacup to steady herself.

Lord Shelford glanced between Mr. Kempton and the colonel. "What's this? I need to join you next year and take my brother's place in your yearly tradition."

Romford nodded his agreement. "I don't know what kind of swimmers you are, but you were all excellent with an oar. I saw you race more than once. You did well as team captain, Loughton, and your rowing scull never lost the University Boat Race to Oxford, did it?"

Loughton shrugged. "Our Blue Boat did all right."

The duke laughed. "We were more than that. He made us practice six days a week, all weather, before every race."

"It's a wonder any schoolwork got done at all," Kempton said.

Rachel darted a glance sideways. She knew Curtis had always been athletic, but she didn't realize that he had captained such a prestigious team at Cambridge. Once again, the more she knew about him, the more she felt intimidated by his social standing.

Kempton set down his cup. "The only time Woodford ever lost anything was when Loughton graduated top of the class, despite taking those difficult medical classes."

"Is that where you learned how to mix a rum toddy?" Woodford asked.

Mr. Kempton's eyes took on a mischievous twinkle. "Speaking of which."

Woodford chuckled. "Don't tell me."

Kempton nodded. "Loughton fell ill after our icy plunge."

Rachel set down her tea.

"Not from that." Curtis pushed his cup away. "It was something far worse—Crimean Fever."

Lord Romford laughed. "Can't handle a dip in the winter water, eh? Making excuses. I shall join you, too, next Christmas, and someone recruit Dunmore. We'll lay wagers on who catches cold. My money is on Loughton."

"He attended a family with ill children," Kempton said as the men laughed. "It had nothing to do with his swim. We all caught cold, truth be told."

Romford chuckled. "You are a loyal friend."

"Did he get drunk trying to cure himself, as usual?" the duke asked.

"I handle my alcohol fine," Curtis said. "I choose to abstain."

Lord Shelford bellowed a laugh. "Spencer always said you have a fine singing voice."

The duke looked at Mr. Kempton. "Has he learned any new tunes?"

"Ask Miss Wickford." Mr. Kempton turned to her. "What was he singing?"

The table fell silent. The laughs died away, and every eye was trained on her. Should she tease him? Deny it? Was this Mr. Kempton's awkward attempt at matchmaking? She tried to think of a way to avoid answering.

"Out with it, Rachel," Eleanor said. "I can always tell when you're trying to hide something."

Nothing for it. "Well. He was convinced he was dying."

"Never happened," Curtis said. "You and Kempton concocted this story in the lobby."

Alice laughed. "It's true, Curtis. You were convinced you would perish. Mrs. Glenn was there, and so was Kempton."

Mrs. Glenn sniffed. "Soused. Completely out of his mind."

"Chills and aches all over," Mr. Kempton added. "Drank a rum toddy to cure that."

Curtis looked between them, indignant. "I handle my illness as well as my alcohol."

"Which is poorly, I'm afraid, Colonel. He pounded on our door at two in the morning," Rachel said, "with an urgent message."

The duke nodded his head. "It was always urgent when he was drunk."

"I'm never drunk," Curtis protested, grinning.

Rachel paused. Every eye was on her. "He desperately wanted to tell me something before he died. His temperature had just begun to spike, and the fever had taken hold. He was completely out of his mind." She turned to him. His eyes darted to her mouth, as if waiting to see her mouth twitch. It didn't, and his face grew serious. He knew she couldn't lie. Perhaps he was beginning to believe this might have happened.

"What was it?" Lord Romford grinned from ear to ear.

Rachel cleared her throat and began to sing, a perfect imitation of Curtis's wavering, soused singing voice. "*I am the very model of a modern major general. I've information animal, vegetable, and mineral. I know the kings of England, and I quote the fights historical. From Marathon to Waterloo, in order categorical."*

The table erupted in laughter. Rachel watched Curtis relax. She would never tell anyone what else he'd said, nor would Mr. Kempton.

"Let me guess," the duke said. "The entire score?"

"He's memorized the whole play," Mr. Kempton managed between gasps.

"Never happened," Curtis said, grinning. "They were conspiring before we arrived."

Rachel smiled at him. "He's got a fair voice for sea shanties, too."

Lord Romford and the duke nodded. "Was it 'Roll the Old Chariot?' He can go for hours on that one."

Rachel bit her lip. Finally, she nodded. The table erupted in laughter again. Curtis was studying her, sizing her up.

"You're sunk, man," Lord Shelford said. "You can deny it to your mates, but you can't call three gentlewomen all liars."

"Top class nurse," Kempton said. "Miss Wickford got him through a rough patch. Cold compresses and the lot, so I could sleep."

Rachel tried not to squirm in her chair as the duke and Lord Romford grinned at her. She could feel Curtis's eyes on her. "Although the colonel thinks I should not be nursing anymore. But really, it was just a fever. Nothing that a few hundred pots of tea didn't cure."

She'd brewed every last leaf they'd bought in Italy, and she'd sat with him all day, while Kempton sat up with him all night. Her whole heart had gone out to him, and then he'd done an about-face when he awoke from the delirium.

"Not nurse? Why not?" Eleanor asked. "That's all she does."

"Rach-Miss Wickford risks too much," Curtis said. "She may have contracted Crimean Fever herself—"

"And how would she have done that?" Lord Shelford grinned.

Curtis glared at him.

The duke cleared his throat. "That would be serious, indeed, Loughton, if you had anything other than your usual case of Rum Toddy. I don't think Miss Wickford can catch *that* from you."

Romford caught Kempton's eye, and they laughed. Even Alice and Mrs. Glenn stifled giggles beneath their napkins. Rachel desperately wanted to get away from this mortifying conversation.

"A walk is in order," Eleanor said abruptly. "I need a moment alone with my dear friend."

Rachel was relieved to get away from the scrutiny. She had no taste for watery tea anyway, and Curtis's sudden scrutiny made her uncomfortable. Eleanor must have seen her unease.

Eleanor drew Rachel's arm through hers, and they began to move out along the great green manicured lawns of the embassy's enormous garden. "Can you believe Guy and his mother manage all of this?"

Rachel knew she was making idle conversation that the others could overhear. They'd have their real talk once they were far enough away.

"Yes, the duke and Her Grace have taken on a lot of responsibility," she said.

They meandered along the gravel paths, until they found a turn. Eleanor glanced over her shoulder before guiding Rachel around the corner. A row of evergreen hedges hid them from view.

Eleanor led Rachel to an iron bench, tangled with iron leaves. A trellis formed a sort of bower overhead. "Now. What happened?"

Rachel laughed. "I haven't seen you since October."

"You know very well. Confess everything, or I shall resort to cruel measures." Eleanor waited.

"I don't know where to begin." Rachel pulled her shawl around herself. The sun hid behind a cloud and the slight breeze suddenly felt chill.

Eleanor glanced over her shoulder again. "Well, the colonel hasn't let you out of his sight since we arrived. He alternates between glaring at Mr. Kempton and staring at you. And how on earth are you not engaged yet?" She clapped her hands. "Have you switched your affections to Mr. Kempton?"

"Why do you assume I would marry either of them?" Rachel asked.

Eleanor laughed. "Because the colonel dotes on you. I've rarely seen a man so in love, excepting my dear Percy, and you've had months alone together to increase that intimacy. Come now, Confess everything."

Rachel sighed. "Very well. True Confession. We have had a disastrous falling out. Curtis is quite angry with me, and there is nothing of the kind in our future, I assure you."

"Curtis?" Eleanor smiled at her. "Not the 'General'?" She peered around the hedges. "Oh! I must explain to Percy that when I take my dear friend into the garden for a private chat, *he* is not invited." Eleanor looked at her intently. "Rachel. You know I have championed the colonel's cause from the beginning. He has been watching us ever since we left the table, and now he's dragged poor Percy across the gardens to find you. Will you be kind to the man?"

And Eleanor vanished, leaving her alone on the bench, ending the talk before it had scarcely begun.

Rachel's heart began to pound. She peeked around the hedge. Eleanor had taken Percy by the arm, and they were returning across the lawn toward the embassy's tall, window-covered building.

But Curtis was striding toward her in great, purposeful steps.

CHAPTER 13

Curtis marched across the lawn. Unless he was mistaken, the woman he loved waited for him just beyond the next row of hedges.

He had been an idiot, completely mistaken for months. If Kempton, Alice, Mrs. Glenn, and Rachel all told the truth, then he'd made a complete fool of himself. It explained Rachel's knowledge that he was Grandfather's heir.

What else had he wanted to urgently tell her? He knew she was holding back to protect him.

It explained her insistence that he did not have Crimean Fever. What if those memories were not hallucinations? He rubbed a hand over his face.

He needed answers, now. Curtis rounded the corner and found Rachel sitting on a bench. Her hair was pinned elaborately in a braided bun, but images of it cascading over her shoulders flashed in his mind.

What had he done? Curtis stopped and cleared his throat. He widened his stance and clasped his hands behind his back.

"Don't you dare interrogate me, General." Rachel left the bench and approached him.

Curtis studied her, willing the memories to return. What was real and what was not? "So, I must have drunk a rum toddy."

"Clearly." Rachel bit her lip. She was maddeningly close. Why had he avoided her for so long?

"If I don't ask, will you tell me?" He tried his most charming smile.

Rachel folded her arms across her chest. "That's a question."

Curtis inched closer. "So, I thought I was hallucinating…"

Rachel sniffed. "You sang a lot."

"Was your hair down?" Curtis watched her carefully.

Her eyes widened. "Kempton said you never remember anything after you drink."

"I might recall more than he thinks." He knew it was a lie, but perhaps he could bluff his way through this. He advanced, running a hand over her neatly pinned coiffure.

Rachel seemed to hold her breath.

"You're beautiful with your hair over your shoulders." Curtis gazed into her eyes.

She slapped his fingers. "Not again. Keep your hands off my braid."

So *he* had undone her braid. What else could he trick her into telling him? "What was your favorite part of the evening?" He searched her face.

She huffed. "If you remembered that evening, then why have you scorned me for the last two months and believed you had the Fever? Why are you following me right now? No, Curtis. Find your kisses somewhere else."

Rachel began to walk away.

"We kissed?" The words tumbled out before he could stop himself. "It wasn't a dream?"

She stopped and turned around, a shrewd look on her face. "You *don't* remember."

"Remind me." He chased her, running to wrap an arm around her waist.

Rachel pushed his chest away. "No. Either you remember, and

you treated me horribly for two months afterward, or you don't remember, and you treated me horribly for two months afterward." She folded her arms again. "Either way, you were a beast."

Curtis collapsed onto the nearby bench. He sank his head into his hands. *What a mess.* He had no idea what transpired between them, but it sounded as though he'd been inappropriately forward. Playing with her hair? Kissing her? How much of the delirium and how many of the dreams were his own doing?

A vague image of himself lying on a couch with his head in her lap came to mind.

Surely not. He could not have been that forward.

And then he'd been so angry with her for refusing to believe that he had the Crimean Fever.

He lifted his head. "Did I, by any chance, lay on a sofa with my head in your lap?" He risked a glance at her.

She glared at him. "So, you do recall? You got what you wanted, a few kisses, and then you discarded me, just like the dozen others." Her eyes flashed with fury. "Blasted scoundrel. You knew you weren't ill. That was an excuse to be rid of me. And you dared asked me not to nurse?" She stormed away.

Dozen others. Confound it. What had he told her? She was right about how many women he'd kissed. He jumped off the bench. "No, snatches are beginning to come back. Nothing more, just your stunning hair and your very comfortable lap."

Curtis grabbed Rachel by the arm and turned her around. Her eyes still sparked.

"I'm sorry, Rachel." He dropped her arm and shook his head, searching her eyes. "It sounds like I was a raging idiot that night. I don't know what else I said or did."

"A great deal," Rachel said.

Curtis tilted his head back, studying the grey clouds drifting above the hedges. "Can you forgive me? I would like to be on good terms with you again, if I'm not condemned to a contagious life-long illness."

Silence. He studied the grass, slightly damp from a light rainfall earlier in the day. "Rachel, please. Will you tell me what I said or did, and what I can do to make amends?"

She folded her arms. "You remember."

"I swear, I don't." Curtis searched his memory for anything else.

She laughed. "You certainly swear."

He gestured toward the bench. "Will you talk to me? Please?"

Rachel narrowed her eyes. "Why the deuce should I?"

Curtis tilted his head back to the sky and blew out a breath. "Because I can't stop loving you."

She considered him a long while. "What's your game? Are you attempting to win another kiss? We are behind a secluded hedge. This is the perfect spot."

Curtis collapsed onto the bench again. What kind of muddle had he made? "I don't even remember the kiss, really. Believe me, I wish I could. It seemed like a fever dream." Since it had cost him so much. It hardly seemed worth it now.

"Kisses," Rachel corrected him. She pursed her lips. "You could hardly stop at one."

Curtis dropped his head into his hands. She must despise him for losing control of himself, and rightly so.

"Did you kiss me back? I mean, was it unwelcome or not?" He searched her eyes. "I would hate to think that I—"

Rachel turned away.

"You're hiding your cheek from me." Curtis ran to face her. "*Did* you return my advances?"

She rotated on the spot, refusing to face him. Curtis hesitated. He did not dare lay a hand on her, knowing he had already done far more than he ever should have, when they were not engaged.

She stood with her back to him, arms folded. Angry. But she *had* enjoyed kissing him, or she would not hide her face. He tried to piece everything together.

"I've been a wretched idiot," Curtis said. "*I* kissed *you*, then I was angry that you didn't believe me. It was all real? No hallucinations, no dreams, no Crimean Fever."

Rachel huffed. "Bang on the mark, you toff."

He tentatively put a hand on her arm. She had loved him in his dreams. She had looked at him with such adoration and longing in the delirium. What was true?

She shook his hand off.

"I didn't remember anything except your hands on my forehead and a cool compress when the fever got too high. And the kissing and your hair and your lap." He grinned. "And you saying you adore me or something like that."

Rachel turned around, her eyes softening. "You still need a good slating."

Curtis took a step closer. "I should not have done what I did or said what I said. You could never harm anyone or endanger them. I blame Rum Toddy Disease for misleading my memories."

Rachel sighed. "You truly thought I was endangering children. And you needed to eat when we spoke. Tea is not enough. You always need to eat."

Curtis inclined his head. "If you'd like to hit me, go ahead." He pointed to his cheek. "I treated you the worst way possible. Flatten me."

She closed the distance between them, slipping her arms inside his coat. She gazed up at him. "I thought you were going to flatten Kempton when he made that crack about me nursing you, Curtis, but he wasn't saying those things unfairly. You were half-rats, and I may have done some things you do not recall. And the things you do remember, well, they are most likely all true."

He wrapped his arms around her waist. "You?" He swallowed. "Cared for me while I was ill? Exactly what did you do? Kempton suggested you were—"

Rachel took a deep breath. Her arms inside his coat toyed with his vest, and he drew his coat around her to bring her closer. Rachel bit her lip. "I did care for you that night. You collapsed on the sofa, and I was trapped. I had very little choice." She smiled at him.

Curtis opened his mouth to apologize.

Rachel put a finger on his lips. "I do care for you. You were completely soused, and you asked me why I would not marry you." She gazed up at him. "I told you something that perhaps made you feel it might not be inappropriate or unwelcome to—"

"What was it?" Curtis interrupted, drawing Rachel to him. She put her hands on his chest. He could see the trepidation in her eyes, but there was something else. Something new. A fragility, a hopefulness, a hint of the admiration he'd seen on the carriage ride home from Bettina's.

"Change. My. Mind," Rachel whispered.

Curtis seized her and drew her in toward him, kissing her with all the passion and desire and longing of the last six months. She responded with equal fervor and no hesitation, and he felt her hands slide up from his chest and around his neck.

There was no room between them, no doubt, no more difference or disputes. This was perfect accord. Curtis intensified the kiss, and time stood still. Rachel was wrapped around him, his coat covering the both of them, yet he drew her in, closer. The end of the battle, a peaceful sea, ceasefire at last.

When at last he stopped to gaze at her, Curtis could only wonder. "I forgot that? It's even better than my hazy hallucination memories."

Rachel rested her head on his chest. "You have a scar, here," she said, running her finger inside the cuff of his sleeve, "from a battle in the Crimea. Am I right?"

"I wish you had reminded me earlier." Curtis relished the feel of her in his arms, her fingers now tracing a line up his arm and resting again on his chest. He smiled down at her. "You've known for months? We should marry by license, as soon as we return."

Rachel slid her arms out, but he kept the coat around her shoulders.

"It's chilly. Stay here with me." He led her over to the bench.

She laid her head on his shoulder. He could only grin, like a greedy child caught stealing too many sweets.

"You *have* changed your mind," Curtis said. "Haven't you? Disavowed your vow never to marry?" He watched her face.

"It's a lot to consider, all at once," Rachel said. "You've been set against me for two months. You thought me a menace and a completely irresponsible creature, and I've accepted that. It's hard to understand what is happening."

"But I've changed my mind, and you've changed yours." He grinned. "I love you. That never changed."

"But the rest worries me. You change your mind rather often," Rachel said. "What's to say you won't change it again as soon as we arrive in London? Lay down another dictum or believe you're dying again?"

Curtis eyed the slightly wet grass.

"Don't even consider kneeling on that," Rachel said.

He laughed and took her hands. "Will you let me propose? I want to do it properly. You know I want to marry you."

"Not yet." She traced the lines of his face. "You think that now, but wait until you return. Your grandfather won't want a confounded country girl for his grandson. There are fifty other women waiting to take my place, and you've already kissed twenty of them."

Curtis covered her hand with his own. "Ten. Fifteen, maybe."

Rachel huffed and withdrew her hand. Curtis pulled her head onto his chest.

"It's a compliment to you. I've never enjoyed a kiss so much before or kissed anyone like I just kissed you. Or you kissed me. Depends on how you look at it," Curtis said.

She glared at him. "You need to learn how to give compliments."

"At least I know how to give kisses." He scooted closer to her and raised an eyebrow.

"You're nearly as bold as when you're drunk," Rachel said, but she allowed him to kiss her again. She rested her head gently on him, the coat warming them both. He'd never been so grateful for a cold wind before.

Curtis took one of her hands in his lap. "Will you disavow your vow?"

"I will concede that you are an excellent kisser," Rachel said, "and that I enjoy your company and your shaving soap."

"And?" He brushed her hair with one hand.

She slapped it. "Leave the hair pins alone, and I will consider the idea of matrimony at a future date."

"To me." Curtis shook his hand. "That stung."

Rachel pushed her pins neatly into place. "The hair is off-limits."

"But it's glorious," he said. "Can I take it out again when we're married?" He would do anything she asked.

"*If.*" She left the bench, pushing his coat away. She shivered and wrapped her shawl around herself. She was still determined to do things alone.

Curtis scrambled off the bench and put an arm around her waist. "What do you need from me? When may I propose?" He tested the soil. "It should dry in a few hours."

Rachel peeled his arm off her waist and held his hand instead. "I do not think you have ever stayed in love with one woman for an entire Season."

Curtis blew out a breath. *Bang on the mark.*

"I won't be welcomed by your friends or your grandfather. None of them would consider me worthy to be your duchess, and I'm not sure I am, Curtis. I never imagined I'd marry a marquis." She dropped his hand and rounded the corner of the hedges.

Curtis could see the embassy in the distance. He quickened his pace to walk beside Rachel. "Of course you're worthy. *You're* magnificent. I will change your mind. They'll love you, as I do."

She continued her walk across the lawn, slipping away.

Curtis pursued her. "You adore me, and we're perfect for each other. Even Shelford thinks so, and he's going to be your chaperone. Grandfather will love you."

"Don't enlist anyone else in your cause," Rachel said, and turned to face him. "I am not engaged to you. Are we clear?"

But she agreed that she adored him. Curtis took her hand and stopped walking. "You do want to marry me, don't you? Shouldn't you be rushing to marry me right away? Most women would want to marry a future duke."

Rachel patted his cheek. "Handsome, conceited bloke. You've had too many blasted women chase you. That's exactly the attitude that worries me." She smiled sadly at him. "I do care for you, and I will not blame you when *you* change your mind again. I shall be content with nursing, but yes, if I ever did marry, you are exactly the sort of wretched man I would want to marry. A simple country doctor would do for me."

Curtis eyed the embassy. She loved to tease him, and he would dearly love to return the favor, but too many people could see them. He couldn't kiss her again—yet. "Blast that Dr. Morrow."

Rachel laughed. She was becoming more natural and comfortable with him. The barriers were falling, one by one.

"I won't change my mind or treat you like a beast again," Curtis said. "I can outlast you, and I shall propose on the last day of the Season."

Rachel sighed. "Marriage is more than love. There are considerations that reach far beyond feelings. You've been appointed to a commission by the queen herself, and you move in social circles where I'm unknown. The other women will sneer at me, and I have no desire to be looked down on by everyone except you. I do not fit into your life or your world, and you are far too prone to ordering me about."

She ran her eyes over his shoulders and chest, then back up to his mouth. "You *are* a highly desirable dinner companion, and an excellent kisser, even more so when you're not drunk. If those two things were the only requirements for happiness in marriage, we would be assured of bliss. However, I made a promise to God that I would serve Him first, and I require more than kisses to keep me happy. I need to help the poor and helpless, too."

Rachel moved up the lawn, across the clipped grass, and left him standing in a patch of mud, even more in love than he had been a minute ago.

He loved her for so many reasons. She was bold, honest,

compassionate, devoted to helping the helpless, and she swore as well as he did. She would not admit it yet, but he knew she loved him, too. Yes, marriage required commitment, and sacrifice, and a reasonable amount of strategy. He'd already made his share of blunders.

Shelford had given him advice as they walked down the lawn this afternoon. *"Apologize, Loughton. Doesn't matter what happened. You were in the wrong somehow. Trust me. Advice from a happily married man. Learn how to apologize."*

Of course she fit into his world. His love would be enough. It hadn't changed in six months; it had only deepened. He would wait another five and prove his steadiness to Rachel. In fact—

Curtis grinned. He would go out of his way to show her how steadfast and reliable he was. He would need to consult with Grandfather, as usual, but if all went well, he would be married by the end of August.

CHAPTER 14

Rachel hovered on the edges of the ballroom with Eleanor. Candles burned in sconces on the ivory and gold walls. Tall, Greek statues adorned the tops of columns. Light reflected off the marble-inlaid floor. The domed ceiling overhead drew her eye to a balcony where an orchestra played a lively polka. The thin gold railing was as ornate as the carved archways above it.

She tugged at the new ballgown, an elegant cream silk that accentuated her waist and hid very little of her bust. "I knew you'd make me buy something ridiculous."

"Don't blame me this time," Eleanor said. "The mothers conspired against you."

Rachel's mother had surprised her with an extravagant amount of money to buy gowns in Paris. She'd sent the funds and instructions to Eleanor, with a short note to herself.

"*Aunt Ellen, Lady Barrington, and I all agree. Buy the gowns there. You won't spend the money if I give it to you, so I sent it to Eleanor. I've been saving it for years, so use every last bit. I shall enquire about it at Easter, and there had better not be any excess left over. All my love, Mama.*"

Rachel smoothed the front of her too-perfect gown. Not a single stain anywhere. At least she'd convinced Eleanor to select simple gowns for her. Well, relatively simple. They were from Paris, after all, and they were ballgowns, so they all dipped uncomfortably low. There were no shawls in the ballroom.

She'd insisted there be no tassels or lace or overlays and as few ruffles as possible. Rachel had allowed some braiding along the edges, so popular after the Crimean War. The women's dresses mimicked the men's uniforms. If she had to choose between ruffles, lace, rosettes, or braiding, she'd take the braiding. The puffed sleeves could not be avoided, and Eleanor managed to purchase fabrics with gold threads running through them to get around Rachel's moratorium on decorations.

Rachel squirmed in the confining sleeves and bodice. "You didn't have to comply."

"And have your mother disown me?" Eleanor snorted.

Lord Shelford lifted her hand to his lips. "I have the most elegant wife in London."

Eleanor swatted him. "You're ridiculous."

"And you love me." Lord Shelford scanned the room. "What are we waiting for? My sister is already dancing, and my mother is happily involved in gossip."

Eleanor glanced at Rachel. "I suspect we await the arrival of a tall, handsome colonel in his formal uniform."

"I hate it when you point out how handsome he is," Lord Shelford said.

"I'd like to point out how late he is," Rachel said. "Perhaps he's not coming." She watched the other women dancing. Which ones knew Curtis? Which ones still loved him?

Does he still love me?

The scent of cedar and lavender filled her senses, and she turned instinctively. Curtis had nearly reached her. He wore full formal military dress and had never looked more attractive. The crisp red coat with gleaming buttons, the braid on the shoulders and collar, the trim black trousers, and the clean white gloves. Every eye in the room must be drawn to him, a hero of the Crimean War.

"Did you doubt me?" he asked, and bowed over her hand. They stood awkwardly. She'd seen him move to take her arm, then hesitate. They were in a crowded ballroom, where curious eyes noticed any impropriety. She longed to throw her arms around his neck, but instead she inclined her head toward him and his sister.

"I thought you must have stopped for a swim in the Thames," Rachel said. "Good evening, Alice. How are you?"

"I hate these new dresses. One drop of water, and they're ruined. I'm so much more comfortable at home. Why do I need a Season? Why not next year?" She looked at Curtis. "Mrs. Glenn will be here next year."

He shook his head. "You're nearly nineteen, and you've already been presented at the confounded Court."

Alice turned to Rachel. "Be glad you did not have to attend. I thought I would die of fright or trip when walking backward to leave the queen. At least Octavia accompanied me. I cannot feel fear when I am with your sister, Lord Shelford. She is like Rachel. Perfectly irreverent."

Alice drew a breath. "Do I have to dance? My greatest aspiration is to be a wallflower. Where's Kempton?" She searched the ballroom and dropped onto a sofa.

Rachel and Curtis exchanged a look. Rachel could see a hint of panic in his eyes. How had he managed for an entire month without Mrs. Glenn?

How had Rachel managed without him? She'd gone home to visit Mama first. What a relief to see her after so long and get lengthy updates in person from Dr. Morrow. Mama had shooed her away after only a week, so she could return to Eleanor's townhome and settle in. It had been hard to leave her concerns behind, and indeed, her worries came with her to London. Mama seemed less energetic than last year. She rested more and spoke less. In the quiet moments, when no one else was around,

Rachel's mind traveled back to Mama's frail body trapped on the sofa at home.

But there was rarely time to worry about Mama or moon over Curtis's absence. Rachel and Eleanor spent all their time preparing for Lady Octavia's presentation at Court. It was endless hours of practicing Lady Octavia's curtsey, her entrance, and her exit. Her presentation gown was more extravagant than any bridal gown, and probably cost more than all of the dresses they had purchased in Paris.

It was all a reminder to Rachel that she did not fit into Curtis's life, as she helped Lady Octavia prepare, as she stayed home while Eleanor accompanied her sister-in-law to St. James's court, as she heard the reports that Alice and Curtis had been there, too.

Now, at last, the real excitement of the Season was beginning. More balls and events, and more chances to see Curtis when the nursing school began classes. She had spent the last month desperately missing him, knowing he was meeting with Army generals and preparing Alice for her Court presentation. As each day passed without a visit, she resigned herself to the understanding that the present did not bode well for any sort of future together.

But she could still befriend his poor, terrified sister.

Rachel settled beside Alice. "Is that why you were so late? Nerves?"

Alice laughed. "No, Curtis decided he needed to shave, and trim his fingernails, and I don't know what else."

Rachel bit her lip. "Your *brother* made you late for the ball?"

Curtis grinned. "A gentleman is clean-shaven." He rubbed his face. "You said my blasted whiskers are too long at this time of night."

"You do know that most men wear beards," Rachel said. "They do not keep their sisters waiting."

"And most men are not doctors who need to be especially hygienic," Curtis said. "And you like my cheek smooth."

"How would she know what your cheek feels like?" Lord Shelford asked. His voice was always too loud. Rachel bit her lip.

"Percy, if you're going to be her chaperone and guardian this Season, you would do well to guard her reputation, not ruin it," Eleanor whispered.

Curtis held his hand out to Rachel. "Will you save me the next dance?"

Rachel considered him. A month apart, and he acted as if no time had passed. He was as handsome and charming as ever. "I suppose, since I am not engaged to dance with Lord Romford until the dance after next." She tried to hide a smile, but she was certain he saw it.

Curtis folded his arms, glaring around the ballroom. "Is he? In that case, may I steal your charge, Lord Shelford? I'd like to introduce Miss Wickford to someone without delay."

Lord Shelford grinned. "If I said no? I've been trying to get a good boxing match together." He sounded hopeful.

"I'll meet you at the club tomorrow, if you'll say yes." Curtis glared at him.

Lord Shelford laughed. "Very well. Eleven o'clock. Would you like me to recruit Romford? Itching to get a few knocks in with him, too?"

Curtis nodded and guided Rachel away from the Shelfords.

"Am I worth the risk?" she asked Curtis, relishing the brief moment with him. "A boxing match with Lord Shelford for one dance?" The room thronged with people who pressed in on them from every side, but she was walking on his arm, and they were together.

"I won't know until tomorrow," he said.

Rachel withdrew her arm. Curtis tried to catch her eye, but she steadfastly watched a set of dancers working through a lively quadrille.

"Certainly, *you're* a prize. I'm not sure Shelford's worth my time." Curtis smiled at her. "Might be worth it if I can hit Romford."

Rachel shook her head. "You have got to learn how to give a compliment."

They approached a rail thin, elderly man with shockingly white hair. He was tall, trim, and athletic. His face was rugged and defined. Rachel suspected he used to enjoy mountaineering or fencing when he was younger. He had the lean look of a man used to physical exertion. Another man waited beside him, equally tall, like Curtis, and somewhere in his fifties perhaps. Around the age her father would have been.

Curtis stood beside her, and she suddenly wished she had not taken her arm off his, despite his teasing. She faced two of the most powerful men in England, and her nerves began to get the better of her. Not only were these men associates of the queen, but they were also the ones who dictated Curtis's future, who had bought his commission in the Army, who decided whom he could marry.

Her mind warred with her heart. She knew marriage to Curtis would never work, but she wanted it more than anything. She reminded herself that hope led to disappointment and tried to push the anticipation away, as she had for the last four weeks. She felt her hands shake and glanced aside.

Curtis threaded her arm through his and covered her hand. His touch was light but reassuring, all the force of a thunderbolt in a ray of light. Her nerves calmed, her hand stilled, and she held herself upright, shoulders back, chin up.

Curtis seemed to know when she had collected herself, even without looking, and he began the formal introductions. "Miss Rachel Wickford, my grandfather, the Duke of Lambourne, and my uncle, the marquis, Lord Abridge."

His grandfather sized her up. "This is the one who won't marry you?"

Rachel pressed her lips together. Just as blunt as his grandson.

"Looks just like her mother. Fine woman." He stared at Curtis and the marquis. "Well, leave us."

The duke had known her mother? How? Her hand began to shake again, and Curtis squeezed it. The uncle bowed and left, but Curtis lingered.

"You, too, Loughton." The duke narrowed his eyes.

Curtis bowed and reluctantly let go of her arm. "The next dance, Miss Wickford?"

Rachel inclined her head toward him and turned back to the duke. Out of the corner of her eye, she could see Curtis crossing the ballroom, and she felt unexpectedly abandoned. She hadn't seen Curtis since Paris, and he'd left her alone with the man who could decide her future happiness as well.

The duke sized her up, a shrewd look in his eyes. She maintained a neutral gaze, pushing down the nerves, and pasted on a thin, tight smile.

"Don't try it with me. I know your mother too well. Please, join me." The duke gestured to the sofas behind them. "Long night, and I'm tired of standing. No need to *stand* on ceremony with you." He chuckled at his own joke.

Rachel settled herself beside him on a comfortable couch. The music swirled around them, allowing for a semi-private conversation as the dancers moved through complicated patterns. The duke cleared his throat. "Loughton tells me you know too much."

So, he was worried she would not keep his secrets. Rachel relaxed onto the sofa. She understood people who spoke directly. She would treat him like she treated Curtis, not like a duke. She returned fire.

"He talks too much when he's drunk, Your Grace. He only has himself to blame."

The duke peered at her with a look that could set a woodpile on fire. "That so."

"Yes." Rachel smoothed her wrinkle-free skirt.

"I liked your father." The duke groaned and rubbed his calves. He aimed a string of swear words at his shoes. "Never wear new shoes to a ball."

"I thought Curtis learned to swear in the Army," Rachel said. "Evidently, he learned from you."

The duke studied her. "Does my language offend you?"

Rachel shrugged. If she were going to test the duke, see whether he considered her unsuitable, may as well begin now. "Better your blasted language than hearing Curtis sing one more wretched verse of a sea shanty when he's half-rats."

But he *was* Curtis's grandfather first and foremost, whether or not he was a duke. The duke chuckled. "I like you better than your father. You may call me 'Grandfather.'"

"Curtis and I are *not* engaged," Rachel said.

The duke groaned and leaned back on the sofa. "Then call me 'pompous old fool.' I believe that was your father's name for me."

Rachel considered. "I do remember that term. I didn't know *that* duke was you, Your Grace. He had a great many other names for you, which I cannot repeat in the ballroom. I assure you, *The Scoundrel's Dictionary* was his second Bible. I will merely say that for someone who is reputed to be cantankerous and mean-spirited, you are surprisingly delightful."

The duke put back his head and laughed. His eyes twinkled. "I have missed your father these nine years. Parliament isn't the same without my old rival in town."

"What shall I call you then?" Rachel asked. "He actually called you 'the Old Lion' since your title is 'Lambourne,' when he spoke well of you."

"And when he didn't?" The duke grinned.

Rachel lowered her voice so they would not be overheard. Her first hours at a London ball, and she did not want to ruin her reputation already. "Ugly customer, rummy old cove, confounded swell, the usual."

The duke covered her hand with his. "You don't mince words. I see why Curtis loves you. Why not 'Grandfather?'" He peered intently at her. "Why won't you marry my boy, eh? He's a good one."

Now they had hit upon the real topic. Rachel hadn't expected the duke to be quite so direct. "I'm entirely unsuitable for him. You won't approve of me." She smiled, but she felt the nerves returning. She had expected the duke to disapprove so thoroughly, and she had steeled herself for the pain.

She had tried to resign herself to the idea of never marrying

Curtis. It hurt so much to walk with him through the ballroom, to see him again, to want to marry him and know it was out of her reach. Even if she wanted to, it would never work, and it was better to get the pain over with.

"What?" Grandfather asked, straightening on the sofa. "I thought Loughton brought you over to impress me."

Rachel laughed. "He may have, but I'm here to convince you of the opposite. The sooner your grandson realizes that you will never agree to this marriage, the sooner he can accept the futility of his efforts." And the sooner her heart could begin to mend.

Grandfather relaxed against the wall, tipped his head back, and blew out a breath. He covered his eyes with his arm. He reminded her so forcibly of Curtis that Rachel stifled a laugh. "He underestimated the magnitude of his problem."

"You've discussed this with him?" she asked.

Grandfather nodded. "At length. He's not one for short conversations."

Rachel bit her lip and repressed another laugh. "Truer words were never spoken, but I'm no duchess in training."

Grandfather closed his eyes. "Let me ensure I understand. The only daughter of the finest speaker and most persuasive parliamentarian I knew, Mr. Wickford, the eminent orator and rising star of the House of Commons, whose death we all mourned, is now sitting before me, dressed in the finest style Paris has to offer, putting every other woman in the room to shame, and she is somehow unsuitable for my grandson?"

He trained his intense, searching gaze on her again.

"You're quite the orator yourself." Rachel smiled at him, her thin, polite, non-committal smile. It didn't make sense. Why would the duke accept her so readily? She hadn't even been presented at Court, since her father was only a member of the gentry, not the aristocracy.

The duke continued his unyielding gaze.

"My father died some time ago," Rachel said. "Our estate is not well-managed, and my mother's health is poor. Our days of prominence are long past. My mother has not attended a Season in nine years."

Grandfather raised an eyebrow, an exact likeness of Curtis. "But you do have an ancient and grand estate, which is managed and still profitable, and all the hallmarks of a haughty and unyielding duchess. No doubt, because of your mother's illness, you have been mistress of the house and running the estate yourself for years. You have your father's intelligence, your mother's wit, and an elegant sense of style. So what, exactly, are supposed to be my qualifications for Loughton's wife?" He gestured toward the crowded ballroom. "And which do you lack?"

Rachel held herself still. *Don't betray your discomfort.*

"How many of them can help him pass a bill in Parliament? How many of them can help prepare a report for the queen, eh?" The duke pushed his way up, a little painfully, and Rachel rose to her feet. "Loughton needs a woman with a compassionate heart and a well-trained mind, not a title. He needs a woman who can run a hospital, as well as a household."

Something pricked at Rachel. This was it. The duke's real reason for allowing the marriage. "You want me to marry your grandson for political reasons?"

The duke steepled his hands. "The Army reform effort will take years. Decades perhaps. I won't be around to see it through. He and Miss Nightingale need more people to help them."

Rachel watched the couples dancing. The duke's response seemed so cold and calculating. Did Curtis view her as a means to an end? He insisted that he needed her to set an example and help him with the nursing school. Was she part of a strategy, a tool to be used? Had he chosen her with this intent?

"You want the same reforms, don't you?" the duke asked.

Rachel considered him. "You wish him to marry with no thought of love?"

The duke waved off her concern. "He loves you."

"He's been in love with half of London," Rachel muttered. "Whether he can *stay* in love is another matter."

Grandfather chuckled again. "Oh, I'd marry you if I were any younger. Steal you out from under Loughton's nose." He looked at her, the sparkle in his gold-green eyes as mischievous as Curtis's eyes. "Your mother should remarry. I'm not so old. Now, who can we get elected from your district? That goon who replaced your father is worthless. Votes against me every time."

The Old Lion hadn't contradicted her. His own grandfather had no more faith in Curtis's ability to stay in love than she did. Rachel shook her head. "Do you consider anything except politics, or does your mind dwell only on that?"

The duke thought a moment. "I like roast beef, as well." He trained his tiger-like gaze on her. "Now, can I rely on you to keep quiet about my son's health? I have to protect Loughton and his sister, my title, and their fortune. I need to know what I'm dealing with, Miss Wickford. You know too much, and you won't commit to anything."

Rachel met his gaze. "So, you want to keep me quiet? You want me to marry Curtis to protect Alice from fortune hunters? What makes you so certain I am not interested in your grandson only for his wealth and status myself?"

The duke chuckled. "Because you refuse to marry him." He narrowed his eyes. "Just like your father. If I wanted something, he opposed it. If I say you should marry Loughton, you won't do it. Very well then, I forbid it. I withhold my consent." He folded his arms. "Until *you* convince me otherwise."

Lord Romford approached. Curtis had not yet returned for their dance. She needed a moment to consider what the duke had told her, and she was suddenly less eager to dance with Curtis. All of the relief that the duke approved of their marriage had dissipated with the knowledge that he viewed it as a marriage of convenience, a simple political transaction. An expediency to keep her quiet, protect Alice, and help the family.

Would he really forbid the marriage? If he did, Curtis would be heartbroken, and so would she, no matter that she had tried to prepare herself for the disappointment.

But did she want to be used as a political tool?

Grandfather steepled his hands. "Romford, eh? That man could charm a cow into buying leather. Send Loughton over next chance when you're through. Tell him I've changed my mind about you."

CHAPTER 15

Curtis shifted his weight from one leg to the other. Rachel and Grandfather were talking a long time, and it was well past the next dance.

"At ease, Colonel," Shelford said. "What's wrong?"

He lounged against the wall, folding his arms casually to hide his anxiety. "This isn't quite as easy as I thought."

"Miss Wickford's not returned yet? You think the Season is easy?" Shelford shook his head. "Most miserable time of my life. I assumed you knew that by now."

Curtis tipped his head back against the wall. "Oh, I do. All too well. It must be an excellent thing that they are talking for the entire length of another dance. Getting along and all that."

"They aren't talking," Shelford said, pointing to the couples whirling about in each other's arms.

Hang it all. Lord Romford held Rachel in his arms. They glided around the ballroom floor. How had he beaten him to the chase? Curtis straightened and tried to get a better view of the couples. This dance belonged to him. The waltz. The next would be a quadrille.

Shelford laughed. "Don't let your guard down for one minute, my man, not until she says, 'I do.'"

Curtis watched Rachel dancing with Romford. He would count the minutes until it was his turn. She glided about, her feet hardly touching the floor, her dress swaying elegantly. "I love her for so many reasons, but until tonight, her shoulders weren't one of them."

Shelford clapped him on the back. "I recall what it was like. You'll love those infernal dresses in a few months when you're married."

"If," Curtis said. "How am I supposed to think straight when she dresses like that?"

Shelford looked at him. "You do know who you're talking to."

"A friend," Curtis said. "One who understands."

"And her guardian while she lives in London." Shelford shrugged. "I'm half your height and weight, but I'll still take you on."

"I've heard about your right hook," Curtis said. "Rachel is safe with me."

She appeared through the crowds. Finally. On *Romford's* arm. Had she enjoyed the dance? Shelford should worry more about him than Curtis.

"Your grandfather, the Old Lion, whatever you call him. It sounds as though he had quite a few names for *my* father. Well, he wishes to speak with you." Rachel pressed her lips into a thin line. "You should have warned me *which* duke your grandfather was."

"Did you pick up a few choice words from him?" Curtis smiled. "He knows the best I've ever heard."

"Not something to be proud of," Rachel said. "You're just like him."

Curtis threw back his shoulders. "That's the nicest thing you've ever said to me."

"Because you don't remember when you were drunk." Rachel's eyes went wide, and she clapped a hand over her mouth. She darted a glance at Romford.

Shelford threw back his head and laughed. "Where's Eleanor? I'm going to have a time. If I don't ruin your reputation, you will." He moved away to find his wife.

Romford grinned at Curtis. "Ah, that rum toddy, eh, Loughton?" He bowed over Rachel's hand. "Until our next dance, Miss Wickford." He winked at her and left.

Curtis scowled at Romford's retreating form and moved closer to Rachel. Not scandalously close for a ballroom, just close enough to talk without being overhead. Close enough to remind Rachel that she loved him, not Romford. "And what nice things did you tell me that night?"

Rachel's lips were set in a firm line. She glanced at the matrons standing nearby. Right. This was the not the place to discuss that evening.

A different strategy. Curtis offered his arm to Rachel. "May I have the next dance?"

She seemed upset, not quite herself. Was it the remark she had made, or what he had nearly said in front of the matrons? Or her dance with Romford, or her talk with Grandfather? He wished they could sit and talk, but conversation was impossible in a ballroom.

Sets were forming for the quadrille, and Curtis led Rachel as far away from Romford as possible. He'd rather not share her with him again or with any of the men eyeing Rachel with interest. Lord Egerton and Thorne watched them pass, and Curtis scowled at their greetings.

He scanned the ballroom and noticed Alice and Kempton arm in arm, waiting for another couple. *What a brick.* He had asked Alice to dance, so she would not be a complete wallflower tonight. Kempton was the truest of friends.

He pulled Rachel over as quickly as he could politely manage, threading their way through the crowd, so the four of them could form a square.

He wanted to know how Rachel felt now that Grandfather had reassured her. He wouldn't wait four more months to propose, if he could resolve her concerns right away. He grinned. Perhaps four days, now that she knew Grandfather approved.

He waited for a chance to move to the center and hold Rachel's hand, even a quick touch. The dance flew by, with hardly a chance to talk, but the exercise felt good. The jumps, twirls, spins. Rachel's smile grew wider and more natural. They'd never attended a ball together, and he realized something. Rachel didn't try to hide her feelings when she danced.

Her eyes sparkled, and her cheeks glowed. She laughed when he winked at her. She threw herself into the dance with energy, without any reserve. It was the most natural he'd ever seen her. The music, the elegant gown, her vitality, and the way she had eyes only for him. They didn't need to speak.

The dance ended, Rachel rested her arm lightly on his, and they began to make a circuit of the crowded ballroom.

Curtis acquired two glasses of lemonade for them, and they rested a moment. Rachel's face was beautifully flushed, a perfect pink on her cheeks from the dancing, a sort of exhilaration still singing in her eyes.

"And how was your conversation with Grandfather?" Curtis asked, after setting down his glass. He took a step closer. "Has he set your mind at ease?"

"I'd rather not discuss that here," Rachel said, inclining her head again toward the many gossiping matrons. The spark left her eyes. "Thank you for the dance. It was exactly the respite I needed." She flashed him a genuine smile, though it seemed sad.

"I've missed the gymnasium," Curtis said quietly.

Rachel shook her head, again nodding toward the other men and women around them. "I do find exercise invigorating. I love a good dance, and you are a highly competent dance partner." She smiled at him. "Thank you, and good evening."

She meant to leave him without any kind of conversation. He had to return her to Shelford, and then he wouldn't see her again for the rest of the evening. Who knew when they could ever talk alone. Egerton and Thorne were eyeing her, as if waiting to ask her to dance.

"May I introduce you to some acquaintances of mine?" Curtis took her arm and maneuvered them toward a knot of sophisticated women, determined to establish Rachel's position in Society immediately. He already had Grandfather's approval. Now, he would simply introduce Rachel to Society's most elite and popular women this evening, and his work would be done. Her concerns would be alleviated, and she would finally agree to be his wife.

"It's not entirely appropriate for you to act in the role," Rachel said. "Why should they wish to meet me?"

"Because you are connected with me," Curtis said.

He adopted his most charming smile as the group of women turned to stare at him. Their conversation stopped immediately.

"Lady Agatha." Curtis addressed the most elegant of the women. "How have you been?"

"Colonel. How nice to see you returned from the Continent. We've been most curious about your stay in Germany. When are you coming to regale us with the details?" Her voice left no room for dismissal. She was still the leader of this group, he was certain, if not the leader of all London fashion for young women. If she would accept Rachel, everyone else would.

Curtis bowed toward his old friends. "Lady Clara, Lady Frances, always a pleasure."

He could feel Rachel backing away. He held her arm firmly, putting his hand over hers. Let the other women gossip about his familiarity and wonder about how forward he had been. He wanted them to understand how he felt about Rachel. He kept himself firmly by her side, completely aware that they looked more like an engaged couple than anything else.

"And who is your acquaintance? A relative?" Lady Agatha glanced over at Rachel with an insincere smile, but Curtis knew she would be too curious to snub Rachel. He hoped she held no ill will about the fiasco last year.

Rachel didn't speak or try to ingratiate herself. Curtis grinned.

By Jove, she was magnificent. Her reserve gave her every advantage in the London ballroom. The women would interpret her aloof demeanor as elegance and admire her hauteur.

"A close friend, Miss Wickford. She will be assisting Miss Nightingale. As you know, we are looking for a few select from those at the forefront of fashion to set the standard for the first year of training at the new nursing school. Naturally, Miss Wickford was our first choice. She trained in Germany with Alice these past six months."

Miss South and Miss Herbert whispered to each other. Lady Frances stared pointedly at his hand covering Rachel's, and Lady Clara leveled her steady gaze at them curiously. It was working.

Lady Henrietta eyed her with interest. "And how is dear Alice? I was delighted to see her at St. James's. I did not see you there, Miss Wickford. But, excuse me, perhaps you are older, if you have studied so extensively. This must not be your first Season. I suppose you are looking for a few more on-the-shelf students for your nursing school." She flashed a triumphant look at Rachel.

Curtis assumed his most arrogant demeanor. "I imagine Miss Wickford is too well-bred to discuss a lady's age in a ballroom."

Lady Henrietta glared at him while the other women hid smiles.

"And she will need to train a few others, *mature* enough to handle rigorous studies, to ensure Miss Nightingale's school is a success. You know how ignorant and immature some attitudes toward nurses are."

The women assented.

"Oh, yes," Lady Agatha said. "Positively medieval."

"The General is most urgent in his opinion that those attitudes change," Miss Herbert said. "Quite right, Colonel. My father has charged me to assist with the commission's report, if you wish to discuss it." She smiled at him.

"I suppose those who have few social engagements might find time for your nursing school," Lady Henrietta said peevishly.

Curtis watched Lady Agatha appraising Rachel and her gown, which was more fashionable than hers. Rachel had bought hers in

Paris; the other women certainly had not. He could tell Lady Agatha had not yet made up her mind about Rachel.

Miss South smiled at Rachel. "And who will you be teaching, Miss Wickford? I confess, it sounds like an adventure." She batted her eyelashes at Curtis. "One that the colonel no doubt thinks *me* unable to handle."

"Lady Octavia was, naturally, my first choice," Rachel said, smiling up at Curtis. "She is intelligent and mature. A few of her friends have already agreed to forgo a few of their usual social activities to join us. If you are curious, Miss South, I *do* hope you will join us."

Curtis grinned. The women could not possibly accuse Lady Octavia of being on the shelf at age sixteen or having too few social engagements. Rachel handled it to perfection.

But now that he had spoken with these women, he would have to dance with all of them. "I hope each of you will save a set for me, and we can discuss the merits of the nursing school during our dance. Especially you, Miss South." He flashed an amiable smile. He'd rather dance with Rachel all evening, but if he had to dance, he may as well dance with old friends. Friends who could help the nursing school and help him win over Rachel. "Lady Agatha, Lady Clara, Lady Frances, Miss Herbert, Lady Henrietta?"

Rachel stiffened beside him as the other women reacted. Miss South pouted at him while Lady Agatha smiled invitingly. Lady Clara eyed him up and down, then nodded her head reluctantly. Evidently, she had not forgiven him for last year yet. Miss Herbert grinned, Lady Frances smiled demurely, and Lady Henrietta huffed.

Curtis deemed the time right for a strategic retreat. "Until our dances later."

Lady Agatha's eyes roamed over Rachel's gown again. "Delighted to make your acquaintance."

"Likewise." Rachel inclined her head.

"*You* must come to visit tomorrow," Lady Agatha said, laying a hand on his left arm and sidling up to him. "I must hear all about

Germany." She did not include Rachel in the invitation. It was dangerously close to a snub. Was she jealous of Rachel? Afraid Rachel would replace her? Threatened by her? She need not be. He would have to talk with her first, perhaps.

He bowed and left as quickly as possible. Rachel walked beside him in stony silence as he guided her through the crowd.

"May I dance a second dance with you?" Curtis asked.

Rachel seemed to be searching the ballroom for someone else. "You hardly have time. Six dances will take you three hours at least, and you arrived so late." She snapped her fan open and hid her face.

"If they change their opinion about nursing, others will follow suit," he said, and he knew that a hint of irritation had crept into his tone.

Rachel's fan hid her mouth, but her eyes sparked fire. "Am I to be paraded about, like a zoo animal on display? See, here is the rare, exotic creature known as a 'nurse.'"

Curtis stared at her. "Well, they have never met an Upper Class woman like you. How else am I to change their minds?"

Rachel pursed her lips. "Evidently, by dancing and flirting."

Curtis faced her. "It's not flirting. It's merely dancing with old friends. I would dance every dance with you, if I could."

Rachel narrowed her eyes. "Perhaps you have been a bachelor so long that you cannot tell the difference between conversation and flirtation. I already agree with you about the nursing school, so you need not dance with me any more this Season." Rachel's fan whipped back and forth so quickly it nearly created a windstorm.

Blast. Shelford was right. He had to be on his guard, every moment. Rachel studied him, and the look in her eyes made him wary. She was withholding something from him, something important. Why didn't she want to dance with him?

"What did Grandfather want to speak to me about?" Curtis asked. "Do I need to talk to him before I serve my three-hour sentence?" He grimaced, hoping Rachel would laugh.

"He does not approve of me," Rachel said. "And I'm not sure how I feel about him."

Curtis closed his eyes and blew out a breath. "What did you say to him?"

She lowered her fan and glared at him. "You assume *I* offended *him*. You may as well ask what the Old Lion told me."

Curtis searched her face. This was going horribly wrong. "No, of course, I did not mean to infer that. My apologies. Truly, he will not give his consent?"

She lifted her chin. "You will find another woman to help you pass your bills and write your reports, I am certain. Miss Herbert seemed eager to discuss her father's commission with you. You have managed without me for the past month, and I am sure you will do fine in the future. Enjoy your dances." She began to walk off.

"What did he say?" Curtis tried to take her hand. The shock had not worn off. Why would Grandfather change his mind?

Rachel moved her hand out of the way. "That your marriage is a political expediency. Is that not your aim in selecting dance partners? And why should it not be your aim in selecting a wife? I told you he would not approve, and I was right." She rapped him with her fan, just as Egerton arrived to ask her to dance. "Good evening, Colonel Loughton."

And she was gone, as imperious as the queen herself. She'd make a fine duchess.

His arm ached from the loss of her contact and the smart raps to the forearm.

She assumed he wanted to marry her to help him pass a bill or host a dinner. *Hook it.* He didn't care about that. Grandfather did, and Grandfather knew she was capable. So why would he withhold his confounded permission? It didn't make sense. He'd have to go talk with him tomorrow and plead his case, once again.

Right now was not the time, not while Rachel was dancing with other men. He had to watch and see who asked her next. Was she enjoying Egerton's conversation? He tried to watch her face, but it was as lovely and impassive as ever.

Curtis loved Rachel and wanted to spend every minute of every day with her, because there was no one who understood him better. It had nothing to do with Parliament.

But now *she* thought it did. Grandfather's conversation hadn't helped him get any closer to marrying Rachel; it had set him back. It had made it nearly impossible.

Rachel continued dancing with Egerton, and Thorne hovered nearby. She was too confounded beautiful, and too new to London. She had caught everyone's eye. Now that she disavowed her vow, she would consider marriage to anyone, instead of him, if she believed marriage to him was impossible.

He thought for certain that introducing her to some other women would help cement her social position, alleviate another concern of hers, and put him that much further down the path toward marriage. Instead, she imagined he was flirting with his old flames.

The dance had nearly ended, and Curtis resigned himself to the inevitable. He made his way across the ballroom to begin the next set of dances with whichever woman was available. They were merely old friends. That was all. He would continue to show Rachel these women held no appeal for him. Eventually, she would realize the truth. He loved *her*, and *only her*, because of who she *was*, not what she could do to help him.

But he had to convince Rachel of that, keep the other women at bay, and change Grandfather's mind, before she fell in love with someone else.

CHAPTER 16

Rachel traced a finger along the swirling blue and red design of the leather journal Curtis had purchased for her. She waited in a hard wooden chair near the front of the classroom.

Mrs. Ward, the hospital matron, patrolled the front dais as the students arrived. She looked like the typical nurses most people encountered—born in the lower or middle classes, educated through experience, and trained over years and years of hard work.

Curtis greeted each woman at the door, talking to them animatedly. Smile lines crinkled the edges of his eyes, and he laughed easily. He was in his element. The commander. The colonel. The charming bachelor.

Rachel watched the students settling onto chairs. He had done it. Curtis had charmed them all into coming, except Lady Henrietta. A rock dropped into the pit of her stomach. Lady Agatha, clearly angling for time alone with Curtis. Lady Clara, holding a grudge over some shared history between them. Lady Frances, obviously pining for Curtis. Miss South, trying to prove herself to him. Miss Herbert, desperate for his attention and approval. And in Lady Henrietta's place, Mrs. Isabella Phillips, a stunning young widow, who did not seem the least upset by her husband's death.

In another classroom, Alice and Lady Octavia waited with Mrs. Roper, the other hospital matron. That group of women was even younger than this one.

When she'd imagined training women as nurses several months ago, Rachel had assumed it would be the usual recruits: women from the lower classes, desperate to earn a wage. Indeed, Miss Nightingale had a section of students from the lower and middle classes who would train and then accept paid positions.

So why did Rachel have to train *these* women, instead of the women who intended to actually work? Curtis, General Herbert, Miss Nightingale, and the Duke of Lambourne intended to wage war on society's ideals. Social change wasn't her object in agreeing to help Miss Nightingale establish her school. She wanted to make birthing safe for mothers and help women. On that much, she and Miss Nightingale agreed.

Women like her mother, who needed constant care, could not afford to hire someone from the Upper Class, and women from the highest echelons of the Upper Class did not typically engage in paid work.

There were the poor cousins who became paid companions or lived with their richer relations. Women like Mrs. Glenn, who were genteel and required an income because they were widowed. These were the Upper Class women she wanted to train, not debutantes who would never need to work or see a day's distress. Why was she training aristocratic ladies who might never actually help deliver a child?

These women were elegant and refined, and most of them had titles. They moved in the same social and political circles as Curtis. They were the sort of women who would never accept her as an equal, because she wasn't. She didn't have a title, and she didn't have their kind of wealth or connections. She knew it, and they knew it, even if Curtis wanted to pretend like it wasn't true.

From her position in the corner, Rachel could hear Curtis's booming voice.

"Thank you, Lady Agatha, for attending. I know your duties at home keep you much occupied, but you made time for us anyway. Mrs. Phillips, still in your mourning clothes, and here you are. Miss South, always a pleasure to see you. I am sure you will put the other students to shame with your enthusiasm. Lady Frances, I have always enjoyed our long talks, and I know you will take your studies most seriously. Lady Clara, you postponed your Grand Tour for us. Thank you. Miss Herbert, your father is dedicated to the training of more nurses, and an inspiration to me."

Curtis turned to leave the classroom. At the front, Mrs. Ward cleared her throat.

He inclined his head. "And who could overlook our matron. Women, I leave you in the capable hands of Mrs. Ward. Thank you for your years of service to St. Thomas' Hospital."

He glanced at Rachel, arched his brow, and smiled broadly.

Mrs. Ward cleared her throat again. "Any time you want to leave, Colonel."

"Miss Wickford. Ladies. Mrs. Ward." He shut the door and left the room.

She swallowed. He had a kind word for everyone else, but not for her. It was precisely as she feared. She did not fit into his well-established life in London. He knew these families so well, from years of house parties and Seasons together. The dreams at dusk, the sweet kisses in the shadowland, had faded. All they had left were smoldering looks, the remnants of a dying fire.

Well, she was here for Miss Nightingale, and for her mother, not for Curtis. She would do her part, then return home to Essex to take up a life of nursing. If there was now a hint of sadness and resignation in that future, when there used to be joy, Rachel pushed the thought away.

Mrs. Ward cleared her throat and began to explain the training schedule, Miss Nightingale's regimen, and the expectations.

"She'll get regular updates from me." Mrs. Ward pointed to herself. "The colonel is working on the queen's report for your father, Miss Herbert. Don't none of you bother him."

She glared around the room. "And don't get any ideas about

catchin' him alone. I'll be watching you." She let her eye rest on Lady Agatha a moment longer than the others.

The other women exchanged glances, some with an almost guilty expression. Miss South and Mrs. Phillips smiled at each other. Lady Agatha stared haughtily past Mrs. Ward, who prowled up and down the rows of desks.

Rachel and Mrs. Ward's lectures could not have been more different. While Rachel lectured from outlines with easy-to-follow diagrams, Mrs. Ward told stories of the people she had encountered. Perhaps it was well that the students received a mix of training, theoretical and practical, to prepare them for their assignments or experiences.

As Rachel concluded her last section of lectures, she asked, "Any questions?"

Mrs. Phillips cleared her throat. "You cannot really expect *me* to spread lard on a child's body when it is born."

"Unless you want it to stay unclean," Rachel said evenly. She hadn't expected them to embrace it on the first day, but she was a little surprised by the outright hostility.

"And you *honestly* believe an Upper Class woman could spend that much time caring for an ill relative?" Lady Agatha asked.

"While it is true you may have many other obligations, nursing can be done alongside some of them," Rachel said. "For example, I can still embroider a great deal while sitting at my mother's bedside to attend to her, and my friends are happy to include my mother in their visits."

The women looked at each other when she mentioned her mother. Was it disdain?

Miss Herbert raised her hand. "Could I get a copy of your notes? The lecture was decently organized." The other women nodded.

Decent? Was that a challenge or a compliment?

"I'll leave them here at the end of class each day," Rachel said.

Mrs. Ward dismissed the women to return home. They had to fit their training and schooling around their social schedule, so they left enough time in the afternoon to be at home for callers.

Miss South sidled up to Rachel and whispered, "How do I take notes on old Ward's lectures? I just doodle while she tells stories." She moved away to copy Rachel's notes.

Lady Clara waited behind the others, not talking to anyone. Finally, she moved over next to Rachel. "Will we discuss disorders of the mind?"

Rachel studied her. "Who are you concerned about?"

"No one," Lady Clara said. "Just an interest of mine."

Rachel took in Lady Clara's appearance. Her hands were tightly pressed together, clutching her notes, and her lips were pressed into a thin line.

"Nervous disorders or melancholy?" Rachel asked. "Or another interest?"

Lady Clara looked over Rachel's shoulder. "Have you ever met a person who seems to alternate between both?"

So Lady Clara knew someone, someone in her family perhaps, like that. Rachel nodded. "There is a woman in our village, yes. Some herbs and teas might help with some symptoms. We shall discuss medicine and its effect on the mind. Do you like tea?"

Lady Clara smiled. "I am the rare person who prefers chocolate."

"Even better," Rachel said. "A cup of chocolate can soothe a temperament at times, too. Perhaps we can change the order of the lectures and discuss herbs sooner."

Lady Clara thanked her and moved over to copy the lecture notes. Rachel watched the women, not sure what to make of them.

How many of the women would Curtis go visit? When they left here and returned home, would they have an at-home? Had he sent them all flowers, too, after the ball? It was customary to visit the women one had danced with, as well as send flowers.

Curtis had sent her a tasteful bouquet of roses, carnations, and daisies. Nothing ridiculous, like Egerton's flowers. She intended to dry the roses and keep the petals, but now she wondered whether to keep the flowers much longer. What had the others received?

Rachel shook her head. She didn't want to feel animosity toward the women she was trying to teach. She had to find a different way to approach this new school.

She could not let her past experiences with Curtis taint her ability to train these women. They all had a past with Curtis, she felt certain, and she wondered whether they would despise her because of her current association with him.

She didn't fit into their world, yet she wanted so dearly to influence them. These women could make a difference, if she could persuade them that nursing was a noble and worthwhile profession for an Upper Class woman.

She excused herself and found her way along the hospital corridor toward the classroom where Alice was overseeing Lady Octavia and her friends.

"Rachel!" Curtis's voice startled her. That deep, rich voice that melted her insides. He entered the hallway and approached her with a gentle look in his eyes. "What do you need?"

She looked around. "Why are you here?"

He indicated the room behind him. "General Herbert has given me an office in the hospital to work on the commission's report, where I can also be near Miss Nightingale's school if she requires any assistance."

Rachel cocked her head to one side. "Miss Herbert's idea?

Curtis rubbed the back of his neck. "Well, yes, she spoke to him."

The silence thundered between them.

A pair of desks sat outside his office. Mr. Kempton watched them unabashedly from behind one.

"Whose desk is the other?" Rachel asked.

Curtis grimaced. "Mrs. Ward. Keep your voice down when she's nearby."

"Miss Nightingale's spy," Rachel said, smiling.

"Come into my office." Curtis looked around. "We can talk in there."

Rachel bit her lip. "No, this will do. I was on my way to find Alice. I'd like to switch classes with her, supervise and train *her* students."

Surely, she would have better luck and more influence with younger students who had no previous association with Curtis.

Curtis rested against Mrs. Ward's desk. "But I specifically assigned you to that class. Miss Nightingale approved it."

Rachel tried to keep perfectly still, push down the emotions. "I would feel more comfortable with Lady Octavia and her friends."

Curtis studied her. "But Alice would not feel comfortable with that change. What's this about?"

"I live with Lady Octavia," Rachel said. "We ride in the same carriage. It would be more convenient."

Curtis raised an eyebrow. "Is that the only reason?"

Rachel sighed. "You really wish to discuss this here?"

Kempton grinned at her. "Don't mind me. I'm used to pretending not to listen to your conversations."

Rachel blushed. She could feel her cheeks flame bright red.

"May I, Miss Wickford?" Curtis led her into his office, glaring at Kempton. He whispered as they passed him, "I'll knock your block off for real this time. Not another crack about Rachel and me."

Curtis pulled her inside, shut the door, and folded his arms.

The office was bare, with only a desk in the center and a bank of windows behind it.

"Out with it," Curtis said.

Fine. "How many of them have you kissed?"

Curtis considered. "All of them."

Rachel turned on her heel, left his office, and marched down the hallway. She was done for the day, for the Season, for good.

Curtis ran after her and grabbed her arm to stop her. "It's a compliment. I'm showing you that they no longer hold any interest for me."

Rachel glared at him.

"I need to work on my compliments," Curtis said, guiding her back toward his office. He rested on the edge of his desk and crossed his legs in front of him. "Rachel, I haven't been alone with you in so long." He smiled and opened his arms.

She crossed her arms. "I've been in Town for weeks. I was around. You could have visited."

The smile faded from his face. "Alice required every minute, with Mrs. Glenn gone, attending to dance lessons and tutors on court etiquette for the presentation. I never want to see St. James's Court again." He scrubbed a hand over his face. "But I'll see you every day now that it's over."

Rachel huffed. Weeks, and he couldn't have visited once? True, there were social conventions that had to be followed, and Lady Octavia's preparations had taken every minute of Eleanor's time. Most women took months to prepare for their presentation at Court and their first Season, and Alice, shy, timid Alice, had to prepare in only a few weeks. "How am I supposed to train and teach these blasted women? They have been giving me odd looks all day, and trying to catch glimpses of you, instead of listening to lectures. None of them care about medicine or healing."

Curtis grinned. "No, their interest in nursing is genuine, I assure you. They may just be bored by old Mrs. Ward and watching the hallways for any sign of life. Her lectures aren't the most captivating."

Rachel put a finger on her lips and looked around, as if Mrs. Ward were watching or listening. "She's very informative."

Curtis yawned. "How many times did I have to nudge you to keep you awake in Germany?"

Rachel tried to look out through the smudged window of his tiny office. Someone needed to clean the glass.

Curtis cleared his throat. She refused to admit that her mind had wandered, too.

"We're old friends, that is all. They simply can't make you out. They wonder what kind of woman has captured my heart, because they see how much I love you. *How much I love you.* A compliment," Curtis said.

Rachel shook her head. Curtis loved everyone. "They scowl at me with daggers in their eyes. Why not invite your married 'old friends,' instead of the eligible ones? Surely some moved on with their lives and married."

He considered, then shrugged. "Certainly. Plenty have married, but they're busy with their families."

Rachel shook her head. "You kiss too many women."

Curtis smirked. "Only you, from now on. Never anyone else. Shall I remind you?"

But she would not be deterred by his flattery.

"Let me ensure I understand. Only unmarried women can be nurses? Married women are too busy to be nurses or attend your school?"

Curtis stared at her. He clasped his hands behind his back. "What are you saying?"

Rachel pressed her lips together. "I am repeating your sentiments. You have only sought unmarried women for the nursing school. Why is that? You really think that only unmarried women can act as nurses?"

Curtis considered her, widening his stance, his legs apart and his shoulders back. He looked completely confrontational now. Full Command Mode.

Rachel would not be deterred. "Do you expect that I will cease my efforts, *if* I marry? Put my time into solely running a household, hiding away in confinement, and raising my children? I would not be able to help you at the school. That is what I told you from the beginning. Nurses should never marry. We are in agreement, after all."

Curtis moved his arms around Rachel's waist, and leaned back against the desk. "No, no, no. Married women can be nurses. You're right. We should expand our selection, include some other leaders of Society. You should marry me, Rachel, and continue to nurse and teach."

It felt good to be in his arms again, but she could hardly enjoy the sensation when she seethed with anger.

"Married women have more need to nurse family members," Rachel said. She was shaking. "Their husbands fall ill and die unexpectedly. Their children are left alone to care for them."

Curtis pulled Rachel into a hug. "I'm sorry."

She let herself relax into it for a moment, and the shaking stopped. Comfort flowed through her. She rested on his chest, and let the peace settle between them. She dared a glance and got lost in the depths of his golden-green eyes. A long, still silence filled the room.

The door slammed open. Curtis let go of Rachel as if scalded, and she swiftly moved across the tiny office.

"I'll not have you alone with her, Colonel, on my watch." Mrs. Ward glared at him. "You'll leave my nurses be."

"Apologies." Curtis leaned against the edge of his desk. "We were, ah, discussing her duties."

Mrs. Ward laughed. "Her duties don't include letting you run your hands all over her."

Curtis blew out a breath.

"And I'm married, Colonel. So if you have any problems with married nurses, you best state so right now." Mrs. Ward linked her arm through Rachel's. "You were right to complain, dearie, and I would have let you change classes. The colonel is heartless, and you're best off not marrying him."

"How long have you been eavesdropping, Mrs. Ward?" Curtis asked.

She arched an eyebrow. "I don't eavesdrop. I can't help overhearing loud voices."

Rachel turned to leave, but hesitated. He seemed to understand now. "About getting new students and changing classes, Colonel."

He met her gaze. "I cannot change your assignment, Miss Wickford. We've already begun the training for the year, and Miss Nightingale has approved the plans. She is in charge of the school. I'm sorry, but it's too late to enroll additional students."

He *wasn't* sorry. He hadn't even asked Miss Nightingale or Mrs. Ward to change the assignment or admit additional women to her class. Every time she let down her guard or began to hope, he disappointed her. Every time they disagreed, he laid down an edict or issued an order.

"Is that so, *General?*" Rachel lifted her chin. "And will I receive additional women to train? Married women?"

"Perhaps next Season," Curtis said. "You could be among them." He grinned at her.

If she were married, what would prevent him from changing his mind and requiring her to stay home?

"*I* will not be here next year," Rachel said, sweeping past Curtis and Mrs. Ward. She would avoid him for the rest of the Season and leave as soon as she could. She felt an ache in her stomach as shadows obscured the dream.

"As you wish," Curtis said, the frustration evident on his face. "Suit yourself."

Rachel heard the office door slam behind her. She could see nothing as she stormed down the hall. Floors and walls and ceilings blurred together. *The nerve.* Curtis had no idea what a predicament he had put her in. She had sacrificed so much, left Mama alone for months, in order to train other women.

And they wouldn't listen to her. They didn't respect her. It would all be useless. Curtis had the same answer for every problem: marriage. Marry him. It wasn't that simple. If only it were.

"Rachel!" Mr. Kempton called, rushing down the hallway after her. "Come to dinner. Alice needs you."

Rachel paused. "Miss Loughton. I believe she asked you to call her that. I will not eat dinner with that—"

"Oh, don't take it out on me," Kempton said, catching up to her. "It wasn't my idea to ask Lady Agatha to attend the school."

"Why is she a *particularly* poor choice?" Rachel asked, narrowing her eyes.

Kempton took off his top hat and inspected the silk lining carefully. "No *particular* reason."

"You're a worse liar than I am. Tell me, and I'll call on Alice this afternoon," Rachel said. "Lady Agatha was last year's flame. Am I right?"

Kempton spun his top hat and flipped it back onto his head. "Promise not to hit me?"

"That's really more Loughton's style, the blasted bloke, not mine," Rachel muttered.

Kempton grinned. "Well, yes. Lady Agatha was the end of the Season, Lady Clara mid-Season, and Lady Frances at the beginning. Miss South and Miss Herbert, the year before that. Mrs. Phillips and Lady Henrietta, the year before..."

"Of all things," Rachel said. "Thank you for the illumination, Kempton. That is quite enough information. I will visit Alice, for her sake and for yours. Not for that confounded swell." She drew a breath and marched down the hall to the sound of Kempton's laughter.

❧

Rachel and Eleanor presented their cards to Curtis's butler, King. They'd waited until near the end of visiting hours, in case Alice needed extra time to talk with them.

As soon as her other guests left, Alice took a deep breath. "I detest this," she said. "I liked living with you better, Rachel, and you, Eleanor, when you were in Germany." She slumped on her sofa, and her crinoline hoop shot up.

Her eyes grew wide, and she straightened.

"Don't mind me," Eleanor said. "Stay comfortable. We're old friends, too."

Alice relaxed again, shoving the hoop back so her skirt could collapse around her. "I don't know why we have to wear these awful things."

Rachel and Eleanor laughed. "So that we do not have to wear mountains of petticoats."

Alice stretched. "I'm so glad visits are over at last." Her eyes grew wide again. "Oh, dear."

Eleanor smiled gently. "I assure you, we feel it a great compliment that you do not view us as guests in your home."

"Yes, exactly!" Alice sighed. "I am so relieved you are not offended. Only, I've lived with Rachel for ever so long, and with you for months before that. We positively feel like family." She beamed. "I am quite determined to make a match, now, you know, Rachel, and I've given up on my vow never to marry. Have you?"

Eleanor stared at Rachel. "Did I miss something?"

Rachel shook her head. "Nothing, merely a passing conversation. It's so much easier for nurses to remain unwed."

Alice laughed. "That conversation meant a great deal to my brother, I assure you, Rachel. It's no small matter for me to change my mind, and I'm sure it is not easy for you."

Eleanor studied Rachel. "I thought you and the colonel were getting along well enough in Paris, and he could not wait to dance with you at the ball."

Rachel traced the flowing design on the sofa and avoided Eleanor's eyes, as well as her unspoken question. "I am glad to hear that you are pursuing your Season with vigor, Alice."

She paled. "Oh no. I'm a complete disaster. I only meant that I should not be *opposed* to marriage. I meant to encourage *you*."

Rachel bit her lip. "Thank you, but the colonel and I are fighting our own war right now, and he may be more at peace with my decision than you realize, Alice. In fact, he quite agrees with me now."

Alice studied her with an unusually shrewd look on her face. "How was the first day at the nursing school? Who did you have in your class?"

Rachel traced the design on the sofa again. The texture of the raised thread swirled in circles along the smooth fabric. "Lady Agatha, Lady Clara, Lady Frances, Mrs. Phillips, Miss South, and Miss Herbert."

Eleanor laughed. "No wonder you are put out with the colonel."

"Yes, why would he encourage *them* to attend?" Alice asked.

She clapped a hand over her mouth. "It's a good thing Curtis sent Mrs. Glenn away. She'd be appalled at my behavior."

Rachel stared at her. "Sent her away? I thought she *wished* to visit her sister."

Alice shrugged. "She did, but her sister could just as easily have come here. She often does. Her sister loves to visit London."

"Do you miss her dreadfully?" Rachel could tell Alice barely held back the tears.

Alice left the sofa and threw herself around Rachel's neck. "I have missed living with you. Germany was such a treat."

Rachel hugged her. "I've missed you as well. You must come visit Eleanor and me."

Alice wiped her eyes and returned to her sofa. "At least Kempton's installing another gymnasium upstairs. A little smaller, with a lower ceiling. Oh, you must come try it!"

Rachel nodded. "I wish I could. I'm afraid there are a few more rules now that we are back in Town, and a bit more propriety must be observed."

Alice smiled. "Naturally, but you'd love it, Eleanor."

Eleanor clapped her hands. "Tell me when it's finished, and we'll come for 'tea.'" She winked. "I'll be careful what I wear that day."

"As soon as it's done." Alice watched them stand. "Must you go? I'm expected to have dinners regularly and invite Grandfather, and I'm not sure what menu to order for the next one. I don't know who to invite. Curtis spends all day working on the report, and then all night working with Kempton on other matters. Could you—"

Rachel took Alice's hands. "Shall I come back in the morning, before we go over to the hospital? We can work on your menu and guest list and ride to St. Thomas' together?"

Alice hugged her again. "Thank you."

Rachel couldn't leave Alice in the lurch, no matter how angry she felt with Curtis. Why would he send away her best source of strength and support during her first Season? She'd thought it couldn't be helped, but it sounded as though he'd made the decision to take Mrs. Glenn away from his sister when she needed her chaperone the most.

Rachel encountered new sides of Curtis all the time in London. The charming social politician. The Old Lion was wrong. A wife would only hamper him. Curtis wouldn't know how to advance his agenda without directing his efforts on the debutantes.

And did he really think a married woman could not also be a nurse? Who did he think spent the most time in the sickroom? Wives and mothers.

She'd done well to fight her feelings, school her emotions, and test him, because she did not like what she saw. The kind, doting brother had become thoughtless and self-absorbed. The doctor with whom she shared the birth of Bettina's beautiful twin daughters now thought that unmarried women made the best nurses. Where did that leave her, if she married? And the man who swore he loved her was spending his time wooing the other women of London for a political cause.

He'd been as commanding and overbearing as she'd feared, and she was relieved to still be free. Yes, she was right, but her heart ached to know it. She had never wished more to be proven wrong.

CHAPTER 17

Curtis slumped over his desk as the early morning sun filtered through the drawn curtains. Rows of numbers. Sheets of papers. Too much information. The commission on army sanitation was staggeringly complex. He needed someone to think for him. He could only concentrate on one thing: Rachel's voice echoing in his head, telling him she would be gone next year.

King opened the door of his study. "Carter will be most vexed."

He straightened. "It's not wrinkled yet. Did he send you to check on me?"

King cleared his throat. "Your appearance reflects on him, as your valet."

"In that case," Curtis said, "I'll change back into my confounded shirt sleeves." He moved toward the open door. "I'm not getting any work done anyway."

King blocked the doorway. "Miss Loughton is expecting a guest."

"Now?" He sized up his butler. "Stand aside."

"Mrs. King and Cook don't want you wandering around undressed when Miss Alice has a guest in the house." King pointed toward the desk. "Stay in the office."

"Honestly. Who runs this household?" Curtis collapsed into a chair by the fireplace.

A knock sounded at the door. King glared at him. "Keep your coat on. Wrinkled looks better than shirt sleeves."

Curtis heard Alice's squeals of delight and footsteps in the corridor. Her friend had arrived, and he hadn't eaten breakfast yet. True, he should have eaten hours ago, but he could not wrap his mind around this report.

He'd given Alice an extra year to prepare for a Season. She should have been ready last year, but Father's death was too fresh. Mrs. Glenn had worked with her, but Alice was still too impulsive and unpolished.

He rubbed a hand over his face. What was he to do? He thought sending Mrs. Glenn away would force Alice to rise to the occasion. Instead, she had become more helpless. He couldn't reprimand her in front of her friend. How was she ever to learn the boundaries and conventions of Society or become a gracious hostess, when she could hardly remember her own mother?

What kind of friend agreed to come right after breakfast? Perhaps Lady Octavia. Should he encourage her to spend less time with her? He was responsible for his sister, and he couldn't allow a friend to influence her with poor judgment. Alice visited her friends so rarely, though. He would ascertain who the friend was, then decide.

Alice always spent the morning in the breakfast room before they left for St. Thomas', so Curtis made his way down the corridor. Sunlight filled the glass-enclosed breakfast parlor. Alice and Rachel sat together, their heads bent over a sheaf of papers. Curtis stopped in the doorway. He would encourage *this* friend to visit more often.

Curtis sauntered over to the sideboard, took a plate, and filled it with a hearty helping of ham, stewed tomatoes, and roasted potatoes. He settled across from the women and began to eat.

"That is quite a list," Rachel said. "Might I suggest a different way to consider your menu?" She avoided his eyes.

Alice perused the paper in front of her. "But it is a fine selection of delicacies. Mrs. Glenn said I should impress our guests with them. We should display our wealth and the skill of our cook."

Rachel glanced at Curtis. He grinned at her. She hastily returned her gaze to the list. "If I may. My mother also hosted a great number of dinners. She felt it best to make the meal enjoyable for a different reason. Ensure that each person will have a favorite dish and perhaps include one or two unusual foods to showcase your cook's skill. Shall we ask your brother which foods are his favorites, and see whether any are on your list?"

Alice beamed. "I'm certain they are on this list. Mine are." She waited expectantly.

Curtis caught Rachel's eye. They both knew that Alice had terrible taste in planning menus. "I like roast beef or pork, and I hate the fish course. I could skip it entirely."

"Oh. I love the fish course," Alice said, "particularly the hors d'oeuvres."

"Potatoes," Curtis said. "Rolls, pickles."

Her face fell. "I thought, perhaps, consommé, bouillabaisse, souffle, turtle soup, jellies."

"Some roasted vegetables," Curtis said. "Maybe an ice for dessert."

Alice stared at her paper. "None of that is on my list. A citrus ice."

He smiled at her. "Ah, you do know my favorite. Well planned."

Rachel shot him an approving glance. Finally, he had done *one* thing right. Yesterday was a nightmare.

"Perhaps we could include a few more of his favorites on the list," Rachel said. "Your grandfather may favor those foods as well."

"What's this for?" Curtis asked.

"You're hosting a dinner party," Rachel said serenely. "I'm drawing up a guest list. We're selecting the men and women next."

Curtis took another bite. "Honestly, who runs this household?" he grumbled. "What day am I doing this?" He was starting to feel better with food in his stomach and the woman he loved at his breakfast table.

The women ignored him and continued planning. Alice scratched things off her list and scribbled new items.

"Alice, me, Lady Eleanor, Lady Octavia. We'll need six more women." Rachel looked at him, narrowing her eyes.

He swallowed. "Lady Agatha, Lady Clara, Lady Frances, Miss South, Miss Herbert, and Mrs. Phillips." He would not concede. If he were going to convince Rachel to marry him, she had to feel welcome among the other women with whom he associated regularly in his social circles, and the other women had to accept her as an equal.

Rachel pursed her lips. "Very well. Since you *believe* you run this household, we'll need an equal number of eligible men to entice the women to attend. Shall we select some *highly desirable* dinner partners for ourselves, Alice, or ask your brother to select his most handsome acquaintances?"

Curtis hadn't considered that. He didn't want nine other men angling after Rachel.

"Me, Kempton." He stopped. Who were the least attractive men he knew?

"The Old Lion," Rachel said. "Lord Shelford. And now we'll need six *highly* desirable men."

Alice glanced up from her list making. "Lion?"

"Your grandfather," Rachel said. "It's my name for him."

She already had an affectionate nickname for Grandfather. She couldn't be serious about leaving London.

"Oh, Lord Romford, of course. I do enjoy him," Rachel said.

Alice sighed. "Certainly." She and Rachel exchanged a glance and giggled.

Giggled. When had Rachel ever giggled? He'd have to watch that man around Rachel. Lord Romford was what? Thirty-two? Thirty-four? Perfectly eligible and respectable, and he'd taken a great liking to both Rachel and Alice in Paris. Curtis studied his sister. Far too young for Romford. Perhaps she should have had her Season next year after all.

"Mr. Simons, Lord Egerton, Lord Sager, Mr. Thorne, and Mr. Seymour all sent flowers. They'd be delightful. Do you agree with any of them?" Rachel wrote their names on a sheet of paper. "And shall we invite Lord Yelverton?"

"He's so chivalrous." Alice put a hand over her heart. "So attentive."

Curtis set down his fork. "He's a leech. You can never shake him, once you meet him. Why would he send flowers? Why would any of them?"

"Mr. Thorne will do nicely, too." Alice sighed, and regarded her brother with a hint of impatience. "She danced with them at the last ball, and so they sent her flowers. The same reason you asked Kempton to send her the flowers we selected. Did you not notice the bouquets I received?"

"Kempton sent you flowers, Alice?" Curtis stared at his sister. "He didn't just send my bouquet to Rachel? Who else sent you flowers?"

Alice pinked. "We danced."

Curtis had noticed Alice's flowers, but he hadn't checked any of the cards. He hadn't even paid attention to the men Alice had danced with, although he should have. He'd been far too concerned with whose arms Rachel was in.

It hadn't occurred to him that anyone would dare send flowers to her. Hadn't he made it clear enough to all of London that he had marked Rachel for himself? What size and kind of flowers had they sent? Were his nice enough, or did they seem paltry beside Romford's? The man was probably extravagant. Egerton certainly would be ridiculous with anything he did.

"But will they promote your cause well enough?" Rachel smiled at him. "Or shall I consider some of the others? These men might be the most pleasant, but also most in need of persuading."

Curtis coughed on the swallow of tea he had just drunk. "Others? How many flowers did you receive? And which were your favorite?"

They continued to ignore him. Alice checked Rachel's list. "This sounds delightful! If we are to have a dinner, these men are the least terrifying and most handsome. I'll begin to copy out the invitations."

Rachel checked the list again. "Review the menu with Cook first and talk with Mrs. King. You'll want the candlesticks and silver gleaming. On no account must you allow Mrs. King to set the table with tall flower arrangements. They stifle conversation and make one feel claustrophobic. The table must be ornamented simply to allow the guests to see one another. Have you ever felt trapped beside a dull dinner partner and been unable to talk to anyone else, because of the awful table décor?"

Alice nodded.

"Yes, and let King know when carriages will be arriving."

Alice and Rachel both eyed Curtis's apparel with distaste, though he noticed that Rachel's eyes lingered on the tight fit of his vest.

"Carter will need to order him a new coat and trousers. Oh, there's hardly time. He'll need to pay extra and have it rushed. I don't know why he didn't get one in Paris." Rachel eyed his collar and cuffs. "At least make sure he changes right before the dinner begins. He cannot keep his cuffs clean. Ink."

She spoke of Curtis as though he weren't there. He inspected his coat. It was last year's fashion, though it fit him well, and there was, indeed, ink on his cuffs. Rachel liked him in this coat, and he saw no need for a new one. "Carter and I visited the shops in Paris. We bought new neckties and vests, and a good deal many other things."

"Yet, you should have bought a new coat in *this* year's style in Paris, and it would have lasted for two or three years in London." Rachel rose from the table. "It sounds like you have this in hand, Alice. Shall I wait for you in the hallway?"

Rachel had taken Alice in hand, and he was grateful. "What about the seating?" He rushed around the table and followed Rachel out of the breakfast room.

He accompanied her down the hallway, desperate to keep her near him for a few moments longer. "Will you step into my study? We can discuss the strategic placement of dinner partners, and I'll accompany you to the hospital.'" He lowered his voice, even though they were nearly to the front door. "Alice won't have any idea how to pair people to walk in to dinner."

Rachel considered him and spoke quietly. "True. She'll dissolve into tears before the dinner begins."

Curtis gestured toward his open study doors. "Join me."

Rachel sighed, but entered the room. He followed her and indicated a pair of gold-embroidered wingback chairs by the fireplace. She perched on the edge of one, barely there.

He collapsed into the matching chair across from her, tipped his head against the headrest, and stretched out his legs. He closed his eyes. Rachel, at home again. The early morning fire crackled, and his stomach was full from breakfast. He'd make this conversation last as long as he could.

"Lord Romford with Alice," Rachel said.

"Grandfather with you," Curtis replied. "No argument. I know he'll insist, so it's pointless."

She sniffed. He opened his eyes and leaned forward, resting his elbows on his knees. "It is the greatest honor I could show any of my guests, Rachel. You'll have to endure it, whether or not you like him. We're trying to show the *ton* how highly he respects you."

She grimaced.

Every day, she let down her guard a little bit more. She was playful with him now. No more emotionless faces. Curtis laughed. "Clearly, you have a few choice words for my grandfather."

She smiled slowly. "The Old Lion doesn't *respect* me. He wishes to use me as a political tool. I am attending this dinner for Alice's sake, and hers alone. Not because I am a prize pony to be trotted out for show."

Curtis inclined his head. "I enjoy the vision I see before me."

Rachel pushed up from her chair.

He waved a hand. "No, don't go. I'll stop teasing you. Back to the seating arrangements. Lady Agatha with me, I fear. She is the leader of fashion and must be given her dues."

Rachel sniffed again.

"Should we allow Lord and Lady Shelford to go in together?" Curtis asked. "No one minds at a private affair such as ours."

"Agreed," Rachel said. "No one would mind. But it is yours. Your dinner, not ours."

At least she was attending the dinner and planning it. She was sitting alone with him in his study. There was hope.

"Lady Octavia with Lord Yelverton? I'm sorry for her, but it can't be helped. Someone must bask in the glow of his attention, since you insist on inviting the calf. He moons about if any woman bats an eyelash. Once he fixes his eye on a woman, he's done for," Curtis said.

Rachel still sat on the edge of her chair, as if she hadn't decided whether to stay and talk to him. He knew he should ask, but he couldn't help it. He had to know, even if the question made her storm out of the room. He watched Rachel to see whether she would betray any hint of emotion. "He sent you flowers?"

She leveled a stare at him. "My head is not turned by a bit of mooning. If it were, we would have been engaged months ago." She didn't leave. She was teasing him, instead. Well, glaring, but it felt like teasing, too.

Curtis grinned. "I suppose I'm not one to speak."

Her glare softened, then she smiled. "And he is only *moderately* desirable as a dinner partner, despite his extravagant bouquets." Rachel settled back into her chair. "Octavia doesn't mind a man mooning over her. She takes it as her due. Mrs. Phillips with Mr. Simons. He's gentle. Miss South with Lord Egerton. He can handle her enthusiasm."

Curtis nodded. He did not care who walked with anyone, as long as Rachel walked safely with Grandfather and away from the other eligible men. "Agreed. Lady Frances with Mr. Seymour."

"No," Rachel said. "He's a bit full of himself. I prefer Lord Sager."

He raised an eyebrow. Lord Sager had managed to ask Rachel to waltz with him. Curtis had suffered through that dance with Lady Clara, and spent the entire time watching Sager flirt with Rachel.

"For Lady Frances," Rachel said serenely, but her eyes twinkled. She *was* teasing him. "Although he is also moderately desirable."

"But not highly?" Curtis grinned at her.

Her eyes flitted to his chest then quickly over to the fireplace. She still thought he was attractive. Curtis relaxed into the chair, his hands behind his head. "Miss Herbert with Mr. Seymour, then," he said. "She can put any man in his place."

Rachel smiled at him. "Agreed. That leaves Mr. Thorne with Lady Clara. I'm sorry Alice cannot go in with him."

"What about Kempton?" he asked.

Rachel widened her eyes. "Oh dear. That's eleven men and ten ladies. We'll have to leave him out this time."

"We can't. Alice will be absolutely silent." Curtis couldn't imagine how Alice would get along without Kempton around.

"He has his own family and other friends," Rachel said. "He cannot always be at her beck and call. She would do well to remember."

He stared at her. He relied on Kempton like a brother. He was always there when he needed him.

Rachel bit her lip. "*You* might do well to consider that."

"I could not slight him," Curtis said.

She studied him. "He might like a break from your constant company. He sees you all day at the hospital and every night for more work and social engagements. We can include Lady Henrietta in the party and have twenty-two instead of twenty." She considered. "This is already far too large for an ordinary dinner party, and Alice shall be invited to attend dinners at the homes of each person invited to the party. We should invite 'no more than the Muses and no fewer than the Graces.' We are well past that number."

Curtis shook his head. "No, spare me. Do not invite Lady Henrietta. You do not need to tell me that she changes the dynamics of a dinner party. I shall have to offend Kempton instead."

He hoped she would allow him to talk a little longer. He had missed her so much, and they hadn't spoken in so long. Not really since Germany.

He bent forward and rested his elbows on his knees. "How am I ever going to teach her to do this, Rachel? She never saw my mother give a formal dinner, and I'm both brother and father to her now. She's had years to prepare, and yet she still does not understand the nuances of things, like pairing couples, that are simple and effortless for you. You've barely met these people once or twice, and you understand them better than she does, who has known them her entire life."

A familiar wave of emotion passed over him. He tipped his head against the back of the chair, closed his eyes again, and let out a long breath. "When I was in Constantinople, at the Scutari hospital, I was in charge of so many lives, but it was different. I sat behind a desk, implementing orders, scheduling rotations, making sure Miss Nightingale's procedures were followed."

The emotion rose, like a tide, and he waited for it to pass. "The nightmares still haunt me. Men lying on stretchers in the hallways, covered in sores and blood." He uncovered his eyes and sought Rachel. "I'm tired of being responsible for so many other people."

She watched him silently, her eyes full of that quiet understanding and compassion he relied on.

He held out a hand. "Come, see for yourself."

He pushed off his chair and drew her up. He led her around the desk, seated her in his leather chair, and bent over her. He pointed to Miss Nightingale's latest missive. "Of the eighteen thousand soldiers who died in the Crimean War, sixteen thousand died of illness, not injury. *Sixteen thousand.* If we'd known how to clean our hospitals sooner, they needn't have died, and still I'm fighting for reforms. Grandfather says it will take years after this report for the Army to change its operations."

He showed her paper after paper, chart after chart. "I can't make sense of it all. The queen appointed nine of us, but Miss Nightingale will actually write the final report. Hundreds of pages, using her statistical analysis, and men are still dying while I sit behind this desk."

Rachel studied the papers, putting them into piles. "You have them grouped, don't you? The way we organized our notes in Germany into separate journals."

Curtis stared at her. It was so obvious.

"How have you divided your portion of the information for the commission?" she asked.

He rubbed the back of his neck. "Dash it all, I haven't. I'm drowning. *You* organized the notes in Germany, not me. I merely copied them."

She studied the notes, picking them up and sorting them. He stepped back, letting her work. "I'll see whether Alice is ready to leave yet," he said. Perhaps if he left her alone and gave her some time, she could make sense of things.

After several minutes, he returned. "Alice will be down in two minutes. She's finished with Cook and King."

Rachel startled. "Will this work?"

Curtis sifted through the piles. In ten minutes, she had made order of something he'd been unable to organize for months. An urgency to make amends swept through him. He couldn't wait until August to marry her. He needed her in his life every day, every minute, starting now.

Rachel pointed to the stacks. "Do you have a few key ideas we could promote during the dinner party? Have you arrived at two or three simple conclusions that could be easily conveyed in a casual manner to the others, in the course of conversation? Perhaps one idea from each of these groups?"

"Not yet," Curtis said. "I will before the party. Or you could help me?" He gazed at Rachel, placing one hand on the back of her chair, and bent over the desk. He would kiss her, if she'd let him. "My cuffs are stained, but at least I shaved this morning."

She glanced at the open door. "Alice must be ready to leave by now, and the *other women* will be expecting us at the hospital." She pressed her lips into a thin line.

Right. She wouldn't wish to kiss him, if she were thinking about all the others he had wooed. He still had to prove himself.

He straightened, tugged at the bottom of his coat sleeves to cover the ink stains on his cuffs, and took her hands. "Thank you for listening to me. Grandfather expects it will take the rest of his life and a good deal of mine to fight this battle, and Alice doesn't understand. She doesn't want to hear a word of it."

Rachel smiled. "At least you have Kempton."

"I'm glad I have you. Thank you for your help with the notes and with Alice. I don't know what I'd do without you." Curtis hesitated. He wanted to hold her, to apologize for his temper yesterday, but he didn't wish to renew the argument.

She dropped his hands. But was it reluctant? Her face was unreadable, but she was still there, unmoving, inches away.

Did he have her in his life as steady and sure as the sunrise? Or would she vanish at the end of the Season, like a mirage? He should apologize. Shelford said to always apologize, and he hadn't done that.

"Rachel," Curtis began. "About yesterday. I'm sorry."

She stepped back, the spell broken, a look of surprise on her face. "Thank you, Curtis. I—Shall we—" She swallowed, her eyes drifting away from his, searching for something. He didn't know what. She bit her lip. "Shall we see about the carriage?" She turned and went into the hallway.

He would have to wait and see.

CHAPTER 18

Rachel had talked to Kempton at the hospital, and he had graciously agreed that Lord Romford was more desirable as a guest than he was. Rachel still felt sorry to leave him out of the dinner party.

"I've got other friends," Kempton had blustered. "My own family doesn't recognize me. Perhaps I'll surprise my mother and stay home that evening."

Rachel knew Alice would rather talk with Kempton, but perhaps she needed to exert herself and leave the comfort of only associating with close friends. At least she already knew Lord Romford reasonably well from their week in Paris and his friendship with her brother.

On the evening of the dinner party, Rachel arrived before the other guests. King welcomed her with a wry smile.

"He's in his shirt sleeves, isn't he?" Rachel asked. "Carter's going to kill him."

King merely closed the door behind her. "Or the missus. My wife runs a tight household."

"And Cook?" Rachel peeled off her cloak and handed it to the butler.

He accepted it. "All's in order."

"Except Curtis." Rachel looked around the hallway, as if she could inspect the dining room from there. "The silver? The table-cloths? The table decorations are not gauche?"

King lowered his chin and peered at her. "In order."

"And Alice?" Rachel made her way to the drawing room.

King opened the doors for her. "Ah. Perhaps all is not quite in order."

Rachel wandered over to the window and gazed out on the murky twilight. Nightfall arrived later and later, now that it was spring, but it was still a long time until the golden summer evenings.

She could make out the outline of other majestic townhomes, arranged in neat rows along Park Lane, marble steps leading up to column-lined entrances. The entrance to Hyde Park was only a short distance down the street, and the Duke of Wellington's grand home only a few doors away at the corner.

Her parents once rented a townhouse in Grosvenor Square, before Papa's death. She remembered springs and summers in Town, with political dinner parties. Such a different life, before Mama's accident and Papa's death.

The scent of shaving soap warned her that Curtis was approaching. She breathed it in and closed her eyes, resting her head against the window. She wanted to live in the shadowland outside, where dreams lingered, and reality never intervened.

A light touch on her elbow startled her. "Alice cannot decide which dress to wear."

Rachel turned to face Curtis and caught her breath. She knew he'd look handsome, but she wasn't prepared to have him so close. He wore an immaculately pressed coat, stretched across his broad shoulders, with a starched collar. The bow tie was perfectly crisp. His face was smooth, recently shaven, and his eyes were an ocean of green tonight.

Rachel bit her lip. "Shall I advise her?"

Curtis drew her arm through his. "Stay with me. She'll be down shortly." He grinned at her. "Your dress is a regular stunner."

She winced. "I'd rather be in the gymnasium." She tried to lift her arms above her head and could only raise them halfway.

Curtis's eyes dropped to the bare skin around her neck and shoulders, and he cleared his throat. "So would I." He swallowed and shook his head. "That dress *is* stunning."

"But confining," Rachel said.

Curtis led her to the center of the room. "Then it is well that our task is greeting the guests, not scaling rope ladders."

Rachel tugged at the bodice of her gown. "I'd rather climb a wall."

Curtis blew out a breath. "So would I, but will you help me? Alice won't be able to greet anyone. If you could stand beside her, show her how to do it?" He gazed down at her, his eyes searching hers, traveling over her face, and flicking back up to her.

Rachel nodded. She didn't trust herself to speak at the moment, either. Her resolve had melted the moment he touched her elbow.

Curtis glowered. "If one more man sends you flowers, I shall have to take stronger measures. If one more woman tries to catch me alone, I shall sic Lord Yelverton on her. I want them to see you standing beside me. It sends a clear message of my intentions."

It was as if the argument at St. Thomas' had never happened. He still wanted to marry her, despite her accusations and concerns, and assumed she wanted to marry him. He had apologized for his flare of temper, but would he change his behavior?

She didn't know how she felt about Curtis right now. Her feelings were in turmoil, up one minute and down the next. She saw such contradictory sides of him that she hardly knew what to think.

Best to stay calm, stay quiet, and help Alice's party succeed. She could think later, when he didn't smell so good or stand so close.

Rachel held herself erect, her chin up. "We have so little time to talk in the hospital. Nurse Ward is quite strict. I hardly know the women you've invited." She'd seen her mother and father greet guests in their home. She tried to imagine herself as serene and gracious. It didn't matter which political party someone belonged to; her mother treated them with the same equanimity.

Alice eventually arrived in the drawing room, moments before Grandfather. She wore the pale gold dinner dress Rachel had encouraged her to buy in Paris. Alice looped her arm through Rachel's. "Thank goodness you are here. Will this dress do?"

Rachel nudged Curtis in the ribs. He coughed and looked at her, a question in his eyes. She inclined her head toward Alice.

"You are lovely tonight, sister," Curtis said, rubbing his side. He put his hand on Rachel's back and whispered, "So are you, my dear."

Alice looked over and stared pointedly at his hand. Rachel hardly had time to react before the duke arrived, and Curtis quickly removed his hand from Rachel's back. The Old Lion cackled with delight when he saw her. "Oh, she's a queen. Look at her disdain, Loughton." He bowed over her hand. "You can't teach that, my dear."

Eleanor arrived next with her husband, then the other guests. Lady Agatha's tall frame and quiet manner reminded Rachel of herself. Even their taste in dresses was remarkably similar. They both wore cream dresses shot through with gold thread. Lady Agatha's dress had more decoration, was far too low cut, and had far too many ruffles, being a few years behind Paris fashions, but Rachel could tell that she and Lady Agatha were alike in several uncanny ways. Both had dark hair and dark eyes, a heart-shaped face, and a natural sort of reserve.

Rachel bit her lip and fought an urge to wrap her arms around her middle. She pressed her hands together and forced her legs to remain where they were, despite a sudden weakness in the knees.

At least Curtis was consistent.

Lady Agatha headed straight for him, and he bowed over her hand. Rachel held her mouth in a thin, tight smile, the one she had practiced so often, even though her throat burned.

"And how is your sister? Have her symptoms improved? Have you changed physicians?" Curtis held Lady Agatha's hand.

"I must see her myself. You take too much of her care on yourself."

How long was he going to hold her hand? Was it really necessary to hold it so long?

"You are always so kind. She would welcome a visit." Lady Agatha smiled at him. *Was there longing in her gaze?* She turned to Rachel. "We've all wondered where you came from, Miss Wickford. I've so wished to make your better acquaintance. Miss Loughton, a pleasure to see you again."

Alice inclined her head. She had not moved away to speak with anyone, but waited with them to greet guests.

"Essex," Rachel said, not believing a word that Lady Agatha said. "Not far from London. A few hours ride." She had no desire to further an acquaintance with her.

Lady Agatha looked between Curtis and Rachel. "I am grateful for this course. I do worry what others would think if they knew how much of my sister's care I give." She met Rachel's eyes and tilted her chin up to match Rachel's proud look. "This gives me an opportunity to learn without risking my reputation. If someone as elegant as yourself can set the standard, no one will question me."

Rachel wanted to laugh. *Elegant?* She was a simple country girl. "*You* are the leader of fashion, Lady Agatha. You set the standard and others will follow."

"Is that your secret?" Lady Agatha regarded her. "Is it that easy?"

Rachel met her eyes. "Why should you fear?" She thought of the talking points that she and Curtis had prepared. "No one is as highly regarded as Miss Nightingale. The entire country regards her with gratitude. An Upper Class lady can care for her own as well as a stranger. Why should she not be educated and do so, if she chooses to use her time in that manner? Miss Loughton is a fine example."

Lady Agatha smiled sadly. "But *you* do not risk your own reputation, nor does she. You do not know what I do for my sister. Very few do."

Rachel took her hands. Perhaps they had something in common. "I have assisted in nineteen births and cared for an ill mother for nine years."

Lady Agatha squeezed her hands. "I should like you and Miss Loughton to take tea with me some afternoon."

Rachel wasn't sure she was ready for that. "Our classes keep us so busy. We shall be together nearly every day. We shall talk again at St. Thomas.'"

Lady Agatha moved off, and Alice let out a deep breath.

Rachel could feel Curtis watching her. Was he disappointed that she had ignored Lady Agatha's offer? She hoped it did not feel like a snub to Lady Agatha. She had not intended it in that matter. Surely, the woman was not sincere. She was merely attempting to assess her competition.

Rachel studied the next woman approaching them. Mrs. Phillips stretched out her hands to greet Curtis.

"Colonel! You've been gone an age and left me bereft." She indicated her stylish black mourning clothes, which were rather daringly worn.

"Thank you for attending our intimate dinner party. I did hope you would find it discreet enough for a widow."

"Psh." Mrs. Phillips looked around the room as if bored. "He was twenty years older than me. I'm hardly heartbroken that he's gone. It's already been a month."

Rachel schooled her expression to hide her shock. Beside her, she could see Alice staring. She nudged Alice.

"But still, it was unexpected, and you must have felt some affection for him." Curtis was still holding her hands. Finally, he let go.

Mrs. Phillips shrugged. "He wasn't my first choice." She looked at Curtis and pursed her lips.

Rachel felt sick.

Curtis moved closer to her. "Nor was I, Isabella. We both know that." He drew Rachel forward. "Have you met Miss Wickford? I don't believe you are attending balls yet."

"More's the pity," Mrs. Phillips said, extending a hand. "Pleasure." She sized Rachel up.

Rachel scrutinized the woman without apology. Her direct gaze might be considered a bit rude, but the widow was hiding something, she'd bet on it. The blasé attitude seemed affected, not genuine. It must be something important to affect such shocking behavior. She examined the woman's features carefully as the widow and Curtis exchanged meaningless banter. Mrs. Phillips's gaze flitted back to her every now and then and quickly away again.

She was expecting a child. That was it. The corset didn't fit quite right. She was a thin woman, but there was a slight roundness to the face. She must be several months along. She seemed so vibrant, yet there was an exhaustion lurking beneath the affected gaiety, too, that hinted she might be expecting a child.

The conversation lagged.

"Did you and your husband have any children before he passed?" Rachel asked.

The question clearly caught Mrs. Phillips off-guard. She was silent.

"She did not, in four years of marriage," Curtis said quietly. "It has been a matter of private consultation with many physicians and great personal pain. I'm sorry, Mrs. Phillips."

His tone reproached Rachel for her rudeness.

"No, Colonel, it's quite all right. How did you know, Miss Wickford?" She stared.

Now Curtis was confused.

Rachel dropped her voice. "Some women prefer a midwife and others prefer a male physician to attend. Curtis and I—"

Mrs. Phillips's eyes flew to his face and back to Rachel. Rachel realized her mistake. She was usually more careful in company, but she had forgotten in her surprise that the widow was hiding her condition. Not one of these women had called him by his Christian name.

"The colonel and I have delivered two births together. I attend to the mother myself, and he can assist if there are complications. Some women insist on having a male doctor, and he is experienced." She smiled. "He is also adept at carrying firewood and scrubbing floors."

"She calls me her assistant, but *I* oversee the births," Curtis said. He had recovered quickly.

Rachel tilted her head up at him. "He thinks he does."

They gazed at each other. An overwhelming force swept through her, a thrill that was both exhilarating and unnerving. Curtis's green-gold eyes danced with a storm of love, daring her to defy him. In the middle of everything, of Mrs. Phillips flirting with him, with Lady Agatha throwing herself at him, he had the temerity to look at her like that?

Mrs. Phillips cleared her throat, calling their attention back to herself, and whispered, "You cannot imagine my terror, being alone with my dear husband unexpectedly gone, and no idea whether I carry his heir or a daughter. I shall have to raise the child alone, and I have never given birth. What if I lose this child, as I have the others?" Her eyes filled with tears. "Of course I wished to join the nursing course. How else am I to learn about delivering a child?"

"You're much more advanced than you were when you lost the others. Am I correct?" Rachel whispered.

Mrs. Phillips nodded.

Rachel knew she was terrified. It explained the outrageous behavior. She wished they could speak privately, so she could put her mind at ease. "Contact me if anything is amiss. I suspect you shall have a healthy child in three or four months. It's nearly time to stop wearing a corset. We shall talk more later."

Mrs. Phillips narrowed her eyes. "This is quite secret, as you may well imagine. The heir has not yet been informed of my condition."

Curtis rested a hand on her arm. "Miss Wickford is discreet and well experienced. You need have no concerns, but perhaps it is time to consider legal issues or inform the heir. We must talk further."

Mrs. Phillips threw back her head. "Of course," she said loudly, and moved away.

Rachel glanced at Curtis.

"Don't ask," he said, rubbing a hand over his face. Alice giggled.

Miss Herbert had been hovering on the edge of Rachel's vision, and she moved in quickly as soon as Mrs. Phillips glided off. Ribbons and bows covered her dress, the most extravagant in the room, and the crinoline hoop beneath her skirt would surely knock Rachel off balance when she arrived. Far too wide. Miss Herbert liked attention, that much was clear.

Rachel calculated in her head. *How much longer?* Surely, dinner would be served any moment. She would be seated between Lord Romford and the Old Lion. Only one more awkward conversation, hopefully, then she had an entire dinner of interrogation at the hands of the duke to anticipate. What an evening.

She inhaled deeply to steady herself. Cedar and lavender. She loved Alice a lot to endure this wretched dinner, but there *were* a few advantages.

"I shave twice a day when I'm going to see you," Curtis muttered aside.

Butterflies danced in her stomach. Standing so near, side by side, it was easy to imagine a lifetime of this. Their easy friendship and the deep attraction.

"Why did you not tell me to bring my case book? Are we scheduling home visits or holding a dinner party?" Rachel whispered back.

Curtis grinned at her and straightened to greet Miss Herbert.

"Colonel, how goes the report?" She shook his hand like her father, General Herbert, might, and held his a little too long. Curtis pulled his hand away.

"Complicated. And how is your father?" Curtis flashed a winning smile at her.

"He's swamped, and so am I. It's the wives and daughters who write the reports." She tilted her head playfully, her wide skirt swaying as she moved.

Curtis indicated Rachel at his side. "Your father must see the system Miss Wickford is implementing to organize my notes."

She had implemented no system, but now she was committed to produce one and teach it to someone else.

"Oh, I am the one who needs to see it, not my father," Miss Herbert simpered.

Rachel couldn't believe it. Another house visit. Another call. Curtis was still involved in the lives of every woman.

"Miss Wickford and I must show you which journals to purchase," Curtis said. "And then you must come to my office, and the three of us can go through the notes to coordinate with your father."

Miss Herbert studied Rachel. "I'm very thorough, but very overwhelmed. I should be most grateful for your assistance. Could you spare the time, Colonel? Miss Wickford? Miss Loughton?"

Her smile included all of them, although Miss Herbert seemed desperate to catch the colonel's eye.

"Certainly." Rachel returned the smile. Were all her new London friends to be Curtis's old flames?

Lady Frances approached with Miss South. Finally, someone with a reasonable dress. While Miss South was covered in flounces and bows and tassels, Lady Frances wore a simple and elegant silver evening gown with hardly a trace of decoration, something that Rachel herself might pick. "Thank you for the invitation, Colonel. It's been so long since we've seen you." She peered up at him hopefully.

"Didn't think you'd want to include *me*," Miss South said, with a hint of belligerence in her tone. The feathers in her hair moved every direction as she spoke.

"Ah, but Miss Wickford drew up the guest list and insisted on both of you." Curtis turned to Rachel.

Blasted man. He had insisted, not her, but now she was trapped. Again. She smiled her most gracious smile at both women. She indicated Alice. "Miss Loughton made the list, of course. The colonel jests. I merely advised her that I should so much love to get to know both of you."

Lady Frances immediately reached out and grasped her hands. "And I have been longing to ask you to tea! Haven't I, Lydia?"

Miss South nodded. "We don't care a fig for the colonel, but we do love to meet new friends. Alice, do join us. I have missed *you*." She tossed her head and flounced away, the feather in her hair bouncing with every minced step.

Lady Frances laughed. "Promise you'll come soon with Miss Loughton. Any time I'm at home. I'll give you my card. I have so many questions for you. That old bat, Ward, simply won't let us gossip at the hospital."

She seemed the most promising of the group. She was clearly pining for Curtis, also trying to catch his eye, but she seemed reasonable in every other regard.

King announced dinner. Rachel used the diversion as an excuse to avoid answering Lady Frances. Alice stared wide-eyed at Rachel.

Rachel whispered, "Have you forgotten the pairings, dearest?"

Alice nodded, her eyes glistening with unshed tears.

Rachel nudged Curtis in the ribs and whispered, "*You* remember the pairings. Will you please rescue her?"

Curtis immediately took Alice's arm. "May I help with the pairings? I would love to talk with everyone. You don't mind me interfering, do you, Alice?"

She shot Rachel a grateful look, and the siblings moved off to begin inviting couples to walk in to dinner.

The duke came to take Rachel's arm. "Come, Miss Wickford, shall we lead the way before the others leave the drawing room?" the Old Lion asked. "I have a matter to discuss with you, and I'd rather not be overheard."

CHAPTER 19

Rachel walked down the hallway with the duke, far ahead of everyone else, while Alice and Lord Romford went last to ensure each person had a partner.

"You're far too delighted with yourself," Rachel said to him.

The duke patted her hand, which rested on his arm. "You're majestic," he said. "I watched you put those women in their place."

"I didn't," she protested.

He merely chuckled. "I know what I saw. Come now. Let us talk privately before dinner. Loughton gave me a list of arguments to work into the conversation." He continued to chuckle as they advanced along the corridor.

Rachel entered the dining room on his arm. Light paneling and mirrors ran the length of the room. She inspected the candelabras and flower arrangements, which dotted the oval table at intervals, set for twenty guests. King had done as she asked. She'd have to remind Alice to thank him later.

The duke halted abruptly. "King. Who authorized the use of these vases?"

King glanced at Rachel. "Alice selected them."

"Stow it, King. She's never seen them. My son hid them the day her mother died. She wasn't old enough to remember them. I haven't seen them in ten years at least."

He trained an intense glare on Rachel. "Do you have any idea what this will do to Loughton when he sees them?"

Rachel lifted her chin. "Remind him of happy memories, I imagine. They are by far the most tasteful vases. Wide and low. They're almost like a dish. I asked Mrs. King to show me everything she had. The others are far too tall."

The duke narrowed his gaze. "You have no apology?"

Rachel bit her lip. "Would you rather be trapped with a miserable dinner partner for two hours? They should be used. I'm sorry if the memories are painful for you, Your Grace, but yes. A vase is an empty vessel that you've filled with memories. Fill them with new memories."

His eyes glittered with the same intensity she'd seen in Curtis's eyes so often, and then softened, as quickly as his grandson's did. "Must have taken a great while to polish the tarnish off, King. Very good. Everyone else has those gauche bronze ornaments right now."

He led Rachel toward the gleaming mahogany table. "They were her favorite for a reason. They are the best in the house. I haven't been able to see over the candles for the last month." He chuckled. "You can't tell me Alice selected those vases, and you can't tell me Loughton thought of those arguments on his own."

Rachel stopped in front of her seat, relieved that the conversation had taken a different turn. "I deemed it prudent to guide the dinner discussion, should the opportunity arise."

The duke pulled out the upholstered chair. "You're as conniving as I am. I'm proud of you, that's all."

Her relief quickly turned back to unease. She considered his words as he pushed her seat in to the table. She spoke quietly after he seated himself next to her. "This dinner was meant as an opportunity to influence political opinions. Alice clearly stated your intention to me."

He looked around the room. "You've exceeded my expectations

for one so young, dear." He spread his napkin on his lap. "But down to business before the others join us. You've been discreet. I'll give you that much. I haven't heard one whisper about my son's health. Can I assume that will continue?"

She glanced toward the door. "Certainly. I am no tell-tale."

Curtis had just entered the room with Lady Agatha on his arm. The others followed, and soon the food appeared on the table.

The duke offered her a roll and began to dish food onto her plate.

Rachel didn't intend to impress him. He praised her for being calculating and scheming, while she'd never considered herself as anything but practical and level-headed.

"But you have made a liar of me." The duke studied his food. He dropped his voice. "I told my cook to prepare something for me when I return. Anytime I eat with Loughton, she knows I'll arrive home hungry. I may actually eat my fill this evening. Who approved this menu?"

She smoothed the napkin on her lap. "I'm sure I don't understand you."

The duke trained his eyes on her. "I'm sure you planned this dinner. It's appetizing. The things I've had to eat this last month when I've dined with my niece and nephew..." He shook his head.

Rachel hid a smile behind her napkin. "Not a fan of sardines on toast, Your Grace?"

He muttered, "So, you've been to one of Alice's dinners, too?"

"I concede nothing," she said.

"So Loughton tells me." The Old Lion peered at her. "But roast beef will go a long way toward changing my opinion of you, if that is your aim." He speared a roast potato, dipped it in gravy, and took a bite.

"Then I should have ordered pork," Rachel muttered.

The duke's strict demeanor cracked, and he grinned. "Always in opposition. I wonder, were you like this with your father?"

Rachel played with the napkin in her lap. Of course she was.

Papa had taught her rhetoric, and she always took the opposing view from him to refine her skill.

He contemplated her. "If I always disagreed with your father, and you did as well, I wonder if your politics agree with mine." He took a bite of roast beef and seemed to relish it.

She hid a smile beneath her napkin. She knew she was more reform-minded than her father. She probably did agree with the duke. If she were a man, which political party would she join? His or her father's?

The Old Lion peered at her. "Now, tell me about this seat in Essex. It's troubled me for years. Who can we get to replace that buffoon?"

Rachel took a long sip to avoid answering the question, but she knew the duke would not be deterred. "Lord Barrington's eldest, Matthew, is quite busy with the Dunmore estate."

"He'd vote against me, like his father. Who else?" The duke speared another potato.

She sighed. "Lord Chelmsford's younger brother, Peter, will assist his father-in-law in his mining firm. I believe you must be content with the wretched bloke who already has the seat."

She took a petite bite of the roasted vegetables. If the duke liked the beef, she would eat the side dishes.

"Tell me about the father-in-law." The Old Lion had clearly decided to dispense with any trivial dinner conversation, and there was no avoiding him. On her other side, Lord Romford had engaged Lady Agatha in a long anecdote.

"Mr. Maldon, the mining magnate." She chewed as slowly as she could to avoid another question.

"Perfect. *Mister*. Wealthy. Wants a title, I assume?" He glanced at her.

Rachel nodded.

"Any political persuasion?"

She shook her head. "I'm sure he'll join whichever party will give him a baronetcy." She considered. "If you can persuade Mr.

Maldon to your side, Peter may be able to get Walter—Lord Chelmsford—to vote for you."

The duke continued to talk exclusively to her, ignoring Lady Frances on his other side. "True. Two votes at once. Promising. One in the House of Lords and one in the House of Commons. Pursue my interests in both houses of Parliament. You have a gift, girl. Now, who can help him run an election campaign? Who are his closest friends?"

Rachel resigned herself to a prolonged discussion. "Lord Barrington or my mother."

"Your mother?" The duke's face split into a smile. "How close are they?"

She set down her fork. Mr. Maldon was courteous, solicitous. Always present, when he wasn't in London. She spent more time with Lucy's Aunt Ellen and Mr. Maldon than anyone else. "Quite close."

"Like a father to you, eh?" The duke grinned. "Excellent. She understands how to win a seat for a member of Parliament. *You* are a gift from heaven. Do you know how long I have waited for a chance like this?"

"Nine years." Rachel set down her fork. She felt disloyal to her father to be helping the duke, to be trying to elect someone to her father's old seat in Parliament who would join his opposing party, even if she herself actually agreed with their politics. She wasn't sure she wanted his praise.

The Old Lion inclined his head toward Curtis. "I told Loughton to court your friend Lady Shelford last year, because she was from Essex. Hoped we might be able to turn old Barrington's vote."

Rachel dabbed at the corners of her mouth. "So, when he met me and Lucy?"

"I'm sure the location of your estate only added to your other charms." The duke studied her. "Hang it all, don't get your dander up because you happen to be the perfect fit for him."

She had no appetite. It had been a political ploy all along. Curtis knew from the beginning that his grandfather needed to secure votes and influence in Essex. Lucy was engaged, so Rachel was the natural choice. She'd almost convinced herself that Curtis truly loved her, but he'd sought her out for political purposes.

"Enjoy your roast beef, Your Grace." She turned to Lord Romford, who had finished telling Lady Agatha his anecdote.

"Tell me what this scheming is about," Lord Romford said. "I shall be sure to vote for your old friend." His smile was genuine and kind.

Rachel relaxed. "Please, do tell me whatever amusing story you've been rehearsing. I should like a break from serious conversation at the moment."

Curtis glanced over at her, trying to catch her eye, but she would not meet his gaze. She would not enumerate the salient points of his commission report or attempt to persuade Lord Romford to anything. She wished to leave the dinner party as quickly as possible.

As soon as dinner ended, and the women retired to the drawing room, Rachel begged Eleanor to leave the party. She asked King to send for the carriage to avoid seeing Curtis.

"Thank you, Alice," Rachel said. "You handled everything so well. I'm sure the rest of the evening will be a success."

"Must you go?" Alice whispered, looking around at the other women.

Rachel nodded. "Lady Frances seems kind. Sit near her or Miss South."

Rachel and Eleanor waited in the hallway. Rachel had asked King to merely send for Lord Shelford, without telling Curtis that she was leaving. She felt a hint of unease, but did not wish to provoke a confrontation. Curtis would demand to know why she was leaving early, and she wanted to vanish quietly without an explanation.

They made their way home in silence. When they had taken off their wraps and given their things to the footmen, Rachel still could not feel easy. She took her shawl back. The weather in late April was sometimes warm, sometimes cold. Like her feelings toward Curtis.

Rachel played with the ends of her shawl. "Do you have a moment?"

Eleanor and Lord Shelford exchanged a glance. Lord Shelford indicated the drawing room. "Shall we?"

Rachel and Eleanor chose comfortable chairs near the fireplace while Lord Shelford stretched on a sofa.

"What is it, dearest?" Eleanor peered at her.

Rachel took a handkerchief out of her pocket and began to twist it in her hands. "Do you know, I've been asking myself the wrong questions. I've been so worried about whether I would fit into Loughton's world, that I never wondered whether he'd fit into mine."

Eleanor shifted on the chair and rearranged her skirt. "Fair question."

"You and Lord Shelford—"

"Percy," he called from across the room. "Just call me Percy."

Rachel continued. "You come from the same world. Your father is an earl, and so is Percy. They're both Peers, and it's the same set of friends."

Eleanor relaxed into her chair. "I see. And you? Your father was a member of the House of Commons, and the colonel is preparing a report for them, so you're involved in the same sort of political life."

Rachel stared into the fire. "No, that's not what I meant."

"Why not?" Eleanor asked.

Rachel sighed. "I grew up in our neighborhood and spent most of the time there. Mother hasn't been to London for almost ten years. Curtis isn't a member of Parliament—"

"He could be," Percy interrupted. "If you wanted him to run for a seat."

"But my life is in the country. Quiet, caring for my mother. God wants me to be a nurse, to help her." Rachel watched the flames dance.

Eleanor smiled. "Or your life is here in London. It's only your mother and Lucy's Aunt Ellen left home in Essex during the Season. Lucy and Peter are returning from their Grand Tour soon. I'm here, as well as my parents. Even Mr. Maldon visits regularly on business. Your friends and your life are changing. You could change as well. Perhaps you already have. Perhaps God has a different plan for you, using your nursing skills *and* your rhetorical talents."

Rachel tucked the handkerchief away and pulled her shawl around her shoulders. "I don't know who I am when I'm in London. The duke sees me as masterfully shrewd and calculating. I don't want to be that version of who I could be. I like my other self, the one that cares for Mama and helps Dr. Morrow and is kind."

"I like you," Percy called out from the sofa. "Loughton loves you. Excellent match the other day. Fine boxer. Him, I mean, not you."

Eleanor laughed. "You're an excellent politician, Rachel, as were both of your parents. My mother is, too, and I'm learning to be. There's nothing wrong with being deliberate in your actions. That does not make you manipulative. It's merely wise. You can be kind, and still be a politician."

The fire burned bright, fierce and relentless. "But I don't like the way Curtis treats the women at the nursing school. It's like he's still in love with them. I can't treat other men that way just to persuade them to a cause. I don't dance with Lord Romford and Mr. Thorne to secure their votes, and I can't bear to watch him flirting and dancing with the others, holding their hands too long, seeing them still in love with him."

Eleanor and Percy were silent.

"You see it, too, don't you?" Rachel asked. "I'm not imagining it. He's so used to being a bachelor that he doesn't understand how to be anything else."

Percy snorted. "I told him to learn to apologize. We need another conversation, this time without the boxing gloves."

"He doesn't know how to stop loving people," Eleanor said. "Percy's the same way. Loves everyone he meets."

"Except Loughton," Percy said and yawned.

Eleanor caught Rachel's eye. "But he loves them. He's not *in love* with them. There's a difference, Rachel, and he is only *in love* with you."

Rachel bit her lip. It was easy for Eleanor to say that. Had she really seen the way he'd looked at Lady Agatha and Mrs. Phillips? She couldn't imagine being married and having her husband spending time in intimate places, like a sickroom, with other women.

She wanted to keep him all to herself. She was jealous, and she could admit it. He would never be the kind of husband who adored her and only her. Eleanor said that Percy was the same, but he wasn't. His adoration of Eleanor, and only Eleanor, was plain for all to see.

Percy didn't spend time alone with other women. Curtis had arranged to visit Lady Agatha in front of her. She felt sick. She could not share him with every other woman he'd ever loved. Yes, he might love her, but he also loved several other women.

She admired him. She had never shared such a deep connection with anyone. She respected him. She wanted to help him with the report, the nursing school, and Alice. She wanted someone to help her with her worries, and she didn't want him to carry his burdens alone. They believed in the same causes, and she had to admit that she enjoyed politics.

Perhaps that frightened her. It was too easy. She didn't wish to become the cold and calculating person the duke already assumed she was.

There were too many unknowns, too much risk, and she did not know him well enough. Love wasn't enough, and attraction wasn't enough. What if he demanded that she give up nursing after she married? Who would care for Mama?

He would assume full and absolute control of her life, if they married, and she did not know whether he could be relied on. God had called her to do the work of nursing. He might have also led her heart to Curtis and led her heart to marriage.

But she didn't trust him. He changed with every mood and every setting. He wasn't at all the sort of doting, quiet, steady husband she had imagined for herself. He was constantly in motion, full of energy, and eager to challenge her.

The more she learned about him, the less she felt like she really knew him. Had he pursued her because she lived in Essex? Because of her father's political background? How cold and calculating had his own methods been?

He didn't know how to help Alice, and his methods sometimes seemed unfeeling and uncaring. What if he grew cold toward her as time progressed?

And a letter from Mama and Dr. Morrow had arrived today. Mama was ill, getting worse, and required help. She might have to hire a nurse, since Rachel was away, and Rachel's first aim in learning about medicine had ever been to help her mother.

"Eleanor, Percy, can you help me?" Rachel asked. "I need to go home."

CHAPTER 20

Curtis stared at the handwritten note, not a hint of cologne on the cream Italian stationery. Alice sobbed in a corner of the drawing room. *"Dearest Alice, my mother's illness has grown more serious. I must return and care for her. Please tell your brother, so he can make arrangements at the school. I will miss you. —Rachel"*

He dropped onto a sofa. *Gone.* Everything went so well last night before dinner, when Rachel was able to talk with some of the other women. She'd seemed to enjoy dinner well enough. He couldn't imagine a better evening, until Rachel had vanished, like the mirage he'd feared she was.

She'd left him to carry the weight, just when he thought he didn't have to do it alone anymore. How would he take care of Alice without her to prompt him? How could he help Miss Nightingale's school without her to assist the matrons and set an example for the other women? How could he work on the commission's report without her to guide his thinking and organize the notes?

He couldn't face the prospect of a life without Rachel. It left a hole too large to fill. He covered his eyes and let his head drop backward until it hit the wall.

He should be comforting Alice, but he felt completely empty. Achingly empty. Waves crashing onto rocks, but the tide never coming into shore.

Rachel wasn't coming back. What had he done wrong? Thoughts crowded into his mind. There were too many answers. How did he know which, of all the stupid mistakes, was the one that sent her away?

And could anything change her mind? He'd assumed he had until the end of the Season. Still three and a half months left, at least, but now time had stopped. There were no more minutes or seconds. It was stifling, and he couldn't breathe. Only one thing to be done. If she wouldn't see him, he would go see her.

Curtis started with his sister, still weeping in a chair by the fireplace. If Rachel would not return, Alice must have a companion. "Shall I ask Mrs. Glenn to return to London immediately?"

Alice nodded her head, wrapped her arms around his neck, and clung to him.

Curtis hugged her and waited for the sobs to subside. "I'll miss her, too," he said. "I'll send a telegram to invite Mrs. Glenn and her sister this instant."

He strode to his office, grabbed a sheet of paper, and dashed out a few lines for King to have sent.

He scratched out a note to Miss Nightingale next, explaining that Alice would have to assist with both sets of Upper Class trainees. He checked his cuffs. *Ink. Blast it.* Rachel was right. At least his collar was starched. He marched upstairs to change his cuffs.

Then he rode to St. Thomas'. He dreaded this part. He didn't want to face any of the women, and he especially didn't want to tell them that Rachel had left him.

He decided to check with Kempton first. Cowardly thing to do, and Curtis knew it. He cleared his throat. "Did you hear?"

Kempton glanced up from the enormous pile of papers on his desk.

Curtis met his gaze head on. "Rachel's moved home to Essex."

Kempton stared at him. "Must have been some dinner party. What did Alice serve? Jellied pig feet?"

Curtis couldn't laugh.

Kempton came around the desk and clapped him on the back. "When does she return?"

Curtis shook his head. "She doesn't."

"And?" Kempton prompted. "When are we leaving?"

"Tomorrow, if you'll go with me." Curtis rubbed a hand over his face. He hadn't bothered to shave, and he wasn't accustomed to stubble.

Kempton went back to the desk. "I'll pack a bag tonight. Are we taking your carriage to the train station?"

Curtis nodded. "If that is acceptable to you."

Kempton studied him. "Why this wretched tone of civility? Did Rachel tell you to be nice to me?"

Curtis shrugged.

Kempton checked his pocket watch. "Shall I get us tickets for the early train?"

Curtis nodded again.

Kempton consulted a timetable on his desk. "Bishopsgate station, Bethnal Green. Leave enough time to get to the East End."

Curtis registered the instructions in a daze. He moved along the corridor and down to the classroom, where the matron, Mrs. Ward, patrolled at the front of the room.

"Eh?" She glared at him. "Ran off my assistant, did you? Miss Wickford did not arrive this morning."

Miss South crossed her arms and narrowed her eyes. Lady Agatha and Lady Clara exchanged a glance. Mrs. Phillips stared round-eyed, while Miss Herbert and Lady Frances began to whisper with each other.

Curtis surveyed the class. "I apologize for the interruption. Miss

Wickford's been called home on a personal matter. Lady Agatha, Miss Herbert, Mrs. Phillips, might I have a word?"

Mrs. Ward sniffed. "Go on, then. You three stay together. He's run off one nurse. I don't intend to lose any others."

Curtis tried to conceive of a way to speak discretely in front of the others, but they surprised him. As soon as they achieved the hallway, they spoke to him.

"Miss Wickford sent me a note, Colonel," Lady Agatha said, giving him a meaningful look. "She and I will correspond privately. Thank you."

"And she sent me a detailed explanation of her organizational system for the notes, with suggestions for where to purchase journals," Miss Herbert said. "We will correspond on our own, if I have questions. I'm not sure *you'd* be able to answer them."

"No, I wouldn't," Curtis said.

Mrs. Phillips turned to him. "I received a note this morning as well. She and I have reached an understanding, and she will visit me in a few months." She winked at him. "You're welcome to accompany her on that visit."

Curtis stared at her, dumbfounded. Of course Rachel wouldn't leave without helping these women. She must have stayed up all night writing notes to her new friends. And Alice. Then why had she left him, without any note or explanation?

Lady Agatha put her hand on his arm. "You must miss her terribly. Will she return soon?"

"I hope so," he said.

Lady Agatha looked at the others. "How much did she tell you of her mother's health in her note?"

They exchanged glances. "Enough."

"It may be some time before she's able to return, then," Lady Agatha said. "Am I right?" She studied Curtis.

Emotions rose to the surface. *Steady on.* He cleared his throat. "That may be so."

Mrs. Phillips shrugged. "Too bad. I almost liked her."

"I could have used her help," Miss Herbert said. "Her system looked quite promising."

Lady Agatha smiled at him. "I hope you come to an understanding with her."

He looked among the three women.

"Marry her," Mrs. Phillips said. "We spoke this morning, before classes, and we all agree."

Curtis laughed. "The three of you agree on something?"

"Six of us," Lady Agatha said. "What do you think we talk about in nursing school?"

"Bachelors," Miss Herbert said. "And anatomy."

Mrs. Phillips winked at him again. "And bachelors' anatomy. Back to class, my dears. Ward's likely to kill us, if we linger much longer." She tossed her head as she headed back toward the classroom, speaking over her shoulder. "I'm sorry, Colonel, you're not the man for any of us. We've sampled the goods, and we quite agree. There are other fish in the sea."

Curtis grinned and bowed deeply as the women left the hallway. He'd like to see Mrs. Phillips remarry and find a husband to help her raise her child, but it wouldn't be him.

He had a train to catch.

CHAPTER 21

Early May 1857

Rachel drank in the familiar sight of home. The peach exterior of her three-story house with rows and rows of windows, the wrought-iron fence, the chimneys lining the rooftop like soldiers.

She pushed away that thought. No, the chimneys looked like something else. She searched the grounds for any change in the scenery, but the carefully trimmed hedges were as neat as usual. As a man's carefully shaved sideburns.

Statues lined the alcoves on the home's exterior, lined up like an army of—

This is ridiculous. Why did everything remind her of Curtis? She gathered her skirts and prepared to descend the steps from the carriage. It was an easy afternoon trip between London and her home. Far too easy to leave, and yet excruciating.

Rachel forced herself to walk calmly toward the house. Mama knew she was coming. Rushing was unnecessary. Running wouldn't cure her mother.

All the same, her heart beat faster. Dr. Morrow's letter had frightened her more than any letter had before. Somehow, she felt as if her very presence would heal Mama, or as if her absence made her sicker.

She should not have stayed away so long. One quick visit at Easter hardly counted.

Mama lay on a sofa in the drawing room near a fire, her eyes closed, her head resting on a pillow, her dark hair neatly braided. Her lady's maid, Joyce, repaired clothes in the corner.

Joyce nodded to her and continued to sew. Rachel slipped into a chair by the fireplace. "Mama?"

Her mother's eyes flitted open. "Rachel," she said weakly. She held out a hand. "Welcome home, dearest. Your note was such a welcome surprise. I didn't expect to see you until August. How was London?"

Rachel handed her mother a glass of water. "I met that Old Lion," she said.

Her mother adjusted the light blanket around her legs. "I miss those days."

"He proposed to you," Rachel said. "If you wish to move to London."

Mama laughed, then coughed. "No, the air is terrible. Did anyone else propose?"

Rachel was silent. "To you or to me?" she finally asked.

Her mother laughed again, then coughed again. "Stop making me laugh," Mama said. "To you, obviously, dear."

"It depends on what you call a proposal," Rachel said.

Mama rested her head against the sofa. "Whatever it was, tell me about it. Everything. You can imagine how distorted Eleanor's account has been, filtered through her mother."

Now Rachel laughed. "Colonel Loughton did express a wish to wed."

"A wish? He's sent at least ten blasted telegrams begging for permission to ask your hand in marriage, to court you, and I don't know what else. One on Christmas Day, one from Paris, one the night before last. He seems to think he's rather close to the brink rather often, and then he never quite follows through."

Rachel rose from her chair and crossed to the glass doors, which looked out over the gardens. Her mother pushed up on the sofa.

"Very proper sense of decorum. He didn't want to ask you without my permission. We're getting to be regular correspondents," Mama said.

"Without my knowledge." Rachel pressed her lips together and turned to face her mother.

Mama raised her eyebrows. "Don't adopt that tone with me, Rachel Mariah Wickford. I'll correspond with anyone I like."

"When was he going to tell me?" Rachel cocked her head.

Her mother sat up fully on the sofa, smoothed the light blanket on her lap, and cocked her head as well. "When you stop being ridiculous and allow him to propose. Why should he tell you before that? It would make no sense to tell you he had your mother's confounded permission to propose before he actually did so."

Rachel crossed her arms. "I'm not being ridiculous. I'm prudent and wise and correct in my judgment of his blasted character."

Mama crossed her arms. "Are you? Then why are you here with me instead of in London with him?"

"You wanted me to come home," Rachel said. "You're ill."

Her mother reclined back onto the pillows. "I love you, and I'm glad you're here, but I never intended for you to drop everything and leave London. Just because I am ill, it does not follow that you are the only person who can care for me."

"I want to," Rachel said. "How can I pray and ask for your health each night, if I'm not willing to come nurse you? Faith requires action, and I've devoted my life to nursing and to taking care of you."

Mama held out her hand. Her voice was tired and thin. "And I want you here. I missed you terribly while you were away, but there was a reason we were apart. You were learning more about medicine, and you were training others. I don't want you to return home only to hide from your difficulties. Are you acting because of your faith or your fear?"

Rachel grasped her mother's hand and spoke quietly. "But what if you die while I'm gone? I had no warning with Papa. One minute the sun was shining, and I was on top of the world, at the crown of my favorite oak tree. The next moment, he lay collapsed on the ground, a dark, unmoving form in the middle of a bright circle and no matter how much I cried, I could not bring him back. I had slivers in my feet from sliding down the trunk so quickly, and my throat was raw from yelling for you."

Her mother squeezed her hand.

"Every time I feel like I'm on top of the world, I look around for something to collapse. I wait for a letter from Dr. Morrow, and I feel for slivers in my feet. I don't want to miss something. I want to be here when you need me," Rachel said.

Mama reached for the glass of water and took another sip. "Your colonel isn't so unsteady. He seems persistent and reliable to me." She shook her head. "Oh, Rachel. Every time you're happy with him, you anticipate the ways that he will disappoint you. Whenever you start to feel any level of comfort with him, you dig around until you find some measure of dissatisfaction. You have never been able to allow yourself to feel joy, since your father's death."

Rachel fought back the tears. "But joy vanishes when I least expect it."

"Like you leaving London when the colonel was planning to propose?" her mother asked. "He thought you were almost ready, months ahead of the end of the Season. He wished to know where to get married to accommodate my ill health."

Rachel couldn't bear the thought of how much pain she had caused Curtis. The tears spilled onto her cheeks.

"I'm sorry I hurt him," she whispered. "It would never work between us."

Mama lay back. "Do you love him?"

Rachel nodded as the tears rolled down her cheeks. She could feel the sobs building.

"Does he love you?"

She nodded.

"Is he a decent, honest, respectable man with an income to support you?"

She nodded again. "He swears like a sailor."

"Like your father did." Mama laughed. "Like you and I do. That counts in his favor, not against him. Then what is the obstacle? No man is perfect. In fact, I will tell you a great secret. Men are imperfect, all of them."

Rachel bit her lip. She tried to school her emotions and control her voice. "I'm jealous and afraid." With that, she burst into sobs, threw herself onto her mother's lap, and cried as she hadn't since her father died.

Rachel hardly slept that night. Curtis wandered in and out of her dreams, thin and starving. "*But Alice ordered the wrong dinner,*" he wailed.

The dream version of Curtis wandered London like a madman, climbing a knotted rope ladder to deliver a report to the House of Commons atop a sailing ship's platform in wrinkled shirt sleeves and ill-fitted trousers.

Next, he appeared at a formal dinner in his red coat. It was Alice's birthday, and he was presenting his sister with a pair of boxing gloves and a tennis racket. "*Shelford said you'd like these.*"

Alice turned to her with accusation in her eyes. "*Why did you miss my birthday?*"

Curtis turned to her. "*Why did you leave me alone?*"

Kempton picked up the tennis racket and laughed and laughed.

Rachel tried to climb down the oak to get to Curtis, but her slippers tangled in the branches. She had forgotten to take them off, and the ribbons were stuck, and she couldn't get to him. She couldn't move. She could only watch Kempton swinging the tennis racket, and Alice holding the boxing gloves, and Curtis, with his face upturned, searching the branches of the oak for her.

Rachel woke and gazed out her window at the desolate shadows tangled in her favorite tree. Wispy clouds eclipsed the moon's light, casting dappled patterns onto her coverlet. *When is Alice's birthday? I must make things right with Curtis, with Alice, with Kempton, with Miss Nightingale and Matron Ward and the women at the school, but I don't know how. I'm entangled in my cares and concerns, and I don't know how to leave them behind.*

The dream felt real, as if Curtis were calling out to her across the miles. She could feel his heart speaking to hers, through the shadows of night. The feeling was urgent, and real, and she nearly left her bed to dress and call a carriage, though morning was yet hours away.

Had he died? Was he injured? His heart was reaching to hers, begging her to hear him in dreams, because Curtis could not speak to her in person.

Rachel shook herself. She was not a fanciful person. She was level-headed. Steady. Not given to imagination or visions. She could not sleep the rest of the night, but tossed in her bed. What if something happened to Curtis, and she had never reconciled with him? Was it her own heart, pleading with her to find him, to tear off the slippers and risk a few slivers on the way down?

※

A crisp stack of telegrams welcomed Rachel. She sipped her morning tea and ate a slice of toast. Lady Agatha insisted that she would not allow Curtis to visit unless Rachel attended her sister as well. She wished to confide in a woman who understood the burden of caring for a relative, and the colonel wouldn't understand. He was too heavy-handed.

Agreed. Lady Agatha must have known him well. Rachel took another sip of her tea and opened the next telegram.

Mrs. Phillips. Four telegrams from her, each more outrageous than the last. She nearly blushed for the telegram operator who had sent them. For a woman who desired to keep secrets, she had no idea what discretion meant.

Mrs. Phillips insisted on visiting her tomorrow in Essex and taking up residence there. With her. Or renting a home. She had to be near Rachel for the entirety of her confinement, and no one else would do. Rachel could deliver the baby, and she did not need a male doctor to interfere.

Then Miss Herbert's telegram. Short. Orderly. Complaining about the colonel's lack of progress, and her father, and the amount of work. Thanking her for commiserating. Also insisting that she had no use for Curtis, if Rachel was not there to organize his notes.

And then Lady Clara, Lady Frances, and Miss South, sending their regrets, their complaints about the matron, and their entreaties that she return to the school.

Rachel took a bite of the marmalade-covered toast. She'd believed each of the women had enrolled in the nursing school for the sole purpose of pursuing the colonel, but as she met each woman and got to know them, she realized that they each had a genuine interest in medicine.

Was it possible she mistook their intentions? Did her own insecurities and jealousies lead her to view their interactions with Curtis wrongly?

It was possible that he and the ladies at the nursing school were, indeed, simply old friends who knew each other well. Curtis was wrong to banter and flirt as he did, but did she still do the same herself, at times?

Rachel sipped her tea as she gazed out the windows. Sunlight streamed into the dining room, and she could see the shadow of the old oak tree across the lawn.

Mr. Thorne and Lord Romford. What might an outside observer think of her behavior toward them? Was it entirely innocent? And Mr. Kempton. How did she treat him? Playfully, casually. If the colonel watched her banter and smile with him, would he have cause to wonder whether she was attached to him?

He had. In Paris. When she and Mr. Kempton spoke privately, Curtis had let jealousy get the better of him, too, yet her interaction was entirely innocent. At the dinner with Lord Romford. At the ball with all the other men. She did not think she was flirting, yet Curtis had reacted strongly to the idea that the men had sent her flowers. And why had they sent flowers? Had she encouraged them enough that they believed they might court her themselves?

Her light-hearted or friendly conversation with the other men did not mean that her heart was set on them. On the contrary, she loved Curtis and ached to be with him. Only one man held sway over her heart the way he did, and she knew he loved her in return. Maybe, just maybe, Eleanor was right. He loved everyone he met, but he was only *in love* with her.

Dr. Morrow visited after breakfast. Mornings were the most painful for Mama. She felt better by afternoon and seemed almost energetic by evening.

Mama rested in her bed, not yet ready to walk into the drawing room. Joyce plumped the pillows behind her and helped her sit. Rachel adjusted the curtains to let in just enough light. Nothing had changed in this room in the nine months she'd been gone. In the last nine years.

She focused on her new embroidery pattern as Dr. Morrow talked with Mama. A clean linen. A new design. She'd start over, carefully choosing the colors and controlling each stitch she made.

"This London doctor of yours seems quite enthusiastic about your mother's case," he said. "Wants constant updates."

Her needle slipped. A mistake already. She picked at the thread to undo the knot. "By Jove, not you, too, Dr. Morrow. Mama, are you allowing him to correspond with the colonel?"

Mama shrugged. "*London* doctor. Why would I turn that down?"

Rachel laid her hoop on Mama's side table. She'd never be able to concentrate. "When I get a hold of him—"

Mama turned her gaze away from the doctor. "Are you planning to see him again?"

Rachel's stomach did a flip at the thought of seeing him again. "I'm staying with you, Mama. I only meant that he should not presume to correspond without my permission."

Her mother tilted her head. "*Who* is in charge of my health? *Me* or *you*?"

Rachel conceded the point. "You."

Dr. Morrow settled into a chair.

"Tell her," Mama said.

Rachel braced herself. "What? Why did you wait until he was here?"

"Because you seem to respect Dr. Morrow's opinion." Mama sighed. "It's not bad news."

Rachel rested her head on Mama's bed. It had been a difficult week, and she wasn't sure how much uncertainty she could take.

"Mrs. Wickford plans to sell your home. She can no longer maintain it without your help," Dr. Morrow said.

Rachel reached up to take Mama's hand. "I've returned home for good. We shall stay here together."

"Listen," Mama said. "Hear him out. I'm too tired to explain." She closed her eyes.

Dr. Morrow glanced around the room. "Mrs. Palmer has offered your mother a place to live with her."

Rachel stared at him. "Aunt Ellen? Live with the Maldons?"

Mama turned to face Rachel. "Ellen and I are both lonely. Lucy is moving to London, and you should remain there to help Miss Nightingale. You can use the proceeds from the sale of the estate to rent a townhome for the rest of your life. Mr. Maldon will buy this estate for Lucy and Peter, so they have one of their own when they visit."

Of course. It made perfect sense. Mr. Maldon wished to secure his footing as a member of the gentry. Buying an estate for his new son-in-law would reinforce Peter's aristocratic roots, rather than his status as a mine owner.

But to leave Mama and live on her own in London for the rest of her life? She would be able to work at the nursing school indefinitely, all year, if she wished. And see Curtis again.

Rachel went to the curtains and looked over the side lawns, the flowers, just now forming their spring buds, and new leaves covering the trees. "What about your health? Aunt Ellen is hardly qualified to care for you."

Mama blinked drowsily. This conversation was wearing her out. "Joyce does well enough. If I rest and sleep, I require little assistance."

"Curtis says you rest too much. You need an indoor gymnasium to stretch more." The words tumbled out without thinking. She pressed her lips together. "Sorry, Mama."

"He's already sent the specifications to Mr. Maldon." Mama yawned.

Rachel watched the old gardener pruning the hedges in the distance. The neat, orderly rows of bushes ran the length of the gravel pathway leading into the gardens. "Naturally. Officious, interfering man."

"It's quite kind of him," Mama said. "Mr. Maldon has begun work already. I believe he's corresponding with a Mr. Kempton?"

Rachel drew the curtains back further to let in more light. She could see the pond in the distance. "Honestly." Kempton was corresponding secretly, too. What else had she missed during her months away? "How much do you see of Mr. Maldon when you're with Aunt Ellen?"

Her mother folded down her coverlet, avoiding Rachel's eye. "A fair bit."

Ah. "The duke believes we require a new member of Parliament to replace the buffoon that replaced Papa. I suggest Mr. Maldon. Perhaps you could help him mount a campaign."

Mama closed her eyes. "What did the Old Lion really call him? I'm sure it wasn't 'buffoon.'"

Rachel rested her head against the door frame. "I'm not sure how I feel about selling our home. I came home to care for you."

"I'm selling it *because* I care for you," Mama said. "You cannot live with me forever, Rachel. I'll decide what's best for my health and my daughter. Reconcile yourself to my decision. Ellen and I are quite content with one another's company, her lap dog, and more maids than either of us know what to do with. Mr. Maldon quite spoils us."

Rachel folded her arms. "And if I insist on remaining in this house, you shall not be able to sell it."

Her mother adjusted her head on the pillow. "I shall sell it whether or not you live here, dearest. You may beg Lucy and Peter for a wretched room, if you wish, but I am decided. I have no need of this great estate, and you belong in London."

Mama's will was stronger than her feeble body. If only her body matched her spirit. Rachel would spend more time with her. "Do you recall the gymnasium I told you about? The one we had in Germany? I can show you how to do the stretches, once the pulleys are installed."

Mama murmured faintly, "Oh no, the colonel says he'll come and do that himself."

Dr. Morrow took her arm and accompanied Rachel out of the room. She shook her head. If she ever saw Curtis again, she didn't know whether to slap him or kiss him. He presumed too much. He interfered too much. He cared so much. She'd slap him, then kiss him, then slap him again. Then kiss him again.

Rachel and Dr. Morrow walked arm in arm past the drawing room into the front entryway. *Curtis.* She stopped abruptly, and her mind went blank. She could feel her heart racing as she took in every detail of his appearance.

He waited in the entryway with Mr. Kempton, knocking his top hat against his leg. His clothes were wrinkled, his face had two days' growth of beard, and his eyes had great circles beneath them. He looked the way she felt—like a shipwreck.

How to make amends? Where to begin? Rachel cleared her throat. Perhaps now was not the time to slap or kiss him. Perhaps she would start, as she always had, by teasing him. "Dr. Morrow, may I present that illustrious London doctor who keeps harassing you without my knowledge, Colonel Loughton, and his likewise duplicitous associate, Mr. Kempton, who sends the telegrams without informing me?"

"Rachel," Curtis's voice cracked. His eyes traveled over her, as if she were unreal, then landed on her arm, linked with the doctor's.

Mr. Kempton extended a hand. "Pleased to meet you, Morrow."

Dr. Morrow shook his hand and looked at the colonel.

Curtis stared at Rachel, without noticing the doctor had extended his hand to him as well. *Why had he come?* Her heart continued to race.

Dr. Morrow dropped his hand and nodded to Rachel. "Consider your mother's proposal. I have no objection, based on her health. Mr. Maldon and his staff will take care of her. Good day." He left quietly.

"Didn't you have a few choice words for the doctor?" Mr. Kempton asked. "If you found him with Rachel?"

Rachel gestured toward the drawing room. "Have you been swearing the whole way from London, or just since you left the train?"

She selected a comfortable chair and tried to take everything in. Curtis was here, in front of her, looking like a complete disaster. She couldn't breathe, and he wasn't talking. How were they ever to reconcile?

"Oh, for heaven's sake," Mr. Kempton said. "Do I need to go snore in the corner again?"

That seemed to shake Curtis out of his stupor. "Again? When was the last—Don't tell me. The rum toddy. Wait. You were awake when we—"

He looked between Rachel and Mr. Kempton and groaned. "Could I have done things any worse?"

Mr. Kempton studied him. "Certainly. I will make a worse muddle of things when I marry."

Rachel was still trying to decide whether she was angry that he had been so imperious, taking charge of her mother's health without consulting her, or whether that showed great concern and care, as well as audacity and eagerness and determination. Should she be angry that he had corresponded secretly or flattered that he took such pains to ensure he consulted her mother?

"You haven't shaved." It was the first thing that came out of her mouth.

Curtis collapsed onto a sofa and put an arm over his eyes.

"Kempton, take a walk," Rachel said, watching Curtis. "I'm sure your legs are cramped after that long train ride. My gardens are lovely and quite extensive."

Mr. Kempton saluted her and left the room. She and Curtis were finally alone, and she still hadn't decided whether to slap him or kiss him first.

CHAPTER 22

Curtis didn't know what to do. He'd imagined so many things he would say or the bold actions he would take, but now that he was confronted with the vision of loveliness that Rachel was, he froze.

Rachel, however, always knew. She rang for tea. She bustled over to a side cabinet, her skirts swaying as she walked, and added some peppermint leaves to the hot water when it arrived.

They waited in silence while the tea steeped. Rachel studied him intently, seeming to take in every detail of his appearance. He shifted uncomfortably.

Finally, she left her chair, joined him on the sofa, and poured out the tea. She stirred in some honey and handed the cup to him.

"Cake?" she asked. "I'll wager you're hungry. We don't have any apples."

Curtis felt himself coming back to life. He ate the cake gratefully, every morsel tasting like manna, and his head began to clear.

"How long has it been since you had a meal?" Rachel asked.

He took a drink of the now-perfectly-warm tea. His favorite. "I cannot recall."

They studied each other. "I rehearsed a few things to tell you," Curtis said. "I cannot recall them, either, it seems."

Rachel perched daintily on the edge of the sofa. "You are a beast when you are hungry." She took a sip of her tea.

He accepted another slice of cake and began to eat. "And many other times."

She nodded.

Curtis set down his plate. "You left without any warning. You left the dinner party, you left London. You left me. What did I do?"

Rachel dabbed at the edge of her mouth with a napkin. "My mother needed me. Eat your cake."

He took another bite, chewed, and swallowed. "I need you."

Rachel set down her plate. "Only to secure votes in Essex."

Grandfather. Hang it all. He washed down the crumbs with another drink of tea. "Are two slices sufficient to change me back into a gentleman?"

She pursed her lips. "You haven't touched the bread and butter."

Curtis ate a couple of the sandwiches and set the teacup and cake plate on a side table. "I'm sorry. Whichever thing I did that drove you away. So many things I've done."

She set aside her teacup and saucer. "I was concerned about my mother's sudden decline in health. Dr. Morrow must have advised you that her condition changed." She narrowed her eyes.

He cleared his throat, pleading with his eyes for her to understand. "I should have told you I was corresponding with him. I wanted to, but I was scared you would push me away further or push me away for good, if I tried to get more involved in your life." He ran a hand over his face. "I worry about her, too, and I wanted to help, but I never should have done it without your knowledge. I should have been your strength. I should have reassured you and let you tell me your worries about her health. You were right to leave. His update concerned me, too."

Curtis picked up the teacup and set it down again. "I've been so worried about what I want and need that I haven't taken care of you like I should. I'm wrapped up in Alice and her concerns, when I should be focused on your mother and your concerns. Of course you were frightened by the sudden onset of dizzy spells and the loss of appetite. It was concerning. I confess, part of my inability to sleep is due to my fears for her, as well as my—"

He blew out a long breath. "How *is* your mother this morning?"

Rachel waved her hand. "Well enough. Obstinate, like you. Too stubborn to be truly ill."

Curtis almost smiled. He gazed at her. "Aren't you going to tell me to stop looking at you?"

Rachel held his gaze. "I'm glad you came. Thank you for your concern about Mama's health."

She was letting him look at her like a lovesick puppy, and she didn't seem to mind. Her expression even had a hint of something in it. What was it? Admiration? Or was it pity?

Curtis ran his eyes over her face, trying to ascertain any hint of emotion. "I want to care for you. I want to spend each day with you, to sit with you, to listen to your worries. I can't take this anymore, Rachel. I want to marry you. Please, tell me what is wrong, and tell me what to do. I will do anything to please you. You know I love you."

He felt emotion rising and tipped his head back to rest against the wall. He covered his eyes with his arm. "It has nothing to do with Grandfather or your blasted estate or confounded politics. I was captivated the moment I met you, without knowing where you lived or anything other than your interest in nursing. I don't give a deuce about anything except your generous heart."

Rachel settled into the sofa beside him. "You wish to know what is wrong?"

Curtis looked over at her. "Everything."

Her chin trembled. "I fear Kempton will be wandering the gardens for hours, then."

He tilted his head to the ceiling. "The abbreviated version, perhaps."

"I have not known my own heart," Rachel said. "I have led you on a chase, unfairly, and I am sorry."

Curtis stared at her. "I don't understand. That sounds like a refusal of my offer, but I know you love me. Your own heart must tell you that, Rachel."

"It does." She smiled at him, as gentle as summer rain.

He took a deep breath. "Then why are you sorry?"

Rachel took his hands in hers. "I'm sorry I was afraid of your grandfather, when he is really an old lamb. I'm sorry I could not see that your compassion for your friends leads you to get involved in their lives. I'm sorry I was jealous of the way you love everyone around you, when it is one of the things that most endears you to me. I'm sorry I was afraid that I would not be enough for you, when you have never once doubted me."

Curtis let out his breath.

Rachel rested her head on his shoulder. "We could have been married months ago, if I had trusted you instead of listening to my fears."

He rested his head on hers. He stretched out his legs and crossed them at the ankles. "I'm sorry for my blasted mistakes. I'm an ugly customer, and you'd be daft to marry me."

"I love you anyway, confound it." She tilted her head up to look at him. "Your grandfather would never have withheld his consent, would he?"

He shook his head. "He asked me to telegram as soon as possible, if I can convince you, and he will arrange a special license." He ran a hand along her cheek.

"*If*, or when?" Rachel asked.

Curtis grinned. "You have him worried. It's good for the old badger."

Rachel laughed. "Old lamb. He doesn't want anyone to know, does he, but he's as gentle at heart as you are."

He gazed into her eyes, pulling her closer. "So? If we speak to your mother, may I send that telegram? Can he put your name with mine on a license to marry?"

Rachel ran a hand over the stubble on his face. "Naturally, the Archbishop of Canterbury is a personal friend of his?"

Curtis nodded.

She held his gaze. "Yes, Curtis. I should like that very much." She considered him. "But I may require a few rules."

"Rules?" He just wanted to kiss her.

Rachel snuggled into his side. "You must eat before every argument, beastly man. Second rule. You must allow Mrs. Glenn to stay with us always. Alice cannot function without her."

Curtis relaxed and put his arm around Rachel. "Agreed. Bread and butter before every fight. And I've already requested that Mrs. Glenn join us in London." His stomach was full, the tea had warmed him, and he held Rachel in his arms. *Us.* He would agree to anything. "Number three?" He gazed at her. When would she let him kiss her?

"No smirking or looking at me like that." Rachel seemed to be trying not to smile.

He widened his smirk. "Can't keep that rule. You're far too pleasant a sight, and you just said you don't mind." He bent over to kiss her.

Rachel brought a hand up onto his chest. "Very well. You may adore me. Number three. No looking that way at other women."

"I don't," Curtis said.

She scoffed. "You love everybody you meet. You *are* a doctor, but you cannot heal everyone. I need you to love *me* more than everyone else. I am absurdly jealous."

"That's the easiest one so far." Curtis stroked her hair with his hand.

Rachel slapped it. "Don't touch a single hair pin until after we're married."

He folded her in his arms.

"Number four," Rachel said, pushing on his chest, and looking up at him.

Curtis gazed at her. "I forgot everything you said, except the word 'marry.'" His eyes lingered on her lips.

"Then you should have shaved." She traced the lines of his face and across his lips. "Four and five. I'll nurse as long as I like, whomever I like, married or not, and you won't send telegrams to my mother or Dr. Morrow or anyone else without consulting me. I must be able to trust that you will not change your mind."

"This is after we marry?" Curtis asked. "You said 'marry.' Make as many rules as you like. Yes. Anything, darling. I need to go send an urgent telegram."

He pulled her closer. "Of course you must continue nursing. That was the reason I first loved you. In truth, Rachel, I am sorry I've not always been at my best, but if you'll trust me with your heart one more time—"

"I really do not care for stubble," Rachel said, but her mouth twitched. She wanted to kiss him.

Curtis grinned. "So you do love me." He straightened on the sofa and lowered his head. She brought hers up to meet him and the reaction was immediate. He kissed her swiftly, taking care not to rub his cheek against hers. Her hand rested on his chest, her head still nestled against him.

He'd buy every bar of shaving soap in London, as soon as he returned, to get a real kiss. He pulled away. "You *are* coming back with me? Wait."

He slid down to the floor in front of her and knelt on one knee. "Will you marry me?" He dug around in his vest pocket. "I brought a ring."

Rachel covered her mouth, then lowered her hand. "Yes."

Curtis stopped searching for the ring. "Really?"

She took his face between her hands and kissed him on the lips, then pulled him onto the sofa beside her. He scrambled up as quickly as he could and wrapped an arm around her. "Why?" he asked.

Rachel ran her hands lightly through his hair. "Because you once told me that fear should not prevent a lifetime of joy. Because I feel like *this* when I'm with you and wretched when I'm not. Because you are a kind brother, a true friend, an admirable kisser, and because you are worried about my mother. Because I am as imperfect as you are, and because I trust you enough to turn my life over to you. Be gentle with it."

Curtis let go of her and continued searching his pockets. "Confounded vest." He found the ring and slipped it on her finger. "Here it is. My mother's."

He stretched out his legs and sighed. "I composed a speech. It was something about how I need you in a thousand invisible ways and the ten thousand invisible ways you worked your way into my heart and my life. I don't remember the rest just now. It was beautiful on the train when I composed it, but it means I love you."

He rested his head against the wall and turned to look at her. Finally, after all this time. Emotion overcame him, and he let out a long, deep breath. "And I will be very, very gentle with your heart and your life and your soul, if you'll have me. There is no one I'd rather entrust my own happiness and eternity to than you."

"You've finally learned how to give compliments." She kissed him. "And I love you ten thousand invisible ways. How many swear words did the proposal include, out of curiosity?" she asked, biting her lip.

Curtis closed his eyes and drew her onto his chest. "If you said 'no,' at least ten thousand. Shall we go find Kempton? And I'd like to meet your mother. Has the dizziness subsided? That Dr. Morrow isn't half as bad as I thought. Much older-looking than I suspected, though I don't believe there's any reason for you to stroll arm in arm with him."

Rachel smiled. "Yes, he's quite old and decrepit at age thirty-six, and not at all desirable. No concern for you."

"He's a relic. Ancient. Seven or eight years older than me at least."

She wrapped her arms around his neck. "Must we find Kempton and my mother right now? I shall not ever have you all to myself. You will always want company about the house, but I love that about you. I shall insist on *one* moment alone with you, my *highly desirable* wretch of a man."

"By Jove, Rachel, you *are* an absolute stunner today," Curtis said, enclosing her in his arms. "Where is the closest telegram office?"

"You realize, we shall be an unstoppable force together," Rachel said, slipping her arms inside his waistcoat. "Are you prepared for this?"

"I've been waiting nearly a year for you," Curtis said, grinning. "Hook it, let's get ourselves a license and be done."

He lowered his lips to hers, careful again not to let his cheek rub against her. She met him with a tidal force, knocking them back against the edge of the sofa. He drew her to her feet as she ran her hands along his shoulders and around his neck, the strength of her kiss only increasing.

He wrapped his arms around the curve of her waist, a flood of feelings cascading through him. The surge of emotion heightened the sensation of his lips on hers. He drew her closer, wave after wave of love crashing into him as his lips caressed hers.

She rested her head on his chest, gazing up at him. She smiled. "Special license, right? How soon can Grandfather get it? I'll go pack my mother's bags. For this, I am sure she can make the journey to London. Shall we invite Dr. Morrow to the wedding to supervise her care?"

"*I'm* her 'London doctor.' I'll monitor her care from now on, here and elsewhere. *He* can advise and implement *my* instructions." Curtis stroked her face gently and held her tight. She was real. No illusion. Daylight and sunshine and a cloudless sky. He leaned down to kiss her again. "You know, I love the tangible parts of you as almost as much as the invisible ways I love you."

Rachel laughed. "I love you, whiskers or clean-shaven, shirt sleeves or coat, in London or Germany or Essex."

He never wanted to let go, but he wanted to make sure he got that license as quickly as possible. "Shall we find your mother first or Kempton?"

Rachel lay a hand on his chest, gazing up at him. "Oh, Kempton, certainly, so he can send the telegram to the Old Lamb. My mother is asleep and will be for another hour or two. Dr. Morrow's visit wore her out. The gardens are extensive, and it may take us some time to find him. Besides, there's one tree in particular I want to show you."

"An apple orchard?" Curtis raised an eyebrow.

Rachel smiled. "Better. My favorite climbing tree. An ancient oak. At least seven or eight years older than you. Probably fifty or one hundred."

Curtis led her toward the glass doors overlooking the gardens. "The loser must pay a forfeit?"

Rachel nodded.

Curtis looked down at the wide skirt and day dress she wore. "Can you climb in that?"

Rachel threaded her arm through his as they gazed over the lawns and sculpted bushes. "No. You are assured of winning." Her mouth twitched as she smiled.

She wanted to kiss him again. Curtis grinned. "Lead on, my love. I am yours to command."

EPILOGUE

Alice heard the front door open, and a woman's voice echoed through the hallway. She relaxed onto the sofa. Rachel was home.

"Did Carter get the boots? Is Curtis wearing that blasted uniform? Does Cook have Alice's dinner ready? Never mind the wedding breakfast, King. The silver? And the tablecloths? My mother is waiting in the carriage, and I will not be late to my own wedding. Those flowers had best not be too tall. Which candelabra did Mrs. King set the tables with?"

She'd never have to plan another social event. After the ceremony, Rachel would run the household. Well, she already did, really. After today, Rachel would officially be Mrs. Loughton, the colonel's wife, and Alice could retreat back into her books and the gymnasium, once Kempton installed it.

Rachel poked her head into the drawing room. "Where is that wretched man? Don't tell me he's shaving again or cleaning his confounded nails. If he's late, Alice, I'll jilt him. Carter!" She stormed out of the room and hollered up the stairs. "Get him down here this instant. He looks well enough! I'm leaving, and you can tell him where to find me. The altar! It's one thing to be late to a ball, but it's quite another to keep his bride waiting."

Rachel's voice faded in the hallway, and the front door slammed. She and her mother must be riding in their own carriage to St. James's.

Alice sighed. This was the best birthday gift she'd ever received: a sister. She'd chosen the pale gold dress that Rachel helped her select in Paris. She could have ordered a new one, but Rachel agreed that this one meant more to both of them than any other dress would. She checked to see that the fabric was spotless, no water stains or wrinkles.

She'd caused enough problems. It had been her own opposition to marriage that had set Rachel against Curtis. She would have felt responsible for her brother's grief and loneliness, if Rachel had refused to marry him. She'd tried to reconcile Rachel and Curtis for months, but she didn't know how to help. The least she could do was be the bridesmaid.

Standing in front of a sea of guests, Alice swallowed. She would do it for them, but her toes felt like lead. If she stood with her back to them, she could pretend that no one else was watching.

Curtis rushed down the stairs into the waiting carriage, his uniform spotless, and they rode to the chapel. Curtis pulled on his white gloves as the vehicle slowed. Rachel had asked him to wait until the last moment, and he complied happily. He brushed imaginary dirt off his shoulders. The braid on his uniform was spotless. "Will she have me?" Curtis asked.

Alice smiled at her brother. "She was ready to harm anyone who came between her and you just now. Carter barely got away with his life. I imagine she is as eager as you are."

Curtis tapped his hat against his leg as the carriage pulled to a complete stop in front of St. James's church. He waited for Mrs. Glenn and Alice to climb down the steps, then bounded past them into the red stone building with its gleaming spire. Mrs. Glenn moved serenely into the chapel, and Alice followed her. Rachel had already disappeared into the bride's room in an alcove.

"You'll do fine," Mrs. Glenn whispered.

Alice made her way to the front and surveyed the gathered guests.

Eleanor and her husband were already there with Rachel's mother and Lord and Lady Barrington, as well as the Duke of Woodford, Lord Romford, Mr. Maldon, and Lucy's aunt. The duke had left the moment Curtis sent him word and barely arrived from Paris.

Lucy and her new husband, Peter Chelmsford, had hurried back from their Grand Tour. Lord Chelmsford, his new wife, Cecelia, and his mother, the dowager Lady Chelmsford had already arrived.

Uncle and Aunt Abridge had taken seats already. That only left Grandfather. What was taking Kempton so long? They'd miss the wedding. She watched the back of the chapel anxiously, and finally Kempton arrived with Grandfather in tow.

"Wouldn't stop fussing with his bow tie," Kempton muttered to her.

Grandfather preened. "I don't fuss." He moved away to prepare for the march down the aisle. He had insisted on giving Rachel away, since her father could not.

Kempton quirked a half-smile. "The Old Lion is worse than your brother." He waited beside her.

"You know what my brother is like when he wears his uniform," Alice whispered back. "I'm late to every ball. I don't mind, of course. I could miss the balls entirely."

Kempton grinned. "You'll be on time now. Rachel will see to that."

Alice swallowed. So many people watching them. "Must I stand here already?"

He shrugged. "Bridesmaid duties. I've been a groomsman often enough. It's easy. Let them admire you." He turned in a circle, preening like a peacock, then he glanced at her dress, the simple white roses woven throughout her hair, and back to her face. His smile fell, and he swallowed.

Alice dropped her eyes to the stone floor of the chapel. What was it about her appearance that caused such a reaction from him? Did she not look well enough?

Kempton put a finger under her chin and lifted it up. He grinned again. "Come now. We're in this together, Miss Loughton." He took her hand and squeezed it. "One wink means Loughton has already started crying, and two winks means Rachel is glaring at him."

Alice laughed.

"Keep your eye on me, and we'll get through this." Kempton spun his top hat, tipped it back onto his head, and moved to the other side of the altar. He looked unusually fine in a crisp black coat with a tall, starched collar and gleaming white cuffs. His white trousers were spotless.

The rector, Mr. Blake, waited for the couple. Curtis ran over from greeting friends, breathless, and took his position next to Kempton. The rector nodded to him, and the music started a few moments later.

Alice watched Grandfather escort her dear friend up the aisle. He had insisted on a special license for the couple, which suited her. She'd get her new sister three weeks sooner than if they had to wait for banns to be read.

Rachel's dress was simple and elegant, a white silk-satin gown with a single rose at the center and a lace overlay across the shoulders. A single cluster of roses decorated the skirt on one side. White roses peeked from the side of her braided bun, and her cheeks glowed with happiness.

Curtis waited for her in his colonel's red coat and full uniform, his face awestruck. He had loved her for nearly a year, and he had agonized over her for an equally long time.

Alice dabbed at the corner of her eyes. Tears came so easily. Kempton caught her eye and winked at her. She bit back a laugh. *She* was the one crying, not Curtis.

Curtis grasped Rachel's hands and knelt before the rector. Standing next to them, Alice could see the way he gazed at Rachel, as if Rachel were a star in the heavens and he wanted to bathe in her shimmering light.

Alice hardly heard the rector's sermon or the vows. She couldn't live in her brother's household forever. She felt extraneous when she was around Rachel and her brother. They often exchanged glances and understood each other without speaking. They clearly wanted to show more affection than they could with her in their presence.

Children would come quickly for the new couple, she was certain, and they would fill all the bedrooms in the house. The upstairs nursery, which Kempton was converting to a gymnasium, would be needed for a schoolroom soon.

Although Alice feared childbirth, Rachel had tried to reassure her. Alice would either have to risk it or find a husband who did not need an heir. The alternative was a lonely spinsterhood, living as a burden in her brother's household.

She dabbed at the corner of her eyes again and darted a glance over at Kempton to see if he would wink once again. He grinned at her and winked twice, rapidly. Alice peeked a look at Rachel, instead of the rector. No glare. He was teasing her, because he saw that she was overcome with emotion. She glared at him, but playfully, since that was what two winks meant. He nearly burst out laughing in the middle of the ceremony.

Oh, if only the Season could be like this, but the Season was dreadful. Dinner parties were formidable, and what if she were invited to house parties in the country without Curtis and Rachel once the Season ended?

She was naturally reserved and preferred an evening with one or two dear friends. She felt tongue-tied and uneasy with large groups of prominent politicians and the socially elite friends that Curtis invited. She got nervous and things got muddled. She forgot names and said the wrong things to the wrong people, or she simply didn't speak at all.

The ceremony ended, and Alice sighed with relief. Curtis pulled Rachel into an inappropriately affectionate embrace. Rachel kissed him far too passionately for a wedding service, and they walked back down the aisle together.

Now what would she do? A future stretched before Alice as long as the chapel's nave. Endless balls, dinners, social visits, house parties, and Grandfather's expectations. What man would pursue her, when she could not even speak without blushing or wanting to burst into tears?

Kempton placed a hand on her elbow. "Relief, eh, Miss Loughton? Thought she might not have him, up to the last." He flashed a charming grin and held out his arm to escort her down the aisle.

Alice studied him. She'd never considered him as a bachelor, just as Kempton. He had wavy brown hair, dark eyes, and a permanent half-smile on his face. He *was* handsome. He was also entertaining and well-liked wherever he went. He always had something to say, and she never had to make conversation with other people when he was nearby. He entertained them for her.

She slid her arm through his, tilted her head up, and returned his smile. "Rachel threatened to jilt him not five minutes before the wedding."

She had to marry *someone*, and Kempton was the only man she could look in the eyes and talk to without falling to pieces. Better than an arranged marriage or marriage of convenience. They were at least friends, and he *had* been trying to kiss her for years.

And he did not need an heir. He knew of her fears and her mother's death. Surely, he would understand if she delayed childbirth or even avoided it altogether.

They began to walk together past the church pews, following her brother and Rachel toward the open doors of the chapel. The eyes of every guest were on them. Did they make a handsome couple? Did they look as well together as Rachel and Curtis?

Kempton just needed a little encouragement. She moved a little nearer to him, wrapping her arm around his and pulling herself close to him. He shot her a look of surprise.

"You know, Kempton, I've reconsidered. We *have* known each

other a long time. You may call me 'Alice.' Did you know I'm turning nineteen today? It's time at last."

Kempton led her down the aisle to the chapel doors. "Happy birthday, Alice, and here you are. You're the one giving *me* a gift." He seemed to be trying to grin, but she detected a hint of uneasiness in the expression.

They walked into the sunshine and the busy street. Alice turned to him with her most encouraging smile. "I've known you sixteen years, and I don't recall hearing your Christian name."

"Frederick," his voice cracked on a high note. "Frederick," he repeated in his regular voice. "My sisters call me 'Freddie.'"

He guided her over to a waiting carriage. Alice kept a firm grip on his arm. "That suits you, Freddie."

He chuckled nervously. He took off his top hat and fiddled with the rim. Alice stared at him. She didn't know what to say.

Freddie swallowed. "Yes. Well, Alice. I. Ah. Will see you at the breakfast."

"Mrs. Glenn and I are riding back with you and my grandfather. Rachel and Curtis will want to be alone now."

Freddie laughed half-heartedly. "Right." He looked around for the duke and Mrs. Glenn, dropping her arm and hitting the hat against his leg. He tipped the hat onto his head, took out his pocket watch, and peered up at the church's clock, comparing the times.

They waited in silence, Freddie checking his watch often, until Grandfather and Mrs. Glenn arrived. Freddie offered her his hand, as always, and helped her into the carriage. Alice allowed herself to hold it a moment longer than she usually would.

He stared at her and collapsed onto the carriage seat next to Grandfather, his legs resting at an angle across from hers.

Alice dropped her eyes to the floor of the carriage, studying his perfectly polished shoes next to her silk slippers. The carriage jolted, and her knee knocked against his, trapping his legs between the side of the carriage and her own. She left them there for a moment before sliding her feet away. She glanced up to see Freddie's reaction. He looked at her with wide eyes.

Grandfather cleared his throat, and she glanced at him. She knew her cheeks were blushing pink. She studied Freddie's immaculate shoes again.

"You made a beautiful bridesmaid, dear," Grandfather said, glancing over at Freddie. "Didn't she?"

"Yes, Your Grace," Freddie's voice squeaked.

Grandfather grinned. The carriage swayed gently as they approached the townhouse.

Alice chanced another glance across the carriage. This would take courage. "I'm looking forward to the installation of the new gymnasium, Freddie. I hope you'll allow me to test out the new ropes when they arrive."

Grandfather peered at him. "'Freddie?' And what do you call my granddaughter?"

Kempton's face had a definite hint of panic about it. His eyes travelled between her and the duke, and he laughed, a high-pitched, nervous laugh. "Whatever you tell me to call her, Your Grace."

Grandfather steepled his hands and considered. He looked at Freddie's coat and trousers, and back to his face. "Where do you live?"

"George's Street, Hanover Square." Freddie cleared his throat. "Not Piccadilly or Grosvenor Square, I am afraid."

"But fashionable, nonetheless." Grandfather narrowed his eyes. "Calling card?"

Freddie fished a calling card out of his vest pocket. Grandfather studied it. "Your address is printed here, not your club."

"Yes, Your Grace." Freddie avoided Alice's gaze.

"Excellent form." Grandfather slipped the card into his pocket. "You may call her as she chooses." He tipped his head against the carriage and closed his eyes.

She sought Freddie's eyes. Usually, he would joke or laugh right now. Or wink at her. It was his role to make light of every situation, and her role not to take him seriously. They had a mutual, long-standing, unspoken understanding never to be serious with one another.

But she had broken that agreement, and Freddie didn't seem to know what to do about it or about her.

He had a half-smile on his face, as if bemused and bewildered. "Alice. Happy birthday, little mouse." He tipped his head back against the carriage and covered his face with his silk topper.

Alice looked over at Mrs. Glenn. She couldn't have a chaperone forever, and she couldn't live with Curtis forever. She only had one option, and he was sitting across from her. He knew she was timid, but she would have to change. She *could* change, for him. The mouse would have to transform to capture the cat. Her hands shook, but she pressed them together.

She'd already frightened him, it seemed, so he could not be so very difficult to ensnare once she set her mind to it. Alice intended to marry Frederick Kempton, whether she loved him or not, and Grandfather already approved.

ALSO BY LISA H. CATMULL

Each of the books can be enjoyed as a stand-alone novel or as part of the Victorian Grand Tour Series.

An Attempted Engagement: Book Four of the Victorian Grand Tour Series

Only one thing stands between Alice Loughton and the man of her dreams: her brother.

Frederick Kempton calls her his "little mouse." She's been shy and quiet ever since he met her sixteen years ago. But when timid Alice Loughton decides it's time to marry, there's only one man for her. The one man who doesn't frighten her. The only man she can talk to without wanting to run and hide. Her brother's hired secretary and closest friend, the one man who can arrange her brother's schedule to give them time for secret meetings together.

But her brother knows Frederick Kempton too well, and he's not about to give his consent for a courtship, not when plenty of other men are pursuing Alice, too. And so, obedient Alice, who has never broken a rule in her life, is forced to take drastic measures, hide love letters by the fireplace, and settle for stolen kisses.

And she's dragged Freddie along with her. Can he walk the fine line between loyalty to his oldest friend and a chance to woo the woman he's secretly loved?

An Inconvenient Grand Tour: Book One of the Victorian Grand Tour Series

She needs to hide. He's tired of being overlooked. It's going to be a long two years.

Eleanor Barrington has one rule: don't draw attention to yourself. She has one goal: marry a Peer to protect her family. When her father decides on a last-minute Grand Tour, Eleanor spends a dangerous amount of time with a man who cannot help with either goal: her brother's best friend.

As the younger son of an earl, Percy Hauxton has to fight for everything. A Grand Tour is the perfect opportunity to pursue his ambition to work for the Foreign Office, but traveling with Eleanor isn't part of the plan.

When circumstances draw them apart and a secret from the past threatens to unravel everything, Eleanor has to decide one thing. Can she marry for love, or does she need a marriage of convenience?

An Engaged Grand Tour: Book Two of the Victorian Grand Tour Series

She's engaged to his brother, but he can't help falling in love with her anyway.

Mining heiress Lucy Maldon is determined to track down her fiancé and make him fall in love with her, even if it means chasing him across the Continent.

Walter, Lord Chelmsford, has no intention of being found.

Peter Chelmsford lives in his brother's shadow. When his older brother decides to go on Grand Tour and leave his bride-to-be behind, Peter accompanies him. While Walter pursues other interests, it's up to Peter to keep his childhood friend safe from his brother.

But can Lucy ever forgive him for stealing her heart and breaking it at the same time?

ABOUT THE AUTHOR

Lisa went with her family on BYU Study Abroad to Vienna when she was twelve years old. The college students voted her "Most Likely To Return Without Her Parents," and she did.

As an undergraduate at Dartmouth, she lived in Mainz, Germany, for three months, then lived in England during part of her senior year of college.

She's lived in seven states, four countries, and moved almost forty times. Lisa enjoys traveling, but her favorite journeys are in books.

She taught English and History for seven years before quitting to pursue screenwriting. None of her screenplays hit the theaters, but she met her future husband the day she moved to Los Angeles.

After leaving L.A., she decided to write books instead of movies. Lisa lives in Utah with her husband and two rambunctious children.

HISTORICAL NOTE

Dear Reader,

Yes, I fibbed. It's more fun that way. I mostly lied about the dates things happened. The Victorian Era is this amazing time period of growth and change, presided over by a queen who had a rich, romantic, loving relationship with her husband. There's so much to steal that I simply can't confine myself to the space of a few months or a single year.

Nurses were looked down on, until Florence Nightingale changed the image. "The Lady With The Lamp" came back from the Crimean War," and gradually Upper Class women began to take up nursing.

Florence Nightingale established the Nightingale Training School and Home for Nurses at St. Thomas's Hospital in 1860. This book is set in 1857, so I fudged a few years. Miss Nightingale's training program took a year, but I compressed it to four months to fit into the Season, which was most active after Easter and ended on the Glorious Twelfth of August, when the hunting season began, and the Upper Class returned to their country estates.

I also changed the location of *Herr* Fliedner's school from

Kaiserwerth, Germany, to Mainz, Germany, because I have lived in Mainz and know the area better.

After the Crimean War, grateful citizens gave freely to a subscription fund, which Florence Nightingale used to create her training school. Queen Victoria appointed a Royal Commission on the Sanitary Conditions of the Army in 1857. I've appointed our colonel as one of the nine commissioners and set him to work on the report, which was delivered in August of 1857 to the House of Commons.

The musical *The Pirates of Penzance* had its London debut in 1880, but Curtis, whose nickname is "the General," needed something to sing. It was too perfect for him, so I had to borrow the Gilbert and Sullivan play.

Kempton, Alice, and Mrs. Glenn argue whether Fanny Brawne was worthy of the poet John Keats. Many felt she was not, after the correspondence from the poet John Keats to his betrothed, Fanny Brawne, was published in 1878. It wasn't until her letters to his sister were published in 1934 that public opinion changed.

Tennis wasn't really a thing until the 1870s, but Alice would have loved it and wanted a tennis racket for her birthday.

I did include the yearly Boat Race between Cambridge and Oxford, which was sporadic before 1856. We're going to pretend like it was already happening every year, and we're also going to pretend like Cambridge won the race four years in a row. Sorry, Oxford. It's fictional, after all.

Marches down the wedding aisle to music also weren't a thing until 1858. One year. Come on, people. I'm using it. Before that, people walked up and back down the aisle without music, then there was often music at the wedding breakfast afterward.

In 1858, Princess Victoria, Queen Victoria's daughter, used the "Bridal Chorus" from *Lohengrin* by Richard Wagner to walk up the aisle as a processional and "The Wedding March" from *A Midsummer Night's Dream* by Felix Mendelssohn to walk down the aisle after she got married. They became the go-to songs to play for marches up and down the aisle. We're still using them today.

As for Colonel Loughton's tiger eyes, Rachel might have seen a tiger at the Regent's Park Zoo.

My favorite bit of research, y'all, was the gymnasium. True story! And the clothes they wore. There are books that detail specific gymnastic exercises, methods, and equipment for training the body and mind, as well as the music to play and the clothes to wear. They even explain how to mark the floor so people will know where to stand. I found illustrations of actual equipment Curtis and Kempton would have purchased in *Instruction In All Kinds Of Gymnastic Exercises As Taught And Practiced In The Institutions Of Germany* by A Military Officer, 1823.

I also found examples of women's exercise clothing in *The New Gymnastic For Men, Women, and Children* by Dr. Dio Lewis, 1868. Watch my social media for images of the real costumes Rachel and Alice would have worn.

Some of my favorite research gems: *The Scoundrel's Dictionary*, 1754, a real book that delightfully catalogues the slang words of the era, *Grose's Classical Dictionary of the Vulgar Tongue*, 1703, and *The Slang Dictionary*, 1869. Delightful reading. I've limited Curtis and Rachel's mild "swearing" to a few choice examples of slang in this novel, but if you want a good laugh, look those up and enjoy!

A last note about anachronisms. The characters seem aware of the germ theory and believe that colds might spread through kissing, sneezing, or proximity to one another. In reality, that thinking is too advanced for 1857.

Enjoy the ride,

Lisa

SOCIAL HIERARCHY IN THE VICTORIAN ERA, 1837-1901

Titles can be confusing because there are three ways to address people: (1) the way one addressed an envelope to them and the way someone announces their name formally, (2) the way one addressed a letter to them, and (3) the way one speaks to them. The graphics on the following pages illustrate the way one would address someone in speech.

I used examples to demonstrate. Victoria and Albert London are the hypothetical people. The title name are also London for our purposes, although the family name and title would not usually be the same.

Notes on the children of the aristocracy

Daughters of a duke, marquess, or earl are called Lady and their first name (Lady Victoria)

Daughters of a viscount or baron are called Miss, but not called Lady (Miss Victoria)

Younger sons of a duke or a marquess are called Lord and their FirstName, but they don't hold a title (Lord Albert)

Younger sons of an earl, viscount, or baron without titles are called Mr. (Mr. London)

Peerage and Titles Explained

Peers are the dukes, marquesses, earls, viscounts, and barons. They are the nobility and the title holders. They sit in the House of Lords.

A duke is called the Duke of a Place, like the Duke of London. Marquesses, earls, viscounts, and barons are always called Lord LastName, like Lord London. They are never called Baron Title or Baron LastName. It is the House of Lords, not the House of Marquesses, Earls, Viscounts, and Barons.

A baronet or knight is called Sir FirstName, like Sir Albert. His wife is called Lady LastName, like Lady London. The female equivalent of a knight is called a dame, and her husband is called Mr. LastName, like Mr. London.

Peers sat in the House of Lords and often attended Parliament. It often began January thirty-first and ended August twelfth, although it ended on July 29, 1856, the year this story takes place. Eleanor and Percy got married on August 1, 1856, after the Season ended for that year.

Although some families were in town in February, most Peers brought their families back after Easter. Parties, balls, excursions, and art exhibits were in full swing during May, June, and July.

Baronets and knights are not Peers and do not sit in the House of Lords.

Men often referred to other men by their title or last name only, like London, instead of Lord London or Albert.

Men and women did not usually call each other by their first name or given name. It was a sign of increasing intimacy or appropriate for childhood friends who had grown up together, like Lucy, Rachel, Eleanor, Walter, and Peter. Women might call each other by their first names once they became friends, like Alice, Rachel, and Lucy.

The oldest daughter was Miss LastName, like Miss London. Her younger sisters were Miss FirstName LastName, like Miss Victoria London and Miss Elizabeth London.

A nobleman often held more than one title. A duke might also be a marquess and an earl. An earl might also be a viscount. The oldest son or heir would be allowed to use the lesser title.

The *ton* was the Upper Crust that socialized in London. It was comprised of royalty, aristocracy, and members of the gentry. Some wealthy business owners or bankers were included as well.

Servants had a hierarchy of precedence, too. In the lower classes, some servants were called by their last names and others were called by their first names. The housekeeper and cook were called "Mrs." whether or not they were married.

And then there were the clergy. Oh, this is as complicated as everything else! It needs another page to explain...Here are some highlights. There are three forms of address for clergy as well.

For example, clergymen were never called "reverend" as their form of address, just as a title. The Reverend Albert London or the Reverend Deacon Albert London would be the formal address on an envelope, but in conversation or to his face he would be simply be called Deacon London or Mr. London, never Reverend London.

The archbishops and bishops sat in the House of Lords.

An archbishop was called "Your Grace" or "Archbishop."

Bishops, diocesan bishops, or suffragan bishops were called "My Lord" or "Bishop."

A Canon, Prebendar, or Archdeacon was called only by their title.

Other clergy in the Church of England were called "Mr." or by their position: vicar, rector, curate, chaplain, or dean. Someone might say, "Come on in, Vicar. It's good to see you, Mr. London," and be talking to the same person. He was the vicar, but he was also Mr. London. He was not Vicar London.

The illustrations on the following pages have the titles on the top and the names by which they were addressed on the bottom or to the side. Remember, this is the way one would talk to them in speech, not the way one would address an envelope. You would not use a formal title like "Earl" in conversation, like "Good day, Earl London," but would instead say, "Good day, Lord London."

Social Hierarchy in the Victorian Era
1837-1901

Presented in descending order of precedence (rank)

Royalty

Aristocracy

Duke	Duchess
His Grace	Her Grace

Marquess/Marquis	Marchioness
Lord London	Lady London

Earl	Countess
Lord London	Lady London

Viscount	Viscountess
Lord London	Lady London

Baron	Baroness
Lord London	Lady London

- The Duke and Duchess are never called Lord and Lady.
- For Lords and Ladies: the last name is taken from their title, not their family name.

Gentry

Baronet	Dame
Sir Albert	Lady London

Knight	*His wife*
Sir Albert	Lady London

Her husband	Dame
Mr. London	Dame London

Untitled land owners

Military officers

Vicars, curates, and church officials

Solicitors

Land stewards and personal secretaries

Governesses, tutors, and companions

Physicians, sometimes called Dr., like Dr. London

- Members of the gentry are called Mr. or Mrs./Miss unless specified otherwise
- Some men held more than one title. A man with a military rank might also be a knight or a baronet.

Middle/Merchant Class

Doctors, surgeons

Wealthy business owners, bankers

- The Upper Class usually called them by their last name only

---

Lower Class/Working Class

Housekeeper - Mrs. London

Cook - Mrs. London or Cook

Valet, butler - London

Lady's maid/abigail - Miss London or London

Coachman - Albert Coachman

Farm workers, tenants - London

- The housekeeper and butler were equals. The valet and lady's maid were equals.

Servants - Victoria or Albert

The poor - Victoria or Albert

Factory and shop workers - Victoria or Albert

Made in the USA
Las Vegas, NV
26 April 2022

48025580R00159